continued . . .

Endurance

"An exciting science fiction tale . . . fast-paced and exciting . . . SF fans will fully enjoy S. L. Viehl's entertaining entry in one of the better ongoing series today."
—*Midwest Book Review*

"[*Endurance*] gets into more eclectic and darker territory than most space opera, but it's a pretty engrossing trip. Recommended."   —*Hypatia's Hoard*

"A rousing medical space opera. . . . Viehl employs misdirection and humor, while not defusing the intense plot development that builds toward an explosive conclusion."   —*Romantic Times*

Shockball

"Genetically enhanced fun. . . . Cherijo herself has been justly praised as a breath of fresh air—smart [and] saucy. . . . The reader seems to be invited along as an amicable companion, and such is the force of Cherijo's personality that it sounds like fun."
—Science Fiction Weekly

"Fast-paced . . . an entertaining installment in the continuing adventures of the *StarDoc*."   —*Locus*

"An exhilarating science fiction space adventure. The zestful story line stays at warp speed. . . . Cherijo is as fresh as ever. . . . Fans of futuristic outer space novels will want to take off with this tale and the three previous *StarDoc* books, as all four stories take the audience where they rarely have been before."   —*Midwest Book Review*

Eternity Row

"Space opera at its very best. . . . Viehl has created a character and a futuristic setting that is second to none in its readability, quality, and social mores."
—*Midwest Book Review*

"S. L. Viehl serves readers her usual highly entertaining mix of humor and space opera. This episode is enlivened by the antics of [Cherijo's] daughter, Marel, and by an exploration of aging and immortality. As usual, I look forward to the next in an exciting series."
—BookLoons

Rebel Ice

"Well-drawn cultures and fascinating aliens."
—*Publishers Weekly*

"It's fast, fun, character-driven, and left me wanting more . . . one of my all-time favorite sci-fi series."
—Fresh Fiction

"Both gritty and realistic." —*Romantic Times*

"A thrilling addition to the series." —*Booklist*

"A wonderful piece of space opera." —*SFRevu*

"Seems very realistic—almost as if the author visited that world and decided to write about it. *Rebel Ice* is a terrific outer space science fiction novel." —Bookwatch

Plague of Memory

"Another exciting adventure in this well-regarded series."
—Monsters and Critics

Blade Dancer

"Fast-moving, thought-provoking, and just plain damn fun. S. L. Viehl has once again nailed it."
—Linda Howard

"A heartrending, passionate, breathtaking adventure of a novel that rips your feet out from under you on page one and never lets you regain them until the amazing finale. Stunning." —Holly Lisle

OMEGA
GAMES

A StarDoc Novel

S. L. Viehl

A ROC BOOK

ROC
Published by New American Library, a division of
Penguin Group (USA) Inc., 375 Hudson Street,
New York, New York 10014, USA
Penguin Group (Canada), 90 Eglinton Avenue East, Suite 700, Toronto,
Ontario M4P 2Y3, Canada (a division of Pearson Penguin Canada Inc.)
Penguin Books Ltd., 80 Strand, London WC2R 0RL, England
Penguin Ireland, 25 St. Stephen's Green, Dublin 2,
Ireland (a division of Penguin Books Ltd.)
Penguin Group (Australia), 250 Camberwell Road, Camberwell, Victoria 3124,
Australia (a division of Pearson Australia Group Pty. Ltd.)
Penguin Books India Pvt. Ltd., 11 Community Centre, Panchsheel Park,
New Delhi - 110 017, India
Penguin Group (NZ), 67 Apollo Drive, Rosedale, North Shore 0632,
New Zealand (a division of Pearson New Zealand Ltd.)
Penguin Books (South Africa) (Pty.) Ltd., 24 Sturdee Avenue,
Rosebank, Johannesburg 2196, South Africa

Penguin Books Ltd., Registered Offices:
80 Strand, London WC2R 0RL, England

First published by Roc, an imprint of New American Library,
a division of Penguin Group (USA) Inc.

First Printing, August 2008
10 9 8 7 6 5 4 3 2 1

Copyright © S. L. Viehl, 2008
All rights reserved

For Frank Frazetta,
whose incredible art opened my
eyes to a universe of possibilities.

ACKNOWLEDGMENT

I would like to thank
Joely Sue Burkhart
for naming *Moonfire*, and for providing
a much-needed kick in the muse for me.

"The deviation of man from the state in which he was originally placed by nature seems to have proved to him a prolific source of diseases."

—Dr. Edward Jenner (1749–1823), creator of the smallpox vaccine

OTR FTE relay 194075/obdistr/source unknown:

Private-party free trader offers level-one unilateral bounty in return for the detainment, capture, or information leading to the apprehension of Terran experimental life-form Cherijo Grey Veil (aliases: Cherijo Reever, Cherijo Torin, SsureeVa, Jarn).

Grey Veil, a bioengineered clone, appears to be a typical Terran female (see embedded images). Educated on Terra as a cardiothoracic surgeon, the organism escaped custody and fled her creator, the late Terran physician/medical researcher Joseph Grey Veil. While serving as trauma physician to the multispecies colony on Kevarzangia Two, Grey Veil applied for and was denied sentient status by the Allied League of Worlds (reference SSD case #4165998-K2-GVC). The organism subsequently sought and was granted asylum by Jorenian HouseClan Torin.

Grey Veil is a highly intelligent and manipulative life-form, implicated in causing the Kevarzangian colonial epidemic, the capture of three hundred ALW ships during the Varallan disaster, the destruction of Hsktskt slave depot world Catopsa, the Oenrallian upheaval, the Jado Massacre, the Akkabarran uprising, and the Vtaga plague. Grey Veil's last known location was serving as a crew member on board the Jorenian star vessel *Sunlace*, TWSID M7774E1691V.

Responders should transmit all related data, signals, and scans to inquirer via OTR FTE obdistr relay; mark S/CGV-LAS 0451 and date. Information directly leading to the location and apprehension of Grey Veil will be rewarded with a level-one bounty fee of four million stan credits.

WARNING: To date Grey Veil has successfully evaded or escaped ALW and Faction custody. She was last known to be traveling under the protection of Duncan Reever, former Hsktskt spy and telepathic linguist, as well as an entourage of battle-trained Jorenian warriors. Grey Veil and her companions are considered extremely dangerous and should not be directly approached or contacted without appropriate forces and safety measures.

One

"Who are you?"

That was a very good question.

I looked up from the chart I was reading and waited to see if the tall, broad, blue-skinned Jorenian male on the other side of the berth had anything more to say. His people, I knew from experience, talked a great deal. When his hands went still and he glared at me with his all-white but still functional eyes, I assumed he had finished. The style and color of his tunic, like my own, indicated that he was this ward's senior medical healer.

His patient's condition indicated that he wasn't a very good one.

"I am a visiting physician. A nurse on this ward indicated this patient was in some distress." I saw no reason to further identify myself or explain the situation. Every time I did, the subsequent reactions of those around me made it impossible for me to do the work. "Was it your decision to treat this female's condition with only native dermal emollients?"

"I do not discuss my treatments with outsiders." His hands moved to accompany his words with cutting bluntness. "We care not for Terrans interfering with our kind. Put down that chart and leave this facility now."

I ignored his hostility toward Terrans as well as his orders, and focused instead on the patient between us. The female lay unconscious, a bleeding rash marring every inch of her pale blue skin. Monitors showed her vitals were slowing, and notes on the chart told me that she had proven unresponsive to conventional antibiotic therapy.

This might be the homeworld of my adopted family, and the natives here important allies, and we all might be dead five minutes from now, but those were not reasons to excuse diagnostic incompetence.

"You did not perform abdominal scans or take a personal history. Nor did you contact her House-Clan to inquire as to the origins of her illness." I would have to note this on the chart and later discuss improving Jorenian triage and assessment procedures with Squilyp, HouseClan Torin's Senior Healer. Providing that we survived treating this patient, of course. "What is your name?"

"I am Tarveka, ClanSon Zamlon, attending healer," he snapped back. "As for this female, she was admitted in a state of delirium, and has since been incapable of coherent communication. The skin rash she suffers from has made it impossible to identify her HouseClan mark"—he pointed to the side of her throat where all Jorenians bore the distinctive black birthmark symbolic of their respective natal clans—"but it hardly necessitates the performance of any internal scans."

The rash had distorted the outlines of the patient's birthmark, turning it into a black smear. "What *did* you do for her?"

"As she is suffering from dermatitis, I performed a dermal scan and took some tissue samples for culture. The results should be back from our forensic lab tomorrow morning." He made an impatient gesture. "Have you nothing better to do than disrupt this ward with your uninformed inquiries?"

I was tempted to point out that his shouting had disrupted the ward far more than my evaluation of his patient, but the greater problem occupied the berth. I almost felt grateful for his initial, inaccurate assessment and the manner in which he had bungled her treatment. He'd probably saved his own life as well as the patient's, and those of everyone else on the ward.

"This female's condition will not be resolved by skin treatments." I switched off the chart display and met his antagonistic gaze. My knees wanted to buckle, but this was not Akkabarr; I no longer had to prostrate myself before angry males. In fact, my new life gave me the right to challenge them. "Do you wish to assist me, or is defending your original, erroneous diagnosis of more importance to you?"

"What say you? *Assist* you? Think you that I am a nurse?" Dark color flushed the skin of his face, and the elegant lids around his all-white eyes narrowed. "You deliberately insult me."

"Only if you are correct about this patient's condition, and I am not." I displayed some of my teeth. "Fortunately, you are not."

"Making new friends, Doctor?"

We both turned as a one-legged Omorr male hopped over to the end of the berth. HouseClan Torin Senior Healer Squilyp's dark pink skin, three upper limbs, and long, white, prehensile facial tendrils formed a colorful contrast to the uniformly blue-skinned, black-haired Jorenians around us. So did his scowl, which he directed at me.

I aggravated Squilyp, but then, I did the same to a lot of my new friends.

The Omorr had brought me with him to the facility this morning to, in his words, "keep me out of trouble." My husband, Duncan Reever, and our adopted Jorenian family, HouseClan Torin, were presently meeting with planetary security officials to brief them on matters of intergalactic importance. That was how they referred to any matter concerning me.

I did not wish to be on this world or among these people. I had no desire to be of importance on a galactic, planetary, continental, or even provincial scale. If no one ever paid any attention to me again, it would not upset me. I simply longed to be with Reever, the only one who truly understood me.

I should have been with him. We had time now to begin our investigation of the mysterious black crystal that my surrogate mother, Maggie, claimed was spreading like a cancer through our galaxy. Reever had already contacted an old Terran comrade who had promised information about the Odnallak, the last survivors of the race that created the black crystal.

Also ever present on my mind were the results from the latest series of medical tests I had performed on my husband. Reever did not yet know that the chameleon cells in his body, which had twice repaired fatal injuries he had received, had also infiltrated every organ in his body.

Reever, like me, was no longer precisely human. Somehow I had to find the words to tell him that.

"Doctor?" Squilyp prompted, tugging me free from the snarl of my thoughts.

"I have disagreed with this healer's assessment and treatment of this patient," I told the Omorr as I offered him the chart. "He regards my professional opinion as a personal insult. We must move quickly to treat this female—"

"She is ignorant and insolent," Tarveka said, interrupting me. "She insulted me, and while I am not Torin, I do not need some bigoted offworlder provoking me into a declaration of ClanKill."

"You *have* been busy," the Omorr said to me.

"I want this Terran removed from the ward," Tarveka said, drawing himself up with great dignity. "At once."

Being labeled as a Terran annoyed me. Although Terra was my natal world, I knew little of it or its native inhabitants. They were said to be isolationists and xenophobes, obsessed with themselves and maintaining genetic purity.

My body might appear Terran in form, but I was hardly human. I wasn't even the original occupant of my body; I had been born to it on Akkabarr after point-blank gunshot wounds had destroyed my former self's mind. I came to life on the day that she died, and was made one of the Iisleg, the people of the ice. Our ancestors had been abducted from Terra and brought as slaves to Akkabarr, but the only thing we had in common with Terrans was our DNA.

I was Jarn of Akkabarr, not Cherijo Torin of Terra.

Her name in my mind made my stomach clench. The Iisleg never spoke of the dead. They belonged to the Gods.

I did not relate any of this to Healer Tarveka. Trying to explain my existence, previous identity, beliefs, and present state of consciousness to a stranger often took hours, and usually required some visual aids. Besides that, if we didn't deal with this patient, and soon, she and everyone on this ward were going to die, including us.

Now I simply had to relay that to these males without sending them both into uncontrolled hysterics.

Squilyp took the chart and scanned the display. "Senior Healer, do you know who this Terran is?"

"Squilyp," I said. "We do not have time to waste on trifling matters. Please don't."

"You are acting like an Iisleg again." To Tarveka, the Omorr repeated, "Do you know who she is?"

Tarveka made an impatient, negative gesture.

"In addition to being a member of HouseClan Torin and the Savior of Varallan," Squilyp said, "the chief physician in charge of rebel forces during the Akkabarran Insurrection, and the named blood kin of TssVar, the new Hsktskt Hanar, she also happens to serve as a member of the Ruling Council of Joren." He paused for a moment to enjoy the stunned look on the Jorenian's face. "May I introduce Dr. Cherijo Torin?"

Trust Squilyp to condense my two lifetimes into a handful of words. I watched most of the healthy dark blue color fade from the Jorenian healer's face, leaving it taut and chalky-looking. "You did not mention that I am also an amnesiac, a dead handler, and a bioengineered clone."

"I will remember to," the Omorr assured me, "the next time you try to provoke someone into declaring ClanKill."

"Healer . . . Torin." Tarveka seemed to be out of breath. "Your pardon. I—I had no idea you would . . . that you . . ." He shuffled back several steps, thumped himself in the chest, and gestured toward the patient. "Please. I would be honored. I will follow. Ah. Any advice, of course. Please."

"It's nice to meet you, too." As a proper Iisleg woman, that was not something I should have said, but my speech patterns were changing. In fact, since regaining memories of my former self through an intense mind link with my husband, I never knew *what* would come out of my mouth. I ignored Squilyp's sharp look as I stripped off my gloves and signaled a nurse. "Prepare the surgical suite."

"Surgery?" Tarveka took a step toward the patient's berth, as if to protect her from me. He also seemed to regain instant control of his lung function and speech center. "How do you intend to treat dermatitis with surgery?"

"The rash is a symptom, not the cause of her condition," I said. "My abdominal scans show a foreign mass lodged in the primary pyloric sphincter, restricting the passage between the lower chamber of the stomach and the small intestine."

"It sounds like a gastric bezoar." Squilyp took my datapad and reviewed the scan results. "Why is the scan so indistinct?"

"The mass is reflecting it."

"I cannot believe this rash to be the result of a concretion in the GI tract," the Jorenian healer said. "With all due respect, Healer Torin, an accumulation of unabsorbed fiber or food is not uncommon among those of us who travel offworld for the first time."

"Synthetics and alien foodstuffs can be difficult for them to digest," the Omorr agreed. "Are you sure it's not the scanner malfunctioning? It shouldn't be this fuzzy."

"It is not a foodball," I said, trying not to clench

my teeth, "or a hairball. Nor is the scanner at fault. It is a—"

"Whatever its composition, we should begin with a gastrointestinal probe, to determine what formed the mass," the Omorr said, giving me a disapproving glance. "There are any number of nonsurgical treatments we can use for dissolution or removal. Enzymatic disruption, gastric lavage—even pulse lithotripsy."

I had to disguise a shudder at the thought of anyone using focused-light lithotripsy on this patient.

"That would be extremely unwise." I tugged back the linen sheet and raised the edge of the patient's gown, exposing her abdomen. "Observe how densely the rash covers her torso. Here"—I indicated the median area beneath her sternum—"the dermatitis disguises a recent vertical cell displacement measuring two-point-three centimeters. A puncture wound, likely inflicted by a sharp object, perhaps a bladed weapon. It ruptured the small intestine, and although the peristalsis has prevented any leakage, peritonitis is imminent." Among other things.

"She was stabbed?" Tarveka murmured, aghast and furious. Jorenians were extremely protective of their kin, and would eviscerate anyone who even threatened to hurt them. "Who could do such a thing on Joren and escape ClanKill?"

"I cannot say, but whatever pierced her body likely deposited the mass into her stomach cavity. She is tachycardic and hypotensive; her condition is deteriorating rapidly." I didn't want to say more in front of the Jorenian, so I turned and addressed the nurse. "I will need a drone surgical assistance unit, a shielded container in which to deposit the mass, and an isolation chamber prepared with full detox for recovery."

"Healer, should I not prep the patient?" the nurse wanted to know.

"I thank you, but I will do that." I went to a diagnostic unit, cross-referenced the forensic database, and entered all the information I had discovered from my scans. The unit compared the data to all such devices known to the Jorenians.

Device not found. Just as I had suspected.

"What are you looking for?" Tarveka came to my side. He looked distressed and still slightly affronted. "Permit me to assist you, Healer."

"I prefer drones in the operating room," I lied. I thought of the communications center, located on the lowest level of the hospital. Sending him there would get him out of my face. "Would you be so kind as to go and inform HouseClan Torin that my return to the pavilion will be delayed?"

"Of course." Hiding his irritation with the exquisite manners of his kind, the Jorenian made a complicated hand gesture of regret and respect, and left the ward.

Squilyp put a membrane on my arm as soon as the Jorenian was out of earshot, and said, "You are not being completely candid. Why do you want a shielded container, and why won't you let a nurse prep her? Why are you accessing the weapons database? You have *never* liked using drones in surgery."

"I will not know for certain until I open her up." The look in his dark eyes made me add, "Don't become alarmed, Senior Healer, but the abdominal wound smells of destabilized arutanium."

His gildrells straightened into stiff, white spikes. "You can *smell* that?"

"During the rebellion, we would always check casualties for the odor," I admitted. "Our wounded were sometimes used by the Toskald that way. I will not know for certain until I open her abdomen."

"But Jarn, for there to be traces of destabilized arutanium—"

"Someone had to plant an explosive inside her body," I finished for him. "One that has yet to detonate. Which is why, when I go into surgery, you must evacuate everyone from this facility."

Squilyp wished to argue with me, but he now knew why we did not have time to debate my decision to operate. He did, however, insist I activate the transmitter in my vocollar and keep the channel open as I worked on the patient. A training monitor in the surgical suite would provide a visual feed for him to observe the entire procedure.

"You may need something," he argued, "and you will not be able to send the drone out to retrieve it for you."

I was not enamored of the idea of being monitored while I worked, but he was right. It would also allow me to quickly relate exactly what I found inside the patient's body, and how much danger it presented to the facility and surrounding area. "Very well."

While I made the adjustments to my vocollar, the Omorr instructed the nurses to begin moving the patients, and then came over to give me an earpiece.

"This will allow for two-way communication," he advised me. "I have summoned Torin security to surround the facility. What should I tell Reever?"

"Tell him that I am working," I said as I injected the patient with neuroparalyzer and secured her body with motion restraints. I rolled the berth over to the surgical suite, but I didn't transfer her onto an operating platform. I couldn't take the chance of jarring her and possibly triggering an explosion.

Squilyp stayed with the patient while I donned a surgical shroud, and then stopped me as the drone surgical assistance unit rolled its instrument tray past us and into the suite. "I cannot allow you to do this alone. I will stay and assist."

The Omorr could be very male when it came to situations like this. He would also die along with the patient if the round exploded while I was operating. Thanks to my bioengineered physiology, I would not.

"You'll get out of here and keep me on remote monitor, or I'll signal your mate and tell her what you're doing," I told him as I fastened a surgical mask over the lower part of my face. "Then I'll signal mine."

"You would not dare."

I looked at him over the edge of my mask and let Cherijo's words answer him. "Try me."

"Of course you would." He sighed. "Very well, Doctor. If you change your mind—"

"I won't." I swept a hand toward the ward exit panels. "Get out."

When Squilyp had left, I grasped the edge of the gurney and eased the patient through the air lock and into the main surgical suite. The drone had followed its programmed instructions and set up for an intestinal laparotomy while I scrubbed.

"Initiate sterile field." As the containment generators created an envelope of clean air around us, I administered the appropriate prophylactic antibiotics and instructed the drone to commence anesthesia before I spoke to Squilyp. "Senior Healer, is the channel clear?"

"It is," the Omorr said over the earpiece as I used a lascalpel to make the midline incision. "This is madness, you know."

"It is a routine procedure with potentially hazardous complications," I corrected. "Cherijo's first surgery after leaving Terra was much like this."

"You remember that bowel obstruction?" Like everyone who knew my former self, Squilyp still hoped I would recover the memories of that life.

"No, I read about it in her entries on Kevarzangia Two. And it was a strangulated colon." I did not personally recall the procedure, but thanks to Cherijo's journals and my husband's telepathic abilities,

I knew many details of my former life. "She did not mention if the surgery was a success."

"It was, barely," Squilyp said. "Another physician named Rogan had misdiagnosed the patient, you told me, and you had to remove the entire bowel, which had turned putrid. She nearly died."

I felt an odd shift in my mind as learned memories blended with my own. "Strangulation obstruction carries a twenty-five to thirty percent mortality rate if surgery is delayed more than thirty-six hours after onset of symptoms. The patient lived. Did I clone a new colon for her?"

"She was an Orgemich," Squilyp said. "That species has twin bowels."

I could just imagine what Cherijo would have said: *I should have strangled Rogan with the gangrenous one.*

Once I had cut the patient's abdomen open, I performed a visual inspection of the stomach and small intestine. Jorenians had the same basic digestive system as most humanoids, with a few exceptions caused by adaptive evolution, such as their dual-chambered stomach, which allowed them to digest their food in stages.

"Color is normal, with some arterial pulsation. I see a considerable amount of distention in the valve, but the tissue appears viable. Thermal scanner." I used the noninvasive instrument to pinpoint the exact location of the mass. "The obstruction is still partially lodged in the pyloric sphincter adjunct to the secondary chamber. That is causing the bulge." I noticed an unusual, dull yellow discoloration around the insertion point in the sphincter, and felt my heart skip a beat.

"Use an isotonic lavage," the Omorr suggested. "You can introduce it through the esophagus and force the blockage to move down into the small intestine."

"Not this time," I said as I studied the scanner readout, although the yellow discoloration already told me exactly what had been shoved into the gut of this female. "The obstruction is a pulse grenade, modified with a contact trigger."

"That's impossible," the Omorr snapped. "Jarn, if she had that sort of grenade in her belly, she would have exploded the first time she took a deep breath or bent over."

"The grenade is encased in an organic material that quickly decays and dissolves once it's placed inside the body," I explained. "The process creates a significant echogenic arc of air around the grenade." I didn't bother explaining the trigger. If I did, he would insist I leave.

"If you bleed the air pocket or touch the grenade with any instrument, it could blow," Squilyp said.

"No." Memories from the rebellion rushed through me. Acrid smoke hanging in frigid clouds. Wet, red ice. Kneeling beside a rebel who had bitten through his lips to keep from screaming. Like all Iis-leg men, he believed that if he showed bravery, he would be given a second chance to live. He had died three minutes later. "I know what this is. What it does."

"Then you know you can't remove it," he added. "Close the patient and get out of there."

"I don't have to touch it." I held out my glove. "Mesentery clamp."

"Jarn."

"We'll have to think up a new name for this procedure, Senior Healer," I said as I clamped off the segment of bowel I intended to vivisect. "What do you think of gastric grenade bypass?"

"I think I should be addressing you as Cherijo," Squilyp said sourly. "You've become as reckless as she was."

"Gastric suction tube. This is not reckless. You should have seen how often we were forced to remove live ordnance from the wounded during the war. Sometimes we had to use blades and our hands, right there on the battlefield." I made a tiny incision, inserted the tube, and constricted the upper chamber of the stomach. That evacuated the contents of the lower chamber. "The patient should be scheduled for gastric reconstruction as soon as she is stable. I will perform the procedure."

"Stop her from blowing us all to the moons," Squilyp said. "Then we will worry about who rebuilds her stomach."

"Indeed. Bypass setter." I applied the large, vise-like instrument to the division between the divided stomach, and tightened the grip until it effectively clamped off the lower chamber. "Fill the specimen container with suspension gel," I told the drone as I brought down the lascalpel and adjusted the beam. Before I made the final cut, I asked Squilyp, "Has everyone left the facility?"

"Everyone but us."

I quickly changed my gloves and sterilized the outside surfaces to remove any possible trace of my DNA. "I am removing the grenade now." I cut the stomach in half, and then did the same to the clamped-off section of bowel on the other side of the bulging valve. Once I had resolved the severed vessels on either end, I carefully extracted the vivisected section in which the grenade remained lodged. Dull yellow streaked the entire section, and silver-blue, viscous liquid streaked the green blood dripping from either end. "Specimen container."

The drone presented the open container to me, and I carefully lowered the section and immersed it in the suspension gel. The smell of the device made my eyes water and sting.

"I'm sending out the drone," I told the Omorr. "Advise security that the grenade is leaking heavily."

"Arutanic fluid?"

"Yes. They must take it to be detonated immediately." With the drone gone, I had to pick up my own instruments, and I groped for a hemostat. "Can you come and assist me now, Senior Healer?"

The Omorr didn't reply, but hopped into the suite a few minutes later, properly scrubbed, gowned, and masked. "How is she?" he asked as I momentarily lowered the sterile field for him.

"Young and strong. If there are no complications from the vivisection or the arutanic fluid, and we can grow her another lower stomach chamber, she will survive. Clamp." I stopped the resection as a muffled blast from outside the facility caused a shimmer in the curtain of energy around us. "Security?"

"Militia." Squilyp eyed the view panel. "They sent in a combat munitions unit with a blast-absorption dome."

Since the building still stood, I assumed they had deliberately detonated the grenade. "How often do Jorenians present as living bombs?"

"Never in my experience." His dark eyes narrowed as he inspected the abdominal cavity for a moment. "Jarn, this was not an accident."

"I agree," I said as I began suturing again. "But who would do this, and why?"

"That is what I would like to know," the cool, unemotional voice of my husband, Duncan Reever, said over my earpiece.

Two

I expected my husband to feel angry over my decision to perform the grenade-removal surgery without his knowledge or consent. I anticipated a lengthy lecture about the risks I had taken and the potential harm that one mistake on my part might have inflicted on me. Reever loved me, and felt very protective of me; he would not accept my decision to operate on a living bomb with equanimity.

As Cherijo might have said, I was in for it.

I came out of surgery to find Reever waiting by the post-op cleansing unit. My husband wore his usual plain black garments, but had pulled his long golden hair back and folded it in a Jorenian warrior's knot. His handsome features remained as expressionless as always, but I could feel waves of tension emanating from his lean, battle-hardened frame.

"Duncan." I considered embracing him, but the patient's blood was spattered on the front of my surgical shroud. Also, he did not look as if he wished to be hugged.

"Jarn."

Unlike most of my friends and allies, my husband thought of me as Jarn of Akkabarr, not Cherijo of Terra. He had fallen in love with me, just as he had with the woman who had occupied my body before me. At times I felt I was the better wife, for the Terran doctor had been too devoted to her work to give him the attention and affection he craved.

At other times I wondered if Duncan had settled for me because he knew that he could never have Cherijo again.

Reever's eyes, which routinely shifted color between blue, green, and gray, now glittered as dark and threatening as snow clouds as he studied me. "What did you think you were doing?"

"The work." That seemed the safest response.

"You were brought here to tour the medical facility," he said, "not defuse a bomb disguised as a patient."

I heard no emotion in his voice, but in his eyes I saw something that reminded me of dark ice cracking at the edge of an expanding chasm.

Dævena Yepa. I was really in for it.

"I had no choice but to operate," I said as I removed my bloodied gloves. "There was no one else who knew how to remove the device."

Reever folded his arms. "Tell me what happened."

As I cleansed, I related my discovery of the

grenade, my decision to operate, and my reasoning for working alone. "There was no time to do anything but clear the ward and operate," I added. "I could not risk a detonation while waiting for assistance. Everyone around me would have died."

I could not be killed, or at least, not easily. My body had been engineered to be impervious to disease and injury by my creator, who had been determined to create the perfect physician.

"As powerful as your physiology is," my husband said, "you cannot regenerate disintegrated hands or limbs, Jarn. Did you first verify if the grenade possessed an internal timer, or a remote signal link?"

"I did, and it did not." Did he think me completely ignorant?

He regarded me for a long moment, and then said, "Tell me the rest."

I had made a bargain with my husband: I would not lie to him, and he would not use his ability to read my mind without my permission. We had both kept our promises, but Reever could also read my expressions and body language. He knew me well enough to know when I was holding back information.

"The grenade is not listed on the Jorenian weapons database," I said, very reluctantly. "It is one that the Toskald developed only toward the end of the rebellion. The grenade is implanted inside a wounded but still-living rebel. The air insulates it against the victim's tissues. It detonates only when the air bleeds out, or the trigger comes in direct contact with other human DNA."

He knew how desperately the Tos had fought in those last weeks; he had been caught and temporarily blinded during one of the worst surface battles. "Why would they use such a trigger, if it does not kill the victim immediately?"

This was the part that I genuinely did *not* wish to relate to him. "To stop the healers who treated injured rebels. To kill the vral."

Reever's jaw muscles tightened. "You are the only Iisleg healer in this quadrant, Jarn."

"Who would try to kill me here?" I asked him as I tossed aside the linen and stripped out of my surgical shroud. "The Toskald have been disarmed and exiled to the surface of Akkabarr. I cured the Hskt-skt plague on their homeworld, and helped to end the war between them and the Allied League of Worlds. The Jorenians adopted me long ago and, in theory at least, I am one of their Rulers. Who else have I pissed off?"

"I will find out," he advised me.

"That will not be easy." The choice of weapon troubled me as much as who had implanted it. "The Toskald had many allies. Perhaps one of them seeks revenge for the outcome of the rebellion."

Reever glanced at the unconscious female. "She may know who did this to her."

"Or she may not." I shrugged into my Jorenian healer's tunic and began fumbling with the unfamiliar fasteners. "If the goal was to assassinate me, they should have chosen other means. There was no guarantee that I would come anywhere near this patient." I shook my head. "Maybe it's just a coincidence. I didn't decide to come here until this morning. No one could have known."

"I don't believe in coincidence." Reever brushed aside my fingers, fastening my tunic as if I were no older than our daughter, Marel. Then he rested his hands on my shoulders. "The trigger was specific. You, Marel, and I are the only Terrans on Joren. This bomb was meant for one of us."

"It was meant for the one most likely to reach inside the female's body and remove it," I pointed out. "That would be me."

"Assassinating you would create worldwide outrage." Reever's fingers tucked a piece of my hair behind my ear. "Every HouseClan on Joren would wish to retaliate."

Jorenians were a peaceful, happy species, until someone threatened a member of their HouseClans, the enormous familial collectives in which their society organized themselves and their kin. It was said that they would not rest until they captured and punished whoever had made the threat. The only punishment Jorenians dealt out for such transgressions was immediate execution.

If one person had been behind this attempted murder, they would be found, declared ClanKill, and eviscerated alive.

"We will not tell them about the trigger," I decided. "They will not recognize it."

"It is not that simple. You are not only an adopted ClanDaughter of HouseClan Torin; you are Clan-Joren," my husband reminded me. "A member of Joren's Ruling Council, and every Jorenian House-Clan's named kin. Any threat to you is a threat to the entire planet. The assassins must have known this."

"No," I said, shaking my head as the possibilities whirled in my mind. "If what you say is true, and the Jorenians discover that the League or another government is behind this attack—"

"It could start a new war." Reever rubbed his eyes, the way he did whenever he remembered the long months of searching for me on Akkabarr. He had joined the rebels, and had been temporarily blinded during one of the battles. That battle had brought us back together, although I had had no memory of him.

I had seen too many battlefields myself. Thousands of faces from those ghastly places swarmed behind my eyes. Stiff, lifeless. Coated with white ice, blue ice, red ice. Torn, smashed, burned. Men and women. Children.

So many had died. Too many.

"No," I said again, the word hurting my throat as it came out.

My husband glanced through the view panel. "It may already be too late."

I looked past him to see Xonea Torin, captain of the *Sunlace*, leading a detachment of heavily armed Jorenian militia into the ward.

* * *

"What say you, Duncan?" Xonea Torin asked after the militia had inspected every inch of the ward. Taller and broader than Healer Tarveka, Xonea had the same solid white Jorenian eyes, with which he could intimidate with a glance. "Was this female sent to kill Cherijo?"

"She was admitted two days ago," Reever said. "The *Sunlace* did not enter orbit until this morning. She could not have known Jarn was going to come here. No one did."

"Then she came here to kill another." Xonea's dark brows lowered. "Who?"

"Her wounds prove that she did not implant the grenade in her own body," I told him. "Nor did she have any external means of triggering the device. She is a victim, Captain, not an assassin."

Xonea didn't appear convinced. "She must have been aware of what had been put inside her body. She could have warned the healers."

I detailed the patient's incoherent condition at the time she had been admitted, and added, "Blood scans still must be performed, but it is likely that they drugged her. They would not want their bomb to talk."

Light from the overhead emitters caught a strand of purple in Xonea's black hair as he turned to eye my patient. "She could have easily given herself the drugs."

"A suicide assassin would never have used a damaged grenade," Reever countered. "They are too unstable and apt to detonate at any moment. The one Jarn removed was leaking arutanic fluid."

Duncan Reever was biologically Terran and, like me, had little notion of what that meant. Reever's xenobiologist parents had abandoned him as a child to the care of the alien natives of the many worlds they had visited. A born telepathic linguist, Reever could absorb most alien languages through mind linking, so perhaps they felt he would be safe. Years of full immersion in alien cultures and societies had instead destroyed his humanity. Eventually Reever's parents had retrieved him and brought him back to Terra to be educated, but it had been too late. Duncan had never learned things like human emotions and social skills, nor did he care to.

My ClanBrother was not a stupid man, and he had seen much of battle and warfare. He knew the tactics of terrorism. Without careful handling, it would not take long for him to come to the conclusions that Reever and I had.

There was one benefit to my husband's emotional handicaps, however. Reever could misdirect and deceive anyone, even a veteran soldier like Xonea.

Some of the lines around Xonea's mouth eased. "As you say, Duncan. What more can you tell me about this grenade?"

"It matches nothing on the Jorenian weapons database," Reever said. "I am inclined to think it was salvaged and rebuilt. Perhaps one of the slave-trader species meant to send a message to House-

Clan Torin for their involvement in ending the Faction's slave raids."

"Slavers." Xonea scowled. "They are cowardly enough to do something like this."

"Indeed." Reever put an arm around my waist. "My wife is weary after the hours in surgery, Captain. I would like to take her to the guest quarters to see our daughter, and have a meal and rest interval."

Xonea gave me a sharp look. "You should have said something."

"You two were so busy talking I couldn't get a word in edgewise." I started to smile at him, and then pressed my fingers against my runaway lips. Reever's memories of Cherijo had helped me make peace with my former self, but I would never feel at ease with hearing Cherijo's words come out of my mouth. "I am a little tired and hungry."

"Very well." Xonea made a quick gesture. "Until we find those responsible, you, Duncan, and Marel will be escorted and guarded by HouseClan warriors."

I started to protest—I was tired of being constantly watched over and guarded and followed—but my husband caught my eye and shook his head.

"I thank you, ClanBrother," I said, and noticed the militia allowing the medical staff back onto the ward. "Please have one of the nurses signal me when the patient regains consciousness. I will need to perform the post-op scans while she is awake and responsive."

One big, six-fingered blue hand made a sharp, negative gesture. "When the female awakes, I will first interrogate her."

"No, you will not," I said, with just as much force. "She was made into a bomb. I have just cut open her body and removed half of her stomach. You will leave her alone."

Xonea gave me an exasperated look. "I will not harm her, Cherijo, but she may be the only one who knows those who made this threat against our House."

"She won't be able to tell you anything if she's hemorrhaging," I snapped. "Until I decide she is well enough to speak to you, she will remain isolated, in recovery, and you will not go near her."

"I must agree with Healer Cherijo, Captain." Healer Tarveka joined us. "The patient's recovery time will be no more than two days."

Xonea's gaze went from my face to Tarveka's, and then he sighed. "Very well. But until I can question her, she is to remain in isolation and under constant monitor." He went over to speak with the warriors questioning the ward staff.

"The drugs I gave her before surgery will wear off in a few hours, not days," I murmured. "She will be awake and alert by nightfall." I met Tarveka's gaze. "You lied to him. Why?"

"I said nothing untruthful about the recovery time." He smiled down at me. "In some rare cases, two days are required for a Jorenian patient to regain full lucidity after surgery."

"Why mislead him, then?" I asked.

"I owe you a debt for saving my patient, and the Omorr believes that you and your bondmate will need this time to make preparations." Tarveka handed me the relay pad. On it was the text of an open relay from an anonymous free trader offering an enormous bounty for capturing me alive.

"Four million stan credits?" I could not believe a bioengineered life-form would be worth so much. "Who would pay such a sum for a female?"

Tarveka looked at our sleeping patient. "Perhaps the more pressing question is, who would try to keep everyone else from collecting it?"

A squad of armed warriors escorted Reever and me when we left the medical facility, and most of HouseClan Torin were waiting to greet us when we arrived at the Torin pavilion. We did not have a private moment to talk until later that night, after we had put our daughter to bed.

"I like it here, Mama," Marel said through a yawn, her eyelids drooping. Fine curls of golden hair framed her small face and spilled over the side of her pillow. "All the food is made of flowers, and there are so many kids, although they're all bigger than me."

Jorenian children did not stay small for long. Fasala, Marel's favorite playmate and the only Clan-Daughter of our friends, Salo and Darea Torin, already stood six feet tall.

"Small females are faster than large ones," I told

her. "Their size slows them down; they can never catch us."

She giggled and then sighed. "I like the silver grass and the way the plants sing, too. And ClanUncle Xonea smiles at everyone here."

Her ClanUncle would not be smiling when he discovered that someone was hunting me.

"I am glad." I bent down and kissed her brow, concealing the fear I felt for my child. My former self had eradicated all material evidence of our daughter's existence in order to protect her, but if they had found me here on Joren, they might well find her. Before I left, I whispered one of the old Iisleg charms to her. "Dream of rain, daughter."

Reever chose to sit and tell Marel stories until she fell asleep, so I went out to the front room and prepared two servers of Omorr tea. I didn't like Jorenian brews, which were far too sweet, or the bitter, dark teas my husband favored. Squilyp's mate, Garphawayn, had given me a mellow, Omorr blend that tasted faintly of mint and spice; it was one of the few teas that Reever and I both found palatable.

Two small, four-legged felines emerged from under the table and came to stand before me. One was a large silver-furred male with luminous blue eyes, named Jenner after an ancient Terran physician my former self had idolized. The other, his black-furred mate, inspected me with her gold-green gaze. Reever called her Juliette.

I had wanted to kill them and eat them, several

times. I was not permitted to slay living things for food, however, and the ensleg were especially fond of living things they called "pets." Reever convinced me that the two cats were harmless, and provided much entertainment and companionship for him and Marel. I still did not trust them; the felines on my world did not entertain or keep company with people. They were usually too busy ripping out their throats and feeding on their dead bodies.

"I know the child fed you after our meal," I advised them. "You cannot be hungry."

Jenner rubbed his head against my leg and uttered a deep yowl, as if to say, *Your ankles seem appetizing.*

"You should be out hunting your own food." I eyed Juliette, who chimed in with a higher, more plaintive sound. Her little belly seemed to hang lower than the last time I had looked at her. I reached down to slide my hand under her, feeling a small, clustered mass inside her abdomen. "Do not tell me you are . . ." I took a scanner out of my medical case and passed it over her, and groaned when it detected five distinct heartbeats; one strong, four faint. "How did this happen?"

Jenner plopped down on his haunches next to his mate and showed me his sharp little teeth as he yawned. *How do you think it happened?*

We had just found homes for the felines' last litter; now there would be another. I uttered the most vicious Iisleg obscenities I could think of under my breath as I took out a container of the dried, smelly bits of protein our daughter called "cat snacks" and opened the lid.

"I should make a snack out of you," I told the felines as I dropped a handful on the floor between them.

"You agreed not to kill the pets." My husband came up behind me and encircled my waist with his arms. "The tea smells good. So do you."

Since leaving Akkabarr, I had been obliged to follow the ensleg custom of cleansing my body at least once a day. Such self-indulgence had never been possible on my homeworld, as drinking and cooking used up most of the meltwater. At first Reever forced me to bathe so often I thought my skin would peel off, but I quickly became accustomed to the curious sensation of being clean all over every day.

"The female has something in her belly." I turned around, pressing myself shamelessly against him as I sought the comfort of his body. "And do you know? It is not a grenade."

"I am happy to hear it." Reever bent his head and kissed the outside curve of my ear. At the same time, his voice spoke in my head. *Jarn, the Torins have put at least two recording drones in the room.* His eyes shifted first to the huge cluster of flowers left in a jar in the center of the room, and then up to the emitters over our heads. *Do not say anything about the patient or the bounty.*

If I concentrated, I could speak inside my husband's mind just as clearly. *Why are they monitoring us? I thought we were allies.*

Xonea will claim it is a security precaution. Reever brushed aside my hair and trailed his fingers down the side of my neck. *I fear we did not completely dispel his suspicions.*

Cherijo had once been Chosen to be the only wife of Xonea's ClanBrother, Kao, now deceased. Unlike Iisleg men, who were permitted at least two wives, and could kill them and replace them as was necessary, Jorenians mated with one spouse for life. My former self's brief engagement to Kao was what had led to my adoption by the Torin. It also made me Xonea's ClanSister, a relationship he regarded as seriously as if we had actually been born from the same womb.

Xonea would do anything he thought necessary to protect me. Even if it meant spying on me and Reever.

Under the circumstances, I could think of only one solution that would protect our daughter and stop the Jorenians from going to war. *Duncan, we have to leave Joren.*

My husband swept me up into his arms and carried me into the chamber where we slept. Ensleg insisted on having separate rooms for eating, sleeping, and cleansing, and to insure they were not disturbed at such activities, put locks on the doors. Personal privacy was one of their concepts that I had found difficult to fathom, but being monitored without our permission made me see some of its merits.

As my husband stretched his long, lean body out

beside me on the sleeping platform, I unfastened his tunic and pushed it back, baring his chest. His skin, several shades darker than mine, felt smooth and resilient under my palms.

We can leave Joren tomorrow. He covered my hands with his. *But we cannot take Marel with us.*

Every muscle in my body tensed at the prospect of being separated from our child. I had never thought I would form a close bond to any person, but since discovering that Marel was the child of my body, I had become fiercely, almost irrationally attached to her.

The Torins will have fewer suspicions if we leave her behind. I pressed a hand over my eyes. *I know it is best, but I hate to be parted from her, Duncan. It is a blade, piercing my heart. If something were to happen—if she were hurt or fell sick, and I was not here to care for her—*

I know how you feel. When PyrsVar took her on Vtaga, I thought I would go mad. A thread of dark, ugly redness colored his thoughts. *We cannot ever risk her being captured and held hostage again.*

Agreed. I rolled on top of him, straddling him before looking around the room. *Did Xonea put one of his spy machines in here?*

He shook his head, his eyes darkening as I settled against him. "I thought you were tired," he said out loud.

"I am weary," I murmured as I bent down to put my mouth on his. "Not dead."

I was not a very good human, and still had much to learn about the ensleg among whom I would live.

Coupling, on the other hand, I had mastered quite soon after agreeing to be Reever's woman.

Coupling did not require much in the way of manners, words, or even thought. Our bodies had been fashioned to fit together, and the fitting of them provided an endless variety of sensation and satisfaction. Among the Iisleg a woman would never dare do the things I did to my husband in our bed, but I had never been a very good Iisleg, either.

I tore at his garments and then my own, trying to bare as much skin as I could before the need overwhelmed me. Since Reever had introduced me to the pleasure we could give to each other, I welcomed any chance to take his body into mine.

Thanks to what my creator had done while meddling with my genes, I did not scar, and despite receiving many serious wounds my skin remained as flawless as a young girl's. Reever's flesh, however, bore the scars of many battles. He had once been an arena slave, forced by the Hsktskt to fight other captives to the death. He had held back those memories from me, but I had watched him fight, and knew my fearless husband possessed frightening speed and inhuman agility.

Yet Reever actively avoided violence.

I knew why. When he had freed himself of the killing sands, he had vowed never to fight again. Still, he had fought for me, more times than I suspected I knew. He had gone into battle on Akkabarr, never wavering, so that he might find me again.

I bent to his chest, and as he slipped inside me, I

kissed each mark, the silver-white keloids like tear trails against my lips.

"I am yours," I whispered between each caress. "I am yours."

Three

Of all the Jorenians I had come to know on board the *Sunlace*, I trusted Salo and Darea Torin most. Darea had been the first to call me by my chosen name, Jarn, and had supported my decision to avert another war by going to Vtaga to help the Hsktskt combat the plague of memory. Salo had stood by me when I went against my husband's and Xonea's wishes to the contrary.

I signaled them that evening, and met with them in our quarters early the next morning. They agreed to care for my daughter while Reever and I went to inspect some nearby planetary systems for evidence of black crystal infection.

Not that either of them believed that to be the reason we were leaving Joren, but they were true friends, and did not question the excuse.

"Reever has gone to secure our transport," I explained as I served them tea. "We have both left recorded messages on the room console for her. We thought it best not to say farewell in person, to avoid having her again attempt to stow away and go with us."

"A wise decision," Salo said wryly. "Your Clan-Daughter can be quite determined."

"Xonea mentioned you will be leaving the pavilion tomorrow," I said to Darea. "Will having Marel with you change your plans?"

"It need not, unless you prefer we stay here," she said. "Whenever we return to Joren, we fly to the eastern provinces, to see friends and my natal kin. It is not a lengthy journey by glidecar, and I believe that Marel will enjoy meeting children from other HouseClans."

"I agree. Nothing pleases her more than exploring new places and people." I looked at Salo. "You must take the usual precautions, ClanCousin. There can be no photo images or vid recordings made of her. Our names must never be mentioned. No off-worlder can know that she is our daughter."

He nodded. "Duncan has created a protective identity for her, which we will use. We are to say that she is blood kin to HouseClan Kalea."

I frowned. "No one will believe that our child is Jorenian. She is too small, and the wrong color."

"Kalea's ClanLeaders, Jakol and Sajora, are half Terran," Darea explained, "and they both have the same color skin. I signaled them last night, and they have agreed to verify the claim, should any inquiries be made."

"That is very kind of them." I forced a smile.

"Marel should eat and sleep well for you, as long as she is not given too many treats between meal intervals. There is a cloth toy that she clutches when she goes to sleep; she sometimes misplaces it, so I put it under her pillow during the day. Her hair must be brushed twice daily, or her curls become tangled—" I stopped, aware that I was babbling.

"You need not worry, Jarn." Darea put her hand on my shoulder. "Your Marel is as dear to us as our Fasala. We will never allow harm to come to her."

"I thank you for that." I heard the door chime. "That will be Squilyp; he is to take me to Reever." I pressed Darea's hands between mine, and nodded to her bondmate. "I thank you, ClanSon Torin."

"Healer Jarn," Salo said, his deep voice gentle as he performed a formal bow. "Walk within beauty."

I was not given the chance to walk anywhere. Squilyp escorted me to a glidecar, one of the ground vehicles the Torins used to travel around their land. I was made to climb inside and sit in it. I tried not to look back at the pavilion as the Omorr engaged the engine and drove away.

"I am not leaving for Omorr until Namadar," Squilyp said, referring to the Jorenian's annual planetary festival to honor their central deity. "I will make routine inquiries with Salo and Darea and assure that Marel is well. Did you pack everything you might need?"

"Reever assembled the supplies and the equipment he requires for performing surveys for black crystal. I have all the emergency medical supplies we might need for the journey." I opened the top of my medical case and took out a tan-colored blob sitting atop my instruments. The Lok-teel, an intelligent mold that among other things absorbed organic waste and sterilized surfaces with its body fluid, crawled up my sleeve and slipped inside my collar, where it nestled between my breasts. "Do you think the child will miss us?"

"Yes, but we will be here to comfort her." He gave me a sharp look. "You will not weep now."

"No." I almost smiled. "I will not weep."

A short time later we arrived at an auxiliary transport dock, where Reever was waiting with the ship he had acquired for our sojourn.

"I was resolved to say nothing, as it is not my place to disapprove of this venture," Squilyp said, his gildrells undulating with his agitation. "But Jarn, I think it foolhardy for you and Duncan to travel alone."

"It is how it must be." I looked out at the ships that were landing and launching. "If my child is unhappy with being left behind, or cared for by Salo and Darea, you will signal me and tell me." He nodded. "I thank you, Senior Healer." I climbed out of the vehicle and started for the gate.

Squilyp hopped quickly to catch up with me. "Wait. You know that the Torins will be happy to send a detachment of guards with you and Duncan. You don't have to tell them why you're leaving

Joren." He stopped me just before we entered the security checkpoint. "You're not listening to me."

"I have done nothing but listen to you since I left Akkabarr," I assured him. "You asked me to trust you, and I have." I looked into his worried eyes. "Now you must do the same for us."

"You could be walking into a trap," he said, his gildrells snarling with his agitation. "Have you thought of that?"

I had to remind him of an unpleasant truth. "Squilyp, when you and Reever and the others were searching for Cherijo, you knew that finding her—me—could reveal the truth behind the Jado Massacre. That what Cherijo had witnessed might goad the Jorenians and their allies into a war with the League of Worlds."

He turned his back on me and inspected the cargo haulers moving freight out to the loading docks. "It is not the same as this."

"It is *exactly* the same." I felt a surge of sympathy for him. "You concealed your feelings, but part of you hoped that Reever would not find me, because if he did, and the truth were revealed, millions might die."

His gildrells became spokes. "I suppose Garphawayn told you all that."

I nodded. "She admired your courage."

"My courage." He glared at me. "I was your best friend. You taught me more about surgery than I can say. Reever spent two and a half years quietly going

mad while he looked for you. But if it had ever become a matter of choice—"

"One life to save millions?" I asked softly. "There
is no choice in that, my friend."

His eyes glittered. "I thought of it, and I attempted to prepare myself to act, but I could not
wish you dead. Since you returned to us, I
have tried everything I know to bring back your
memories—"

"And I am grateful, Squilyp." I took my medical
case from him. "Let Reever and me do this now. For
all those who will be lost if I do not."

Three strong arms came around me as the Omorr
embraced me. Against the top of my head, he muttered, "You will send regular relays, and let me
know that you are well and not being abducted, enslaved, or otherwise harmed. Or I will come after
you myself."

"I promise."

I left Squilyp at the gate, where he stood and
watched me until I reached the docking pad and the
ramp to the scout ship, where Reever was waiting. I
turned and lifted a hand.

The Omorr scowled as he returned the gesture,
and hopped back to the glidecar.

"Husband," I said as I inspected the vessel,
which in close proximity seemed rather small. "This
will be our transport?"

"She's called *Moonfire*," he told me. "The very latest in Jorenian research vessels, scout class."

I set down my case and walked around the nose. "The latest, or the smallest?"

"The latest," he said firmly. "And the fastest."

Although *Moonfire* was hardly larger than a standard ship-to-surface launch, it had a sleek, narrow shape made glossy by hundreds of thousands of dark green, rectangular hull plates. A row of round, deep-space transceiver ports formed an arch over the blue-green viewer panels. The fuselage expanded and divided itself into five curved propulsion thrusters, which cradled a small escape pod. The ship could have easily been mistaken for the bejeweled, clawed hand of some enormous deity.

"It is a beautiful little thing," I told my husband. "But hardly inconspicuous."

"On the contrary." Reever took a small device out of his pocket. "The Zamlon have been experimenting with various types of vessel camouflage." He put his thumb to the device, and a purple halo of light appeared at the scout's nose, illuminating the dark green hull plates briefly before they began to fade. In another moment the ship had vanished from sight.

I blinked, and then looked all around us. "Where is it?"

The corner of Reever's mouth curled in a rare show of amusement. "It didn't go anywhere. Go ahead, reach out and touch it."

I peered at the place where the ship had stood, and saw the very faintest transparent distortion rippling the air. When I reached out, I felt a strange, cool vibration and then the solid surface of the hull. Beneath the shadow of my palm and forearm, a section of the dark green panels reappeared.

"The hull plates are programmed to respond to the environment," Reever told me. "When activated, they project an image that matches the ship's surroundings."

"A ship covered in devious mirrors." I shook my head. "Ensleg wonders never cease."

Reever and I boarded the scout, and as he took the helm and prepared for our launch I stowed my medical case and took a brief look at the rest of the ship.

Moonfire offered two small living chambers, a tiny galley, and storage compartments filled with equipment and provisions. The propulsion systems and environmental controls took up the rest of the space. It would be cramped, but compared to the ice cave krals in which I lived on Akkabarr, it seemed a palace.

I joined Reever at the helm and, at his gesture, sat down in the copilot's seat and fastened the launch harness across my shoulders and torso. I did not touch the wide panel of controls, viddisplays, and databanks in front of me. "To where do we journey first?"

"I have arranged to meet with Alek Davidov," he said, referring to the trader who had once helped him free Hsktskt slaves. "He has many connections among the free traders. He can help us track the one that issued the bounty on you. He may also be able to help us discover who planted the grenade on your patient."

I had not met any other Terrans besides Reever. "Do you trust him?"

He turned to me, as if surprised at the question. "Davidov posed as a slaver for many years. He used his family's wealth to buy and free thousands taken by the Faction during raids. To my knowledge, he has never asked for recompense from any of them."

"Then he is a generous man for a Terran," I said. "Or a complete fool."

"Alek is . . . complicated. Damaged, in some ways, by his experiences." He paused. "I know it is difficult for you to trust strangers, but I once counted Alek as my closest friend."

Friendship was another ensleg concept that did not sit well with me, but I trusted my husband's judgment. Unlike normal humans, Reever could not form emotional attachments, so his trust had to be earned.

As for Davidov, I would reserve my opinion for now. "I look forward to knowing him."

Transport issued our launch slot, and we left Joren without incident. I felt a wave of panic sweep over me as the planet dwindled behind us and *Moonfire* left orbit, but I forced myself to look out at the night snow of stars spreading out before us.

"Do you know, when I left Akkabarr for the first time," I said, "I watched my world shrink, and panicked. I thought the heat from all the ensleg ships in orbit was melting it away. And then, on the journey here, to see all that endless blackness, and more stars than I could count . . ." I looked through the view panel. "I never knew the universe so vast, and myself so small."

Reever input something on the controls. "I never feared space as much as the worlds to which I sojourned," he admitted. "When I was very young, I suffered a great deal of anxiety at the prospect of meeting new species. Each time my parents initiated landing procedures, I would run to my quarters and hide in a different place, hoping it would be the one that they would not discover. Of course, they always found me. Then I would spend the next six months or year among whatever species inhabited that world while my parents performed their research."

What Reever's parents had done to him revolted me. "Did you fear being left with the ensleg?"

"Most of them were friendly and curious, but I hated them touching me. When they did, their languages invaded my head and made themselves plain to me." He made an adjustment on the helm console. "You should have heard them, using translators to welcome my mother and father, all the while secretly hating them and thinking of ways to make them leave."

My heart ached for him. "Did you never speak of this to your parents?"

He shrugged. "My mother did not believe in linguistic telepathy. She was like all Terran scientists, and put trust only in what could be seen, smelled, heard, and touched. What my father thought of me, I cannot say. He would not be distracted from his work by an anxious boy."

I reached out and placed my hand over his. "We cannot choose to whom we are born. We can only learn from their mistakes and try not to repeat them with our young ones." My heart tightened as I thought of Marel's little face.

"I did not wish to leave her behind, Jarn," Reever said bleakly, "any more than you did."

I curled my hand tightly around his. "I know."

According to the signal Reever had received from Alek Davidov, we were to rendezvous with his ship, the *Renko*, near a trade depot world at the very edge of the Varallan system.

"There." I saw the trader vessel stationed above Trellus, a dead world made habitable by the installation of a dome colony. Cargo ships passing through the system frequently stopped at the planet to refuel, pick up supplies, and enjoy the various amusements. Oddly there were no other ships in orbit at the moment. "Should I send a relay?"

"That won't be necessary." Reever touched an emitter on the communications panel that glowed red. "It's Alek. He's signaling for permission to shuttle over."

There must have been a full crew on board the *Renko*, but my husband's friend came alone in a launch to *Moonfire*. It had been part of their agreement about the meeting, that no one else know that I accompanied my husband.

No matter how loyal Davidov's crew were, four million stan credits would loosen any tongue.

As the men connected the two vessels so that Davidov could climb into our ship, I went back to the galley and prepared food and drink. I did not know what the ensleg custom was, but among my people it was rude to welcome a friend without preparing a meal for them. Men were also more at ease with each other if they shared food as well as talk.

It also gave me something to do besides imagine what would happen if my husband's friend had grown less noble since the last time they had met.

"Duncan." Long legs clad in black trousers climbed down the ladder from the upper hatch. Davidov jumped down the last two feet and peered around him. "Is this a fighter made to look like a launch, or do your Jorenian friends have a sense of humor?"

My husband clasped hands with the Terran. "It is good to see you again, Alek."

I stood back, out of Davidov's line of sight, so that I could have a private look at him. The two men might have been brothers, so similar were their height, build, and coloring. Then the subtle differences became more apparent to me.

Davidov had darker, thinner hair, which he wore shorn like an Iisleg female's. Above a wide-bridged nose, two night-colored eyes shifted all around, taking in everything. An angle-shaped scar on his cheek pointed to his left ear. His ready smile thinned his full lips around pretty teeth, but his good humor did not lighten the flat blackness of his eyes. I disliked people who manipulated their facial expressions to make others think they felt something they did not. I breathed in and became even more unsettled.

Although Davidov appeared Terran and healthy, I could not smell him at all.

The Terran seemed to be looking for something other than Reever, his fingers splayed as if prepared to grab it. His next words confirmed my impression. "Where is this woman of yours that I've heard so little about?"

I stepped out of the doorway and came to stand beside my husband.

"This is my wife, Jarn," Reever said. "Jarn, my friend Aleksei Davidov."

"Call me Alek," the Terran said, regarding me as a jlorra might a limping stray. This two-legged snow tiger did not pounce, however, but offered a paw. "You are a lovely little thing, aren't you?"

I briefly touched his hand but didn't answer his inquiry. I was small, but I didn't consider myself particularly lovely. Among the Iisleg, I had been regarded as a skinny runt. Ensleg also had a habit of asking useless questions to which they did not expect answers.

"Show me the rest of this interesting plasteel can," Davidov said to Reever.

I waited in the corridor as my husband escorted his friend around *Moonfire*. As the ship's systems were limited, it didn't take long for the two men to return.

"Terran, obviously, but not the usual sort," Davidov was saying as the men rejoined me. "Jarn, your husband won't tell me how you two met. Did he purchase you from one of his old enemies, or were you so desperate that you had to settle for the likes of him?"

I raised my brows. "Reever and I met during the rebellion on Akkabarr. He was battle blind, and I repaired the damage to his eyes. Later, I threatened to kill him, but he talked me out of it and showed great courage. For that reason, and another, I agreed to be his woman."

"Really." He bent down, putting his face closer to mine to whisper, "Do you have an unattached sister, perhaps?"

He was attempting to use humor to flatter me, but among my people men did not compliment women, and women did not laugh at men. Reever did not respond to jests of any kind, so he also remained silent.

"I can certainly see the attraction between you two," Davidov said, chuckling and shaking his head. "Do you have a corner in this sardine can where we might sit and talk?"

"I have prepared food and drink for you in the galley." I gestured. "This way."

Davidov spent the next hour talking about his recent sojourns, pausing at times only for breath. Reever responded now and then, briefly, but seemed content to listen. I refused to eat and drink with the men and stood to one side, observing. On Akkabarr females did not eat until all of the males were finished and had left the shelter. An act of deference, but also an excellent way to learn what the men would otherwise never tell us.

I no longer had to follow those customs, but I wanted to watch the Terran. Something about him did not feel right. I had no evidence except that each time I looked at him, the hair on the back of my neck stood up.

"After trying *not* to walk on eggs for three months, let's just say I'll think twice before I board another breeding Tingalean," Davidov said, ending another anecdote about difficult passengers he had transported. "But enough about the trade. I've gathered some information about the bounty on your wife." He took a disc from inside his flight jacket and offered it to Reever. "Basically the signal source is untraceable; the originator used Bartermen channels to transmit the first relay. Whoever wants you, Jarn, knows how to cover his tracks."

His tone seemed odd—almost as if he admired the trader hunting me. "You assume a male issued the bounty?"

"Figure of speech." His teeth flashed. "I never assume anything. The Bartermen are also banking the reward and brokering the exchange and, from what I understand, they're doing it for nothing. Free of charge."

Reever inserted the disc in the galley terminal

and switched on the screen. "There is no such word as 'free' in the Bartermen language," he said as he skimmed the data. "Is this all you were able to find?"

The Terran nodded. "Not much, I know, but based on what there is, I'll wager every mercenary in the four quadrants is out hunting your beautiful wife."

Davidov didn't think I was beautiful. He might have wished me to think so, but his body language was projecting something very different. He didn't like me and, for some reason, he resented me. Perhaps it was jealousy over my relationship with Reever. The two men had been friends long before I became involved with Duncan.

Or it might be that Davidov didn't like me simply because of who and what I was. A cloned Terran, created to be the perfect physician.

"I would like to avoid the bounty hunters," my husband was saying.

"We could let it be known that I was killed by the grenade explosion," I told my husband. "Squilyp and I can use a little of my DNA to salt some organic ash. Scanners would then read and identify them as my remains."

Davidov looked intrigued. "A grenade exploded and you weren't killed?"

"The Jorenians would never support such a deception." Reever took my hand in his and squeezed it before he looked across the table at Davidov. "What else have you learned?"

"Nothing more about the bounty, my friend." He produced a sympathetic expression that fell just short of convincing. "However, if you'll allow me to, I'd like to consult with the lovely doctor here about a situation involving one of those shifters you want to find . . . what are they called?"

Reever exchanged a quick look with me. "The Odnallak."

"That's them." Davidov turned to me. "I heard you had some problems with them on Vtaga."

I didn't consider being choked with Odnallak bone dust or discovering that it had caused hundreds of deaths as "some problems." "What do you wish to know?"

"I heard an interesting story about them while I was passing through the N-Jui quadrant." Davidov settled back in his chair. "A long-route hauler and I were having a drink together one night, and after he got pretty well sauced he told me that he'd met one. Spent several weeks onboard a ship with it, in fact. Never knew it was a shifter until the day it left."

"Where did the Odnallak disembark?" my husband asked.

"That's the reason I had you meet me here." Davidov leaned over and tapped the view port. "The shifter got off right here, at Trellus. It's still down there, too. Evidently it's been hiding out on the colony ever since it was dropped off."

Reever frowned. "How could your friend be so sure that it disembarked on Trellus?"

"He brought it here. Damn thing posed as a regular passenger on his ship. He saw it change shape when it thought no one was watching, just before it strolled down the ramp." Davidov grinned. "According to him, they're the only species that can mimic other beings so exactly that you can't tell the difference between them and the real thing."

Some of what Davidov said was true, but the Odnallak were not harmless, and neither was their ability to shift form.

"We should go talk to the colonists on Trellus and confirm this rumor," I said to Reever. When Davidov shook his head, I said, "We will be discreet, of course."

"They won't let you land on the surface," the Terran said. "That's the other part of the nutty situation down there. Right after the Odnallak landed on Trellus, the colony went into complete and total isolation."

"Define isolation," my husband said.

"No one lands, and no one leaves," Davidov replied. "If any ships approach the colonial docks, they're fired on by the colony's battle drones until they leave or they're destroyed."

"How can they live like that?" I asked. "The surface is inhospitable. There is no land on which to grow crops or raise livestock. Even with the best synthesizers and recyclers, they must need some food, water, and other supplies."

"That's where I come in," Davidov said. "My friend recommended me to the Trellusan colonial council before they went into quarantine, and they hired me to make a monthly supply drop. They signal me with what they need, and I send a launch down to deliver the shipment. They have me dump it outside the domes, at a drop point near the old mines."

"Why have the Trellusans isolated the colony?" Reever asked.

"I don't know, my friend," Davidov said, "but I think they're in bad shape. This smells like a disease being quarantined to me."

"When a medical quarantine is initiated, an alert is sent out through the quadrant," I pointed out. "We would have heard something."

"I don't think it's official. You know how paranoid colonists are—always afraid the League will come along and bomb an infected planet from orbit." He gave me a speculative look. "Reever told me you stopped the plague on K-2. You can help these people. If you're willing, I can smuggle you down there in an airtight cargo container."

"It's too dangerous," my husband said before I could utter a word. "At the very least, they may imprison Jarn for violating their isolation."

"But if they are fighting a contagion," I said, "they may also be very grateful for the intervention." I turned to Davidov. "Have they requested any medical supplies?"

He nodded. "Quite a few, considering that they have no doctor or medical facilities on the colony."

I started to ask another question, but saw Reever's expression. He only looked that way when he wished to do the talking, and I lapsed into silence.

"Have you confirmed the reason for the quarantine with the colonial authorities?" my husband asked.

"I can't ask them anything," Davidov said with some annoyance in his tone. "They've shut down their communications array. The only time they send a signal is once each month, to my ship, with a list of the supplies they need. I've tried to return the signal dozens of times, but all they do is jam my relays."

Reever gave his friend a skeptical look. "There are many reasons for refusing to have contact with offworlders. They may be using it as a form of population control, or to follow the dictates of faith. The Skartesh recently founded a colony on one of K-2's moons, to minimize contact with other species."

Davidov laughed. "I can't actually see Trellus becoming a xenophobic religious outpost, can you?"

Each time Davidov smiled or made a sound of mirth, he seemed genuinely amused. Until I looked into his eyes, which were as flat and unemotional as my husband's expression. He also sat very still, as if he controlled every muscle in his body. Had I not seen the man's chest move in and out, I would have thought him dead.

Unnatural, for a man in such an apparent good humor to be so cold-eyed, motionless, and alert.

"No," my husband said. "It's been a haven for every rogue, fugitive, and malcontent since the Hsktskt raided and destroyed the first colony." Reever regarded his friend for a moment. "What puzzles me is your interest in their welfare."

The Terran held up his hands in a gesture of surrender. "Don't shoot the messenger, Duncan. If you want to let all those people down there die, it's no concern of mine. Just thought I'd mention it to the lovely doctor, in case she has the heart you never grew." He leered at me briefly before he got to his feet. "I appreciate the meal, but I've got to get back to the *Renko* and make this supply drop. If I hear anything else about the bounty, I'll signal you."

Four

"We could try to contact the colonists ourselves," I suggested as Reever secured the hatch and returned to the helm. "They may not be jamming every relay sent to them. If they are struggling with some form of contagion, I may be able to give them practical advice."

"I do not think that is the case here," my husband said. "Something is wrong. Alek was trying to deceive us."

I *knew* it. The hair on the back of my neck was never wrong. "What made you think that?"

Reever stared out at the trader vessel, and at Davidov's launch as it disappeared inside the cargo bay. "I could hear the difference in his voice. When Terrans lie, their tone changes, ever so slightly." He looked down at a light blinking on the com panel. "It's the *Renko*. He's signaling us again."

I felt unsettled. "He's already said farewell. What else does he want?"

My husband tapped some keys, and Davidov's face appeared on the panel display. "Alek. Did you forget something, such as the truth?"

"I tried to do this the easy way, Reever," Davidov said, his features now as stony as my husband's. "I want you to remember that."

"If you mean to attack us," Reever countered, "think hard on it first. I came to you in friendship, Alek. I have never shown you otherwise."

"As a gesture of that friendship, I wish I could spend all day explaining the situation to you." A tinge of remorse colored the Terran's harsh voice. "But I'm afraid that time is one luxury that we can no longer enjoy."

"Alek."

Whatever Reever was going to say to him was lost as a burst of pulse fire filled up the viewer panel. As it slammed into *Moonfire*, the force of the blast threw me out of my seat and onto the deck. Reever grabbed me with one hand and lifted me by the back of my tunic into the copilot's seat.

"Strap in," he said as he engaged the engines, and spun the ship around. "I'm going to try to outrun him."

I hung on to the harness straps as a second volley hit the side of the hull. Equipment panels began exploding and showering sparks all around us.

"Why is he firing?" I forced the harness's center buckle together and braced my hands against the console, trying to peer through the energy-scarred viewer. "What did we do?"

My husband's mouth thinned as his hands moved rapidly over the ship's controls and he dodged several other blasts. "We said 'no.'"

As Reever tried to take *Moonfire* away from Trellus, Davidov's ship flew past us, at the same time firing at the top of the hull. I didn't realize my husband was sending a distress signal until the ship's diagnostic unit politely informed him that the transmitter was not functioning. Space tilted and spun as Reever steered around two more volleys fired from the *Renko* and retreated into orbit above Trellus.

"Get back to the escape pod," my husband told me. "I'll release it as soon as you're secured inside. Land on Trellus. If nothing else, they will keep Davidov from taking you."

"The last time I left you on another ship," I reminded him, "we did not see each other again for two and a half years."

"*Jarn.*"

"I am not leaving." I refused to look at him. "Not without you. Never again without you. In life or in death." I had to look at him. "Do you understand me?"

Love made his eyes turn bright blue. "It will be in death if he destroys the ship."

"Then we will journey together into the next life," I assured him, reaching out and touching his cheek. "I am not afraid. Not when you are with me, *Osepeke.*"

Reever started to say something, and then turned

his face and pressed his mouth to my palm. "I love you, *Waenara*."

Osepeke, honored husband. *Waenara*, beloved wife. That was how we would die, together, as we were meant to be.

Moonfire rocked as Davidov fired at the rear fuselage, and the engine array began to fail. Reever turned the nose of the ship toward the planet and began adjusting the controls for reentry.

"I'll attempt to land a few kilometers away from the colony," he told me as he increased power to the ship's hull buffers and stabilizers. "That may help us avoid any security weapons they employ. Trellus has no atmosphere, and the temperature is minus two hundred degrees Fahrenheit, so don't try to leave the ship without an envirosuit."

"I'm not going anywhere without you." I watched the planet swell until it filled the screen.

Trellus appeared to be an ugly, lifeless world of brown, black, and gray rock, covered with jagged cliffs, dead volcanoes, and deep craters from meteor impacts. A silver-white smear of blobs near the equator grew into ovals of ice, and then I realized they must be the colony's pressure domes. The sky pressing all around us, black and cold, looked no different than deep space except over the domes. There I saw flares of gold, blue, and green light emanating from within them.

"I've found a place to set down," my husband said. "Do you see any weapons being deployed by the domes?"

I scanned the elliptical complex of the colony, but aside from the lights there seemed to be no activity. "None yet." Had Davidov lied about that, too?

Reever leveled out the scout as the surface spread out beneath us. Then, without warning, something inside the rear fuselage exploded. Lights and audio warnings created a flashing din for a moment, and then disappeared, along with the lurching sounds coming from the back of the ship.

"Engines are offline," Reever said, hammering the console's keys as he tried to compensate. *Moonfire* began to drop alarmingly fast. "I can't restart them. Assume crash position."

I bent over, covering my head with my arms, and closed my eyes. I felt glad that I had not allowed him to put me in the escape pod. I did not want my brief life to end, but if my death waited on this dead, ugly world, I would not have to enter eternity alone.

We will not die, something said from a corner of my heart. *Remember?*

Sweat slicked my skin, and my heart hammered with frantic fists under my breast. I was no longer on *Moonfire*, but in some black, cold space, unable to move or speak. An ensleg with an animal's head curled claws around the circle of metal on my neck, choking me with it.

You won't die, Terran, the ensleg snarled, scalding my face with burning spit and breath like pulse fire. *Not from the sickness, not from beatings. What will it take to kill you?*

I tried to answer him, but the silencer strapped to my face plugged my mouth.

We're going to crash. He said this bitterly, angrily, as if it were my fault. His claws jerked the collar up, completely cutting off my air. *Maybe that will finish you. Do you wish for death?* He released the collar and reached up to wrench the silencer out of my mouth. *Tell me now.*

I said something in words I did not understand, and then I did.

Don't be afraid, Oforon. It will be quick.

He curled his claws into a ball, and drew them back as if to hit me in the face. Then his eyes closed and he fell to his knees, his head back, a terrible howl tearing from his throat.

I wanted to wrap my arms around him, to comfort him in these last moments. All I could do was rest my cheek against the top of his mane.

The vision blurred, and then vanished.

Moonfire bumped against the surface, once, twice, and then began tumbling over and over, wrenching me in all directions and pelting me with debris broken loose from the interior by the impacts.

"Duncan." I looked over at his seat, but something struck me in my face, whipping my head to the other side.

The seat harness held me in place until the scout toppled over and slammed into something immovable. The force of the final jolt made the straps tear away from the seat. I was thrown backward into one panel and bounced to the deck to slide under another.

I stayed where I was until I was sure the ship's violent landing had finished, and then I crawled out from under the nav console.

The main viewer showed a valley of rocks, dirt, and dust, which may have absorbed much of the impact. Not that it had saved *Moonfire* from being damaged; the interior resembled a derelict being torn apart for the salvage.

A static buzz filled my ears, and blood and smoke blinded me momentarily as I pushed myself up on my knees. I wiped my face with my sleeve, shocked to see it turn red and wet. I pressed the heel of my hand against a gash in my forehead and blinked my eyes clear before I checked the area around me.

"Reever?"

The acoustic shock faded as I listened, but my husband did not answer. I stumbled over a collapsed deck strut and grabbed the pilot's seat and wrenched it around. It was empty, the harness straps in shreds.

"Duncan." I looked all around the helm. "Duncan, are you hurt? Where are you? Can you hear me?"

My husband didn't respond, but a queer-looking thing rolled out from a gaping hole beneath the console. It looked like a child made of machine parts.

Whatever it was, it bumped and pushed its way through the debris until at last it stopped in front of me. "My systems are seventy-three percent functional."

"Congratulations." I stepped around it. "Duncan? Answer me."

I had to stop and clear my way several times before I reached the open hatch leading down into *Moonfire*'s second level, a long and narrow crawl space where different systems could be accessed for maintenance and repair. Reever could have been thrown down there, I thought as I looked over the edge, although the entire compartment appeared to have been reduced to a pit of snarled alloy.

I heard a warning Klaxon, and breathed in. I didn't smell fresh smoke, but the air seemed to be thinning. If *Moonfire* was leaking atmosphere, I would have to put on an envirosuit. But first I had to find Reever.

Metal groaned and shifted, and I hurried toward the back of the cabin. The machine child followed.

My husband lay under a heap of supplies that had been ejected from one of the storage units. His face was bruised, and his bottom lip had been split open, but by the time I reached him he had worked his body halfway out of the pile.

"I'm not hurt badly," he told me, and looked at the machine child. "Access vessel operations array."

"Working." The thing's body made several odd noises.

Blood began oozing into my eyes again, so I tore off the cleaner sleeve from my tunic and used it to bind the gash on my forehead. Then I began clearing away the debris on top of Reever. As I worked, I saw that the screens of all the viddisplays had been blown out, and most of the consoles were either smoking and sparking, or inert.

"What is that thing?" I asked Reever as I helped him to his feet.

"An automatic maintenance drone." He winced as talking made the cut across his lip widen. "The crash must have activated its power unit. The Jorenians use them to clean decks and perform minor repairs."

I glanced around us. "It's going to be busy for a very long time."

The little drone made high-pitched sound. "Vessel operations array accessed."

"How much damage to the ship?" Reever asked it.

A panel on its chest slid away, revealing a small data screen, which blipped and scrolled. "Searching systems database. Engines offline. Navigation systems functional. Primary power cells, ninety-two percent drained. Hull, intact."

"We won't lose atmosphere, but we can't launch without refueling." Reever pulled a fallen wall panel upright and shoved it out of the way. "The crash caused as much damage as Alek did, but something else happened to the engines."

"Just before the engines failed, I heard an explosion in the back," I told him. "Did Davidov go back there before, when you were showing him the ship?"

"He said it was too crowded for both of us, and had a look on his own." Reever closed his eyes for a moment. "He must have planted a charge on the power couplings while I waited for him."

"Power couplings, ruptured. Atmospheric controls, offline." The drone's chest screen scrolled with numeric readings. "Transmitter, destroyed—"

"End status report." Reever inspected my garments. "Are you injured anywhere else?"

"Just my head." I grimaced. "As usual."

He pulled me into his arms and held me for a few moments, then kissed me. "Don't forget me again."

We went over and looked through one of the side view ports. "You are an excellent pilot," I told my husband. "We should have smashed into that range of cliffs over there. Where are we?"

"Vector seventy-eight degrees," the maintenance drone said, "three hundred forty east, plus seven solar, eleven point five kilometers outside colony settlement, Trellus, outer-eitri region, Varallan."

"Stand by," Reever told the drone.

I went to the helm and checked the exterior sensors that were still working before gazing out at the surrounding surface. Outside the ship, curtains and spires of rock dust danced with languid speed, forced into the airless dark by our violent landing.

"We will need weights and tethers if we leave the ship," I said to Reever. "The planet has almost no gravity."

I couldn't see the domes of the colony from here, but there were some shelters at the end of the plain, built between ragged pillars of carbonized rock and what appeared to be gaping black holes descending beneath the surface. Behind them, I could just make out several huge, motionless machines covered in dust.

"What are those things?"

"Ore conveyers and crushers. In the old days, Alek used the abandoned mining operation here to hide his slave runners," Reever told me. "There are thousands of tunnels on this planet."

The mention of Davidov's name made my fingernails dig into the edge of the console. "I would like to drop him down one of them."

"Stay here." Reever picked his way back to the droplift. The controls sparked when he punched them, and the door panels to the air lock only slid open an inch before jamming.

I heard the sound of an incoming relay and straightened. "Reever, someone is signaling us."

"Signal transmitted by trader vessel *Renko*," the maintenance drone said. "Originator is Davidov, Aleksei, Terran, current position ship's owner and flight captain—"

"Shut up," I told it as Reever and I hurried back to the helm.

None of the displays worked, but the audio portion of the relay from the *Renko* came over the console with perfect clarity.

"I'm reading two life signs, and you're moving around the interior, so I know you're both alive and ambulatory," Davidov's voice said over the com panel. "I felt sure you would make it, Duncan. Remember the time you brought down that crippled fighter with all those slaves crammed in the weapons hold? You have to admit, this was a cakewalk compared to that."

My husband muttered something ugly under his breath.

"I regret that I had to be the one to shoot you down this time," Davidov said, "but you will recall that I *did* offer to smuggle your wife onto Trellus first."

Reever tried to relay a reply, but the console did not respond.

"I imagine you have a lot to say to me," Davidov continued. "That's the other thing, old friend. I took out your transmitter before I forced you to land. You won't be able to signal me or any of your friends on Joren. I also used a small charge to rupture your power couplings. I'm afraid that the only way you're getting off Trellus is on my launch. I'll be happy to transport you and the wife, but you have to do something for me first."

"He wants the bounty," I said, my throat tight.

"It's simple: Find the shifter." Davidov's voice grew harsh. "Find it, capture it, and put an end to the games it's been playing down there."

Reever frowned.

"Is he talking about the Odnallak?" I asked, but my husband only gave me a blank look.

"It won't be difficult," Davidov told us. "When it learns about your wife's unique physiology, it will not stop until it can play with her. I suggest you dangle her in a prominent place. One more thing: Don't kill the Hsktskt. I've become very fond of her."

I wondered if Reever's former friend had gone mad. He was speaking as if he had.

"Find the shifter and kill it, Duncan," Davidov repeated. "You and the lovely doctor are the only ones left who can. Because if you don't, I will bombard the surface of Trellus until I kill you, Jarn, the shifter, and every other living thing on this planet. You have thirty solar days. *Renko*, out."

Five

Davidov's threat echoed in my head, which was starting to spin. I tried to take a deep, cleansing breath, and found that I couldn't. My ears suddenly popped rather painfully, as if someone had clapped their hands over them.

"Something is wrong with the air," I told my husband, who was staring down at the ruined helm. His back and shoulders were rigid. "Duncan."

He straightened and turned to me. "The air?" He breathed in and touched one of his ears. "The cabin pressure is dropping." He summoned the maintenance drone. "Report the current levels in the environmental supply tanks."

"Working." The drone made more of its noises, and then said, "Atmospheric supply levels at twenty-seven percent."

"Is the hull leaking atmosphere?" Reever demanded.

The drone fell silent for a few moments. "Negative. Supply tanks two, six, and nine empty and no longer functional. Estimated repair time, three solar days."

"We have to get into suits," my husband said. "We'll run out of air in an hour."

We couldn't stay with *Moonfire* or try to make repairs without air. "Do we have enough oxygen in the suit tanks to walk eleven kilometers?"

"We'll have to carry spare tanks with us."

Movement outside the ship drew my gaze. Shadows, enormous ones, converged on *Moonfire* from all sides.

"We may not have an hour," I told him. "I think colonial security has found us."

The machines surrounding the ship stood ten feet tall, and were covered from top to bottom in heavy, dark blue armor. The armor plates seemed to absorb the light from the ship's exterior emitters rather than reflect it. Tight bundles of shielded power cables ran the length of their frames, feeding into hydraulic boosters and weapons ports.

They had been designed to appear somewhat humanoid, with two upper extension grapplers like arms that ended in four-pronged, claw-shaped grips serving as hands. Instead of two legs, they had three, which formed a jointed tripod base.

"Drednocs." Reever came to stand beside me, and I looked at him. "A type of battle drone developed by the League during their war with the Hsktskt. They were used during the heaviest surface fighting. Very little can stop them."

I recalled what Davidov had said about the Hsk-tskt. "Why would they be used here, on a trade colony?"

"I don't know." He stiffened as something struck the hull outside. "They're fitted with sonic torches and are going to cut their way in. We have to put on suits, now."

We found two intact envirosuits, and I removed the supply tanks from two others. As we dressed, Reever issued terse instructions.

"Do not identify yourself to them," he said, "or relate that we met with Alek, or that he and I have any connection. If they wish to know why we were in orbit, say that we were surveying the planet when we experienced engine trouble."

"Can't we just hide somewhere until they go away?" I asked as I pulled the envirosuit up over my legs.

Vibrating, squealing metallic sounds shook the hull.

"Thermal scanners are standard on all security drones," Reever told me as he fastened the air seals at the back of my suit, and turned to let me do the same with his. "They'll pick up our heat signatures wherever we hide. If they're ATD programmed, they won't harm us." He saw my expression and added, "Security drones are usually programmed to apprehend, transport, and detain."

"Usually." The word hardly comforted me. "How can they be stopped if they are not?"

His eyes went gray. "Let me worry about that."

I prepared to argue the point, but the sounds of grinding metal grew louder. I fastened the breather over my mouth before closing the suit's helmet.

"Can you hear me?" I said over the suit com.

"Yes." He closed the collar gasket on my helmet. "Turn around."

Reever and I had just enough time to check each other's seals before we were flung across the cabin into the breached air lock with every bit of debris that was not secured.

As a viselike device attached itself to my leg, I looked out through the open air lock panels. The security drones had not bothered to board the ship; they had simply reached in with their grapplers extended to drag us out.

And drag us out they did, lifting us from the deck so that our legs dangled several feet from the planet's surface.

The drednoc holding me brought me up to its cranial case and scanned my helmet. "Identify," it said in Jorenian.

I barely remembered in time what Reever had told me. "I am Resa," I said, borrowing my old friend's name again. "Our ship's engines malfunctioned, and we were forced to land here. We are not armed."

I hoped the natives were friendly toward accidental visitors. Before the rebellion on Akkabarr, the harsh winds of my homeworld forced down many ships. Any crash survivors were killed, and their faces, along with those of the dead, were skinned and delivered to the Toskald as tribute.

"Terran, female," the machine soldier said, switching to that language. "You are claimed under colonial charter by Mercy House."

Claimed and *mercy* were two good words. Under the circumstances, ones that I liked very much.

"Terran, male," the drone holding Reever said. "You are claimed under colonial charter by Games Master Drefan."

"I don't think they're going to harm us," Reever said. "We may be considered salvage, or property, until we can identify ourselves to the colonists."

"Wait," I said as the drone holding me and two others began to move in one direction, and the one with Reever and its companions went in another. Both went toward the colony domes, but Reever's drones were headed toward the west section, while mine turned to the east. "We are together, husband and wife. We can't be separated." They did not stop. *"Duncan."*

"Don't fight them," Reever said over my suit com. "They are taking us to different domes. As soon as I can free myself, I will come for you. I will find you."

That was the last thing I heard him say as the drones separated and took him out of com range.

The drone carrying me and two others traveled across the plain to the largest of the eastern domes. We entered the pressurized shelter through a series of airtight corridors. In each corridor we were scanned and subjected to various forms of intensive biodecon, including energy sweep, vacuum, and surface spray. Although the drednocs were not living beings, and would be difficult to contaminate, they were treated as if they were as alive as me.

Something was very wrong here.

At last we entered the main area under the dome. The colonists had built their shelters in various sizes on elevated foundations, forming walkways beneath them. This collection of shelters ranged from single-level dwellings to more elaborate multiplexes.

I was brought to the largest structure, near the center of the dome, and taken on a lift to the lowest level. There the drednocs escorted me to a large empty room, where we waited for several minutes.

My com relayed a warning buzz indicating the low level of oxygen in my air tank. I tried to persuade the machine soldier holding me to release me from its grip so that I could remove my helmet, but it did not respond. My lungs had begun to burn when at last someone living came in.

"What have you brought me today, boys?"

The small, dark female who came to stand in front of the drednocs appeared to be Terran, so I addressed her as such. I had to speak loudly to be heard through my breather and helmet. "Tell them to release me. My air is running out."

"Hang on." She released my collar seal, lifted the helmet away from my head, and removed the breather covering the lower half of my face. She did all this while standing as far away from me as she could.

"You've got air," she said. "So say something."

I dragged in delicious cool air scented with some sort of alien spice. "I thank you."

The other woman wore fitted black garments and a blade belt strapped around her hips. Three small, thin circlets of gleaming silver pierced her face in interesting places: the side of her nose, the top of one ear, and the center of her left eyebrow. Her eyes were the color of a d'narral blossom, pure, strong violet, with dark golden stars around each pupil. She had applied some cosmetics to her face, judging by the enhanced tone of her cheeks, lips, and eyelids. Thick, shiny brown hair fell over her shoulders down to her hips. She looked to be equal in height and weight to me.

"Salvage item four-oh-seven-B," the drednoc reported. "Terran, female, living."

"I can see that for myself, bolt head. Lights." As the emitters brightened, the woman tipped her head to one side and studied my face. "Well, now. You look like you could be my little sister."

I didn't know how common my attributes were among Terrans. I had only shared a superficial resemblance to one Iisleg female: Resa, the healer who had been like a sister to me.

I didn't see myself in this woman's narrow features, but I thought it better not to insult her by stating such an opinion.

"I doubt we're siblings," she told me. "The lizards ate my parents before they could make me a little brother or sister. Perhaps we're distant cousins. What's your mother's name?"

I didn't know what to say. I couldn't tell her that I had been cloned from the cells of a madman and incubated in a machine. No one ever reacted favorably to hearing that.

"None of my business. Gotcha." She lifted the edge of the makeshift bandage I had tied around my head. "Nasty-looking cut." She pinched my cheek, painfully tugging the skin out. "Anyone else in there?"

"She scans clean," a disgruntled male voice said. "Thanks so much for waiting for my signal, Beautiful."

Beautiful glanced at the wall. "She did just crash a ship out there. Her skin is tight, she's lucid, and she hasn't tried to kill anyone. I don't think we need a full workup."

"No, let's permit her to run amok instead," the wall said back. "It'll make life around here that much more interesting."

"You worry too damn much." The female directed the drednoc to release me, and helped me out of the suit. "She's wearing Jorenian gear. Borrowed, or stolen." As I stiffened, she eyed me. "She doesn't like being called a thief. Have you got a name, or should we just call you 'salvage item four-oh-seven-B?'"

Reever had told me not to identify myself, but if

I did not answer her, she might grow hostile. I swallowed to ease the dryness of my throat. "I am Resa."

"Are you?" Something shifted in her eyes. "I'm Mercy. This is my place." She took a step closer. "Now, what are you doing here, besides crashing on my planet?"

"We did not mean to intrude on your territory." I immediately realized that I had said the words in Iisleg, and quickly repeated it in the pure Terran that my husband spoke.

"I understand you," she said back to me in perfect Iisleg. Then, switching to Terran, she added, "Half the slaves I started out with were bred on your ice ball, thanks to some of your friends."

Her hostility puzzled me as much as her references. "It is not my ice ball. I have no friends involved in slavery."

"We'll get to that." She braced her hands against the insides of her arms and tapped her fingertips against her sleeves. "Why did Davidov shoot you down?"

She knew we had not crashed by accident. I tried to think of an excuse, but fear for Reever clouded my head. Then an idea occurred to me.

"I do not know anyone named Davidov," I said. "But my husband might. The drones that came to our ship took him to another dome, on the west side of the colony. If you would bring him here, I am certain he can explain everything."

"If your husband is young and healthy, then Drefan owns him until his salvage debt is repaid.

And you're a terrible liar." She tilted her head. "Davidov and his thugs haven't let anyone near Trellus for the better part of a year. He barely drops enough to keep us alive, so no way would he force down your little ship just for kicks. What's the deal?"

Why would Alek blockade the entire colony? "No one kicked us, and we made no deal. I had thought the colony was under quarantine."

"We are. Davidov's quarantine." Bitterness tainted the smile she offered me. "How did he put it? No one lands, and no one leaves. He's destroyed every transport we've tried to send out, and jams every distress signal we've transmitted."

In the future I was going to pay very strict, devoted attention to what the hair on the back of my neck did. "Why is Davidov forcing the colony to live in isolation like this?"

"No one knows. He won't tell us." She gave me a long, measuring look. "If you're part of his game, I'm not playing it. Cat, forward that crazy bastard's relays in here. I want the ones on the bounty, with the images."

The voice from the wall protested. "Mercy, if you show your hand—"

"What's she going to do?" she snapped. "Cry? Beat up the dreds? Bite my head off? She's maybe a hundred pounds soaking wet."

"So are you," Cat said, his voice growing. "We won't know anything about her until we do a full workup."

"Later. Forward the relays."

The display screen on the wall flickered, and began showing a series of relay vids written in multiple languages. On each one was an image of my face as well as Reever's. I assumed they were from the time he and Cherijo resided on Kevarzangia Two.

When the Terran captions appeared, I saw they spelled out the terms of the bounty being offered for me.

"So, *Resa*." Mercy moved in until her breath touched my cheek, and her eyes bored into my own. "I'll be generous and assume that gash on your head made you momentarily forget that your name is Cherijo Grey Veil. The bounty, though, that's going to be harder to explain."

I sighed. "It is complicated."

"I can only imagine." She folded her arms. "Davidov has been offering four million stan credits to anyone who brings you and your husband to him, but the minute he has you, he forces you to crashland here. Did something change? Why did he want you in the first place?" When I began to reply, she lifted one finger. "Don't make up any new stories. I'm really not in the mood."

"We did not know Davidov was the trader offering the bounty," I told her. "We met with him because he was once my husband's friend, and he claimed to have information about it. He told us that Trellus was under its own quarantine, and tried to talk me into coming to the colony. He offered to smuggle me down during his supply drop."

"That sounds screwed up enough to be the truth. Lights down. So." The golden stars in her violet eyes expanded as the emitters dimmed. "Any particular reason he decided that it had to be you? Maybe you being in so tight with the Hsktskt?"

"I am not tight with anyone," I said.

"You went to their planet." Malice sharpened her voice. "You saved them from that plague. I call that pretty tight."

She did not care for the Hsktskt; that much was evident. I would have to make her believe I didn't either.

"I was forced by the Faction to go to Vtaga." I kept my eyes down and my tone submissive, as if I were answering an Iisleg male. "They threatened to begin the war again if I did not help them. While I was there I was abducted by criminals, several times, and my husband and child were nearly killed."

Mercy didn't say anything for a time. Then the lines around her nose and mouth slowly disappeared. "Obviously you got away."

"I was very lucky." I decided to change the subject. "Davidov told us that the colony had instituted the quarantine. He insinuated that there were medical reasons for it."

"Oh, there's a psychiatric reason," Mercy said. "He's a fucking lunatic." She took the medical case one of the drednocs had brought in and opened it.

"You pack a lot of supplies. What sort of doctor are you, anyway?"

"I'm a surgeon. I specialize in cardiothoracic procedures, but I have worked as a trauma physician and a battlefield medic." I saw her expression change. "Do you need a doctor here?"

"Yes," the wall said.

"No." Mercy began to pace the length of the room. "All right, change of plans. I can't release you into the general population. Too many people have seen these relays. They'll assume you're in with Davidov, and you'll end up dangling from a transmitter or turning into a lump of ice at the bottom of a crater." She raised her voice. "Cat? Get your ass in here."

Before Mercy finished speaking, Squilyp hopped into the room.

I ran to him, but stopped short as I realized the male was not my friend the Senior Healer. This Omorr had a wide, gray-green scar running the length of one arm, which, like the rest of his form, bulged with muscular development. Several black spiral tattoos encircled his outer gildrells. A bronze leather weapons halter crisscrossed his bare chest, gleaming with sheathed Omorr fighting knives. More dark brown leather covered him from the waist down, and a spiked boot encased his one broad foot.

I gaped at him. *"Dævena Yepa."*

"No, Omorr male." He stood his ground while his gildrells flared wildly with nerves. When I opened my mouth to speak again, he interrupted with, "Don't you even *think* about spitting on me."

"She's not from the homeworld," Mercy told him, and patted his arm. "Cherijo, this is Cataced, my Omorr business manager, junior partner, and the chief pain in my ass. Cat, this is Cherijo, mysterious surgeon with very large bounty on her head."

I considered asking her to call me Jarn, but the explanation as to why might make her suspicions about me return. While I was here, I would have to answer to my former self's name. "I am happy to meet you, Cataced."

Cat ignored my greeting and reached out to tug on Mercy's sleeve. "You can't turn her loose."

"They know that scout was in orbit with Davidov before it crashed," Mercy told him. "Everyone saw it crash. Everyone picked up the relays he's been transmitting. We could kill her and dump the body, I suppose. Except she's supposed to be immortal. I wonder if Swap's hungry."

"You can't feed her to your pet worm." The Omorr studied me for a moment. "She's not hideous. We've got an entire house full of females. We alter her appearance enough to make her look like one of the girls."

"And that's going to fool the males in this colony, who have used every girl under my roof countless times since the blockade started, for how long?" Mercy dragged a hand over her hair and gave me an exasperated look. "They come and find her here, they will raze this place to the ground and toss us out the nearest air lock."

"We have to protect her," Cat said, putting himself in her path. "Mercy. Come on. She's a doctor."

"What difference will that make?" she demanded. "She can't do anything but feel foreheads and take temperatures. She's a liability. We have to get rid of her."

"I will leave, and tell no one that I was here or how you helped me," I offered, drawing their attention away from each other. "Only show me where my husband is. I will need him to protect me."

"I can't, honey," Mercy said, at last showing some sympathy. "He was salvaged by Drefan's dreds, and he belongs to Omega Dome until he can reimburse Drefan for the cost of the rescue. It's how we do things here."

"Neither of us are carrying anything of value," I pointed out. "We have some limited assets, but they are on Joren. We cannot pay you until after we leave."

"That's not going to happen," Cat told me. "If your husband is in any kind of fighting shape, Drefan will use him in the games." When he saw my blank look, he added, "Gamers is a bloodsport arena. Simulated battles, hunting expeditions, or any other confrontation where you have to kill or be killed." He flicked a glance toward Mercy. "It's the second oldest form of recreation on Trellus."

"No one actually dies," Mercy assured me. "Drefan uses certain control measures inside each grid. The simulations can't kill or maim any of the gamers."

My stomach clenched at the thought of Reever being forced to fight, even under simulated conditions. "What can I do to free him from the obligation to this Drefan?"

"You? Nothing," Mercy said.

"I can talk to him, and see if we can work out a deal," Cat said. "Drefan owes me. But we want something in return."

"No, we don't," Mercy said instantly.

"Shut up," he told her. To me, he said, "We don't have a doctor on colony, and all of the girls here need medical exams. Will you take a look at them?"

Mercy threw up her arms. "Why don't I set fire to the place myself? Saves us having to wait for the enraged, insane mob to arrive and do it. I never liked this place much anyway. The walls still smell of Rilken."

"Pay no attention to the semihysterical Terran," Cat said. "She thinks everyone is out to get her."

"Everyone has *tried* to get me," Mercy said, her teeth clenched. "Since when did you become such a champion of Terrans?"

"I don't know," he shot back. "I can definitely think of one female I'd like to beat senseless."

She puckered her lips as if to kiss him. "Only beat?"

Their bickering reminded me so much of Squilyp and me while we were arguing over patients that I almost laughed. "I will perform medical exams on anyone you wish." I saw them both frown and added, "Please. Help us."

Mercy swore in a language my wristcom wouldn't translate. "Cat, signal Omega Dome. See if Drefan still has the husband and what he wants to settle the salvage debt. I'll think about whatever he relays back." As he started to reply, she lifted one finger. "Not another word, or I kick her out just on principle."

"Fine. It's your whorehouse." The Omorr stomped out.

"Never hire an Omorr to run your business," Mercy advised me with mocking seriousness. "They're great with the books, they think thieving is beneath them, and what they can do with blades probably makes you look like a fumbling amateur. But soft-hearted? Christ. P'Kotmans are tougher."

I was more concerned with the last thing Cat had said. "This place is a . . . whorehouse?"

"I prefer to call it a brothel." She noted my reaction with a half smirk. "Didn't I mention that before?"

"No."

"Well, then." She made a grand, sweeping gesture. "Welcome to Mercy House, Doc. Home of the oldest form of recreation on Trellus."

The thought of a house filled with females selling sexual services bemused me. The Iisleg had no brothels, as any man could use almost any woman for coupling whenever he pleased. Certain females were made to cater to all men, but the ahayag were not compensated, only used. An Iisleg male certainly would never entertain the notion of paying for sex. The only females he could not have were the wives of certain high-ranking males within the tribes, who were reserved for use by their husband only.

Jorenians did not couple with anyone but their mates, and only after they had Chosen, for the purposes of bonding and procreation. A brothel would quickly go out of business on Joren.

I knew from the data Reever had given me on Terra that my kind had created humanlike machines, called sex drones, which could be rented or purchased by those wishing to couple. They had not been the machines in which I had been created, which only made the idea of them somewhat less repulsive.

Reever preferred to couple only with me, but that was no doubt due to his unusual upbringing.

"There are three rules in my business," Mercy told me as she escorted me down the corridor into what she called the dining room. "The first one is always keep the customers happy. Happy tricks come back."

She had offered to speak in Iisleg, but I asked her to use stan Terran. Now I was beginning to regret that. "You practice deception as well as prostitution?"

"Tricks are what we call our customers," she explained as she prepared two servers of hot liquid, "although certain deceptions of kindness are a big part of the business, too. Here, drink this." She offered me one of the servers.

I took a surreptitious sniff. The scent startled me. "Is this idleberry?"

"Yeah, but not quite as bitter as your people brew it." Mercy sipped some of her own. "One of my girls brought the seeds with her when she was sold off-world. She started growing it in one of our agridomes, and got me hooked on it." She saw my expression and scowled. "This doesn't mean we're best friends. I'm putting everything I have at risk here for you, and I am *very* attached to my personal wealth. It's just something to drink."

"It's not the tea." I thought of how best to ask. "You use slaves here?"

"Most of them *were* enslaved," Mercy said, giving me a direct look. "None of them are now. They're free, paid employees who choose to make this their profession. I peddle sex, Cherijo, not flesh."

We sat down in a comfortable rectangle of cushioned seats, and Mercy propped her feet on the low, oval table set in the center of it. I found myself oddly fascinated by this Terran. Because we shared one body between us, I had never been able to meet Cherijo. I sensed that Mercy's uncertain temper, colorful way of speaking, and possessive outlook were not all that different than my former self's.

This might be the closest I ever came to knowing the woman who had occupied my body.

"You're very far away from the homeworld," I said to her. "How did you come to be here?"

"I wasn't born on Terra." She cradled her server between her hands. "My parents had me in space, on the jaunt here. They and a group of other crazy pioneers were the original colonists on Trellus. We lived in orbit for a while as they were building the first habitat domes and installing the radiation shields." She stared down into her server and her tone changed. "After that, we had six good years."

I heard pain, rage, and sorrow lurking behind her soft words. "And in the seventh year?"

"The fucking Hsktskt came." The server made a cracking sound between her hands, and Mercy rose and carried it over to the disposal unit.

In that time, the Hsktskt only came to a colony of warm-blooded beings for one reason: to raid it. They would have stripped the planet of everything of value, killed most of the inhabitants, and enslaved the rest. That she had survived such a raid meant she had been left behind to die in the ruins.

I knew the Hsktskt's raiding had been born out of resentment toward the warm-blooded species that had intruded on their territory and started colonizing it without their permission. It did not justify what they had done to so many worlds.

No wonder she hated me for curing the plague on Vtaga. To her it must seem as if I had betrayed our own kind.

I waited until she glanced at me, and said, "I am sorry, Mercy."

"Yeah. So were we." She walked around the room, absently picking up things and putting them back down. "My parents died defending this dome. The lizards took or killed everyone else, except me and a couple of other kids who were too small to sell. About half of them starved before the first trader came along. I didn't, and I've been here ever since, and why the hell am I telling you all this stuff?"

"We are both Terran," I said. "One feels a certain bond to another of the species when isolated from the rest. Why didn't the traders who came after the Hsktskt take you back to Terra?"

She uttered a humorless sound. "Traders don't give away passage, not when they can fill the space with cargo they're paid to transport. It wasn't so bad after the pleasure missionaries landed and set up the Shelter. The first training brothel," she added when she caught my expression. "I suppose you don't approve of my business, either."

"I am Iisleg, not Terran," I reminded her. "As long as it doesn't harm others, what a woman does to survive is her choice."

"Well, no matter what they take away from you, you still have your body. The missionaries taught us that." Her expression turned wry. "I'm sure homeworld-raised Terrans would spit on me for what I do."

She didn't seem too concerned about that. "Wouldn't it bother you if they did?"

"Hell, no. I worked my way up through the

ranks, learned every aspect of the business end of the pleasure industry, and saved enough credits to start my own house. All before I was eighteen." She ran a fond hand over the back of one of the seating arrangements. "In some ways it's no different than being a trader or a soldier. Only I don't have to jaunt anywhere or kill anyone."

"Do the colonists treat you fairly?"

"They have to." She lowered her voice to a whisper. "Don't tell anyone, but I'm one of the richest beings in the quadrant."

I finished my tea and stood. "Would you show me around the rest of Mercy House?"

That seemed to take her aback. "You really want to see it, Doc, or are you just being polite?"

"I am being polite," I replied, "and I really want to see it."

"Keep up the honesty thing you're doing," she said. "I like it."

Mercy led me from the dining room out to the main corridor, which ran the length of the house and led off into five different sections. The two largest were reserved for the trade of the house. One had been converted into quarters for the brothel staff, most of whom lived as well as worked in the house. The last two contained kitchens, supply rooms, and Mercy's office and private quarters.

"When I decided to open my own place, I didn't have enough credits to cover building it new," Mercy told me. "I won this one from the previous owner, this Rilken hustler who tried to cheat me in a game of whump-ball. He saw Terran and thought stupid—big mistake. I've been sharking whump-tables with traders for so long I can run a table in my sleep."

I sniffed the air. "Rilkens lived here?"

"Oh, I had the place thoroughly deconned and re-modeled before I moved in to set up shop." She stopped to listen at one closed-door panel. "They might be small, but Jesus, they're slobs. Hang on one sec." She checked the door panel controls, which had the last entrance time displayed, and then enabled the room audio. "Eka, his hour was up ten minutes ago."

"I told him that, Mercy," a strained voice replied. "He won't disengage and I can't shake him off."

"Wait here," Mercy said to me, and overrode the lock on the door. A blast of moist heat came billowing out as she entered the room, and reminded me so much of Vtaga that I half expected to see a pair of Hsktskt inside coupling.

A dusky-skinned, red-haired female dripping with perspiration sat in the center of the room on a reclining couch. What appeared to be a large green octopoid had attached itself to her shoulders and neck. Its tentacles were entwined in the female's scarlet locks, and it expanded and contracted as it made loud sucking sounds.

Mercy took out a device, jammed it against the parasite, and pressed a switch. The octopoid squealed and dropped to the floor to thrash and roll, its tentacles whipping the air in a frenzy.

"Mk-tk," Mercy said, putting her boot on top of the parasite to hold it in place. "We've been over this a hundred times. You can't suck on Ekatarana's derma for longer than an hour. It's not fair to her. She becomes dehydrated."

Mk-tk stopped thrashing and made a snorkeling sound through a nose or mouth shaped like a collapsing cone filled with filament-fine sensory organs.

"I don't care how many credits you throw at me, pal," Mercy told him. "If you can't respect the house safety limits, you can take yourself and your body fluid fetish somewhere else." She lifted her boot. "We understand each other? Or do I dunk you in the nearest liquid-waste disposal and see how you like sucking on that?"

Mk-tk shivered all over, curled into a ball, and rolled out of the room past me and disappeared around a corner.

"Idiot male." Mercy tilted Eka's head to one side and brushed back her flame-colored hair, revealing a large section of flesh mottled with black bruising. "Your arms aren't broken. Why didn't you hit the panic switch when he wouldn't let go?"

"Not like he's an Edpriyin bloodsucker, Merc," the prostitute said. "Besides, after every session with him you let me spend the rest of the day in the tub." She gazed past Mercy at me and frowned. "Who's going to service her? They'll need some direction."

Mercy made a rude sound. "She's not trade. This is Resa, our . . . houseguest."

"Greetings, Resa." Eka stood up and stretched. "I'd stay and chat, but I do need to rehydrate." She rolled four of her eyes and wandered into the adjoining lavatory.

"What did she mean by . . . ?" I paused as I worked out what Eka had said. "Oh."

"I'd better introduce you to the other girls," Mercy said, heading out of the room, "before you end up under one of them."

Six

From the pleasure rooms we walked to the main lobby, where Mercy's unoccupied employees gathered and waited for interested patrons to enter and make a selection from them.

"Normally we take appointments only," Mercy told me. "Since Davidov started the blockade, though, I've allowed unscheduled walk-ins. Sex temporarily relieves anxiety, and these are anxious times."

"Do the other females on colony resent your business?"

"There are a couple of puritans who'd like to shut me down," she admitted. "But I think most of the women on Trellus are secretly grateful for us. We run an honest, clean house, but more importantly, we're discreet."

Mercy greeted several females who were lounging on couches and divans inside the large and opulently furnished room. Some were reading datapads; others were engaged in some form of personal grooming. A few appeared drowsy, as if they'd just awakened. All of them were in a state of provocative dress, and looked at me with varying degrees of interest and not a small amount of apprehension.

"Girls, this is Resa," Mercy told them. "She's not a trick, and she doesn't spit."

"See?" One of the girls nudged another. "I told you there were more like Mercy."

"That's right," Mercy said. "Now forget you saw her and don't say a word to anyone outside the house about her being here, or you're fired. Without severance or reference."

I didn't make a grand impression. A few of them waved or greeted me before returning to their reading, grooming, or dozing.

Eka's unfamiliarity with my species made me curious. "Are you now the only Terran on Trellus?" I asked her as we moved into another room, one filled with security monitors and equipment panels.

"No, there's Drefan, or what's left of him. A couple of mercs from the homeworld stop in now and then, too." Mercy went to one of the consoles and began pulling up various images on the screen. The images showed rooms occupied by males and females who were coupling. "First time they land, they hear about me and come looking for personal service, the bigoted bastards. Pisses them off to find out that I just run the place."

"You don't play tricks?"

She gave me a startled look, and then laughed. "That's a good way to put it. No, I haven't played with anyone but Cat since he and I got together."

It was my turn to feel surprised. "You are wife to that Omorr?"

"I am *girlfriend* to that Omorr," she corrected. "We were going to make it permanent, but the war got in the way, then Davidov."

My gaze went to one of the monitors, and the three males and one female it showed in a very complicated position. "Do you watch all the tricks with your girls?"

"Not because I'm a voyeur, if that's what you're thinking. It's a safety precaution, because . . . we get some rough trade through here." She tapped some keys and the image changed to an exterior view of the colony. She pointed to one of the darker domes. "That's Omega Dome, Drefan's place. Commonly referred to as Gamers. We'll have to go over there for the meet. He doesn't ever leave it."

"Why not?"

"Because he's a proud, stubborn jackass. He's also disabled." She opened a com channel. "Cat, any progress on that meet?"

"We have company," the Omorr said. "He'd like to speak with you."

Another male voice growled, "We want the female. Bring her out."

Mercy closed the channel. "See? I knew it. I *knew* it." She reopened it. "How nice of you boys to stop in. We have an entire house filled with females, so take your pick. Just don't hurt them or remove them from the property, and make sure you have enough credits to pay for what you like."

"I want the female from the wrecked ship," the man replied. "She's the one he'll pay for."

Mercy muted the channel and turned to me. "This walking hemorrhoid and his crew are Gnilltak raiders. Your basic scum of the universe. They've been stranded here ever since Davidov locked down the colony. He destroyed their ship, too. Needless to say, they're not a cheery bunch." She enabled the audio.

"—her now, Mercy," the raider's leader was bellowing. "Or we'll start burning some new holes in your whores. Starting with your pretty boy."

Mercy switched the monitor to the reception room, where a group of armed males had weapons trained on the females. One hulking male stood behind Cat and had a pulse rifle pressed against the Omorr's head.

"Shit," she said softly, tugging at the silver loop piercing her eyebrow before she reopened the channel. "All right, I'm coming out with her."

"I can deal with him," I told her as I removed the Lok-teel from under my tunic. "Give me a moment."

"Oh, no. You're staying here. I'm not going to let them shoot up the place." She opened one of the bins under the console and took out two pulse pistols, tucking both inside her jacket. "They were stupid not to disarm Cat. Between the two of us we can—" She looked at me and shrieked.

"It's all right. It's a type of mask." I went still as the Lok-teel enveloped my head and molded itself to my skull, darkening and refining itself into the broader countenance of an older woman.

Mercy had gone so pale she looked like a negative of herself. "That's really not eating your face?"

"No, it's only covering it." It fanned out over my hair, mimicking it as it turned a pale gold, and crept over my eyes, shaping new ones that were wide, pleasant, and pale blue. Although the telepathic mold had covered my entire face with a mask exactly matching the image I had projected to it, I could breathe and see through it.

Mercy stared, appalled and fascinated. "You're sure that's not smothering you?"

"Quite sure." Once it had finished, I smiled with my new mouth. "This face belongs to a Terran female named Ana Hansen."

"Maybe you should give it back."

"It is only a replica of her countenance, created by the Lok-teel—the thing on my face—to cover my own features," I told her. "I thought it best to use a real person, in the event my identity is checked. Ana is an administrator on K-2."

"But how could it . . . never mind. You can explain it to me later." She took another pistol from the bin and tried to put it in my hands. "Take it. If the mask doesn't work, you'll need it."

"I thank you, but I prefer to use my own

weapons." I showed her my own blade harness. "I have Jorenian field and combat training."

Her jaw sagged. "A Terran, fighting for Joren?"

"I was a battlefield surgeon with Teulon Jado's forces," I clarified. "On Akkabarr, during the rebellion."

"A patcher *and* a soldier. You get more interesting by the millisecond, Cherijo." New respect glinted in her eyes. "When we go out there, let me do the talking. If at any time I do this"—she made a small hand gesture—"attack to disable."

We returned to the reception room, where the raiders were waiting with their hostages.

"You took your time, Mercy." The leader, a large, benign-looking humanoid with a wide frame and soft brown and orange hair covering most of his derma, shoved the end of his rifle hard against Cat's head. The pleasant expression in his liquid brown eyes and the mellow beauty of his voice made his actions seem that much more obscene. "You getting tired of Snake-Face?"

"In your dreams, Pus-breath," Mercy said. She didn't flinch when the raider fired directly over her head.

"My name," he shouted, "is Posbret."

"Whatever." Mercy studied her fingernails. "You wanted to see the female from the crash." She jerked her head toward me. "There she is."

The raider shoved Cat away from him and walked up to me. He had to bend over to look into my face. His breath smelled like the flowers on

Joren, and his eyes tugged at my heart with their soulful beauty. "She doesn't look at all like that clone slut pictured in the bounty relays."

"She is, however," Mercy said, "the female who was in the crash. You can check with my dreds if you like."

Perfumed breath blasted my Lok-teel mask as the raider demanded, "What are you called?"

"Ana Hansen," I lied politely. "I'm an administrator on K-2." I didn't struggle as he grabbed the front of my tunic and lifted me off my feet. Out of the corner of my eye, I saw Mercy put a hand on Cat's nearest appendage, as if to hold him back.

"You don't look anything like the one he wants." The raider's expression turned tragically sad, which I interpreted as a scowl. "What are you doing here?"

I had not prepared a cover story, so I told him a carefully worded version of the truth.

"My husband and I are sojourning together," I said. "We stopped here to visit our friend." I glanced at Mercy, to make him believe that she was the friend in question. "The trader in orbit told us that no one was permitted to land on Trellus. When we ignored his advice, he fired on us. We had to make an emergency landing, and the crash destroyed our vessel. We are stranded here now."

"So are we, curse that mud-sucking Terran up there." Posbret's grip loosened. "Where is this husband of yours now?"

"Drefan has him over at Omega Dome," Mercy

said. "Are you satisfied, or should I draw some stick figures?"

For a moment I thought the Gnilltak might not release me. Then he abruptly let go, and I dropped to the floor. Cat grabbed me and kept me from landing on my face. In doing so the Omorr felt the strap of my blade harness, and gave me a wary look.

"Watch your hide, Terran." The Gnilltak raider shouldered his rifle and left, his men filing out behind him.

While Cat repaired the damage Posbret had inflicted on the house security grid, Mercy sent her frightened girls off duty and cleared the remaining customers out of the house.

"We're closed for the rest of the day because I said so," she told one male as the disgruntled tricks departed. "Keep giving me grief and I'll cancel the free return visit I credited to your account—and call your spouse to let her know how much you enjoy being whipped before you mate."

Before we left for the meeting, Mercy showed me a room in a private, well-monitored section of the house. The furnishings appeared more subdued than those in the pleasure rooms, but I preferred the restful textures and colors. After living for so long on a world of white and blue ice, vivid colors unsettled me. Some combinations even nauseated me.

"These will be your quarters. Mine are right through there"—she pointed to a door panel— "and Cat is across the hall."

I removed the Ana Hansen mask from my face,

and the Lok-teel became a blob again and slid under my collar.

"The room terminal and the emergency transmitter are voice-activated," Mercy continued, "and we'll keep ours connected with yours. If anything happens, you only have to call out and Cat or I will be in here in two seconds."

"What could happen that I would need you so quickly?" I asked, and saw a flash of raw emotion pass over her face. Fear, and something like outrage. "Mercy?"

"Nothing." She handed me a stack of dark blue garments. "We look to be about the same size, so these should fit you. Get washed up and changed while I arrange our escort."

She left me in the room, and I made use of the cleansing unit before I put on the tunic and trousers she had given me. I decided to take the Lok-teel with me, in the event I needed to disguise my features again. After I tucked it under my tunic, I tidied my hair. Duncan preferred it down and loose, and often brushed it out himself in the evenings. Nerves and something else made me begin separating my hair into sections.

My fingers itched to do something. Something I had never done. *Weave.*

Slowly, without any conscious intention on my part, my fingers did just that: They curled around the sections and wove them together, in and out of each other, turning all the loose hair into a cable. A brief search turned up some jeweled clips, which I used to secure the cable's loops to the back of my head.

Not a cable. A braid.

I looked at my image in the reflecting plas above the vanity unit. I had been allowed to keep my long hair among the vral, as they feared me and the effects of my amnesia, but . . . I could not remember learning how to weave it like this.

Iisleg women do not braid their hair. They cannot. They wear it too short.

Dark blue eyes stared back at me, unblinking, unforgiving. *I am not an Iisleg woman.*

I reached out to the plas, touching the slick surface with my fingertips. The woman on the other side did the same, but at the very last moment her hand became a fist and smashed into the plas, punching through it and reaching for my throat—

"Cherijo?"

I blinked, and the shattered plas became whole, and the woman inside it became my reflection again.

Mercy came to stand behind me. She looked as angry as she had when I'd first arrived. "That stupid mule-headed hermit agreed to a meeting, but he wants to see only you. He'll allow you to bring a drone escort for protection."

I noted her white lips and the hands curled tightly against her sides. "Protection from what?"

"Posbret and every other credit-hungry raider on this rock, I suppose." As she shrugged, her gaze dropped away from mine. "You ready?"

I turned my back on the thing in the mirror. "Yes."

Four of Mercy's drednocs escorted me out of the brothel and through the pressurized access ways that connected most of the colony. I argued against so many—surely one was more than enough—but she was adamant.

"Drefan is being particularly unfriendly, even for him," she told me. "I don't know what he's planning, but I want you back here as soon as possible. Husband or no husband. Or Cat and I are coming after you."

I thought the abrupt turnaround in her attitude toward me was rather touching. "Are you sure you don't want me to stay at Drefan's dome? It would mean less trouble for you."

"You"—she poked her finger at my sternum—"are still in debt to me. You come back."

I suited up—another precaution that Mercy insisted on—and followed two of the drednocs into the long, transparent corridor of plas leading to Omega Dome. The other two battle drones followed me, the flickering lights from their chassis dancing across the convex interior of the access way.

Mercy had programmed the drones to respond to my inquiries, so I asked, "How long will it take to reach Omega Dome?"

"At current speed, one minute, forty-two seconds," the drone replied. As it did, the glowing halo of energy around its upper sensor case changed color from purple to green.

"What is the significance of your halo colors?"

"This color indicates this unit is in standard operational mode." The drone's halo turned purple again. "This color indicates this unit is in battle mode."

I looked at the other drednocs. All of their halos glowed purple. "Are you expecting a confrontation?"

"This unit cannot expect," it told me. "Current operational modes were included in programmed orders to escort Terran female designated Resa to Omega Dome."

Mercy had put them all in battle mode before we'd left her dome. I needed to discover what my host feared enough to surround me with four drones ready to kill something. "Is there a threat-identification protocol in your current program?"

"Affirmative."

"Define identification parameters," I said.

"Pass code required."

I had no idea what code Mercy had used to safeguard the information, or why she felt a need to do so. "Cancel previous inquiry."

The drone's halo turned green for a moment as it processed my request. At the same time, I heard a hissing sound and turned toward the air lock we were passing in time to see a reptilian being launch itself at us.

It hit the drednoc I had been questioning, which

fell sideways in front of me, its grapplers slipping on the oily, scaled hide of the attacker. I jumped back, colliding with the drone behind me, and then I was snatched up and held above the fray.

"Put me down," I ordered. The drone ignored me.

The attacker, a huge Tingalean, punched one of its stunted arms through the fallen drednoc's armored chassis. Its limb went through the alloy as if it were worn cloth. With a twist it seized and ripped out the drone's command core. The drednoc instantly shut down and became inert.

The being looked up at me and bared two dagger-long fangs dripping with poison. Its eyes were black and lidless, which made the dark blood rimming them easy to spot. Only a serious head injury caused that sort of bleeding, even in reptilian life-forms.

"I am a healer," I said in a calm, clear voice. "Stop this and I will help you."

Purple light filled the access way as the drone holding me wrapped its extensors around me. The other drones converged on the Tingalean from either side, but it slithered out from under them and struck at the tripod of my drone, trying to unbalance it.

"Stand down," I called out to the drones. "It may be hurt."

The drednocs did not respond to my command but raised their weapons. Pulse fire struck the reptilian in the back, and it screamed before it reversed itself and darted back into the air lock. The door panels slid shut before the drones could follow. After several fruitless attempts to open the air lock doors by the other drones, the drednoc holding me carefully set me down on my feet.

"This was completely unnecessary." I knelt beside the fallen drednoc, but without its command core it couldn't respond or move. "Why didn't you listen to me when I told you to stand down?"

The drednocs formed a triad around me and their inert comrade. "These units are programmed to protect Terran female Resa," one of them said.

"You could have defended me without hurting the Tingalean." I had never seen such a display of hostility, especially from the reptilian. Although their poisons made them some of the deadliest beings in the galaxy, Tingaleans were a notoriously placid, nonaggressive species, who dedicated themselves to remaining as neutral as the Jorenians. "Have there been other attacks like this?"

"Unknown," one of the drones replied.

"Well, who was it attacking?" I asked. "You, or me?"

"Unknown."

There were far too many damn unknowns on this planet.

"Signal Mercy," I told the drednoc who was responding to me. "Relay what happened here."

"Affirmative," it said. "Does Terran female Resa wish to return to Mercy House?"

"No." I stood and went to the air lock, but the

door panel remained jammed shut from the inside. "Take me to—"

Something overhead moved, and bright, hot beams of light sliced down from a maintenance hatch, skewering each of the drednocs. Their emitters burst and sparked as they shook, unable to move, impaled by the light.

I looked up, but the intensity of the light made it impossible to see what had pinned the drones. I saw armor begin to liquefy around the beams, and remembered that Trellus had once been used to mine arutanium. I flattened myself back against the access way wall. The only thing that could remove and process the mineral was an arutanium particle laser, which would cut through anything it touched—including me.

Abruptly the powerful mining beams shut off, and all three of the remaining drones went inert and toppled over, spilling pools of steaming fluid from their melted insides. I didn't wait to see what would come out of the hatch or the air lock, but ran. I was in a section of the access way that offered no exits except to the surface.

It can't follow me out there.

My weighted envirosuit, which had not been designed for speed of movement, dragged at my limbs. I heard a familiar hissing sound behind me and scanned the sides of the access way. I headed for an outer air lock and hurled myself into it, shutting the doors and securing them as the Tingalean had.

Something threw itself into the panels from the other side, denting the thick plasteel. Then a laser began humming.

The suit's gloves made my fingers clumsy, but I enabled my suit's temperature controls and air supply flow, checked my seals, and opened the doors to the surface. Air rushed around me as the Tingalean used the laser to burn through the air lock's seal, and I silently prayed that no one else had entered the access way.

On the surface, I saw that I was only a few hundred yards out from Drefan's enormous Omega Dome, and decided to walk toward it rather than cross the greater distance back to Mercy House. I forced myself not to hurry so that I wouldn't trip, fall, and break one of my seals. I didn't look back at the air lock. The crazed Tingalean had not been wearing protective gear; it had to be suffocating or dead.

A hiss came over my suit com, making my blood freeze as I slowly turned and saw the reptilian in its own envirosuit, emerging from the surface air lock and moving more rapidly than I had thought possible. Under its arm it carried what had to be the mining laser.

It had disabled four battle drones. My chances of stopping or eluding it were unlikely. I pressed the com button on my suit control panel, transmitting my audio to any console within range that had an open channel.

"This is Resa," I said as I kept moving. "Mercy, if

you can hear this, the drones you sent with me are all disabled. I'm out on the surface being pursued by the Tingalean who attacked them. It has a mining laser. I don't think I'm going to reach Omega Dome in time to escape it."

"Dr. Grey Veil?" an unfamiliar Terran male's voice asked.

"Yes. Did you hear my last transmission?" I went around the edge of a small crater filled with jagged rock. "My escort was attacked and—"

"You're alone out there," he finished for me. "We picked up your com signal. You have to take cover now. That cluster of basalt pillars fifty yards to your right will do. Stay there until the threat is neutralized."

I didn't know how he could see me, but I wouldn't waste time finding out. I made my way to the pillars and carefully squeezed into a gap between two of them. The surface began to tremble under my heavy soles, and I saw a long, wide shadow stretch out toward the Tingalean.

This drednoc was twice the size of Mercy's, with a different configuration of extensors and attachments. It looked more like a man—like a mechanical giant of a man—with a larger sensor case, grapplers made to appear like humanoid arms, and two lower appendages that functioned like biped legs. It gave off strange vibrations, and as it passed the pillars, they caused dust from them to slowly rain down on my helmet.

The Tingalean enabled the laser and aimed it at the

pillars, completely ignoring the drednoc. The giant came up and snatched the laser out of the lizard being's hands just as it fired, shifting the beam up into space. The drednoc backhanded the Tingalean, who sailed over the airless surface and landed near the junction of two access ways. It pulled open a hatch and disappeared into it.

"It's gone," I said, trying not to hyperventilate as the drednoc lumbered over to the mining laser and picked it up. It switched off the power cells and continued on its way to Omega Dome. "Drefan, can you hear me?"

"Yes," he said as the drednoc disappeared inside the dome. "You should come inside now, Doctor. Enter where you see the red light."

Just such a light pulsed three times above an air lock, but not the one the drednoc had used. I wriggled out from between the pillars and hurried toward it.

Seven

I went inside and passed through the same series of air locks and decon procedures as I had at Mercy House. Whatever the colonists' problems, they were absolutely the cleanest beings I'd ever encountered.

I expected to be met by another drone, but the being who stepped through the last of the decon chambers was a Chakacat, a feline who walked upright like a person. This one wore an abbreviated leather garment around its hips, and a weapons harness made of four narrow straps wrapped diagonally around its lean torso. I had assumed its species was peaceful, but this one carried power and blade weapons.

I had already met one of its kind on board the *Sunlace*, a former domestic companion named Alunthri. Although that one had been a gentle, intelligent creature who spoke better than some of the Iisleg I had known, it had taken some time for me to become accustomed to the idea of a walking, talking, hermaphroditic feline.

This one had the same silvery pelt and bullet-shaped head as Alunthri, but it was larger, and its muscles more developed. An alien wariness sharpened its clear, colorless eyes as it returned my scrutiny. It also held a weapon trained on me.

"I am Keel, the games master's assistant," it told me, showing small, sharp teeth that matched the golden color of its talons. "Were you injured during the attack, Dr. Grey Veil?"

I shook my head as I began stripping out of the suit.

"Answer me with words, if you please."

It didn't understand body language? Alunthri had certainly read mine well enough. "I am fine." I straightened my garments and eyed the weapon it was lowering. "Where is my husband?"

"Come with me." It extended a paw toward the outer corridor.

The interior of Omega Dome proved to be as austere as Mercy House was luxurious. I noted a shield-shaped medallion in the center of all of the wall panels, and the distinctive emblem inside the three-cornered symbol of protection. A Terran letter "D" formed from the image of a half-waned moon with a sword running diagonally through it.

"The 'D' stands for Drefan?" I asked the cat.

It hesitated a moment too long before it answered me. "Yes."

Clear viewer panels began to appear, and I

looked through one to see two groups of males attacking each other in the middle of a jungle. The ferocity of the battle startled me. "There are people fighting in there."

"Some of them are colonists," the Chakacat said. "Most are simulated combatants. The quality and variety of Omega Dome bloodsport simulations are renowned throughout the quadrant. Our programs are still as close as you can get to authentic combat without entering a slaver arena or joining the military."

"I have been in authentic combat," I told it. "I did not find it entertaining." As we walked on, I passed five more panels before I asked, "How many of these simulation chambers do you have here?"

"Three hundred and fifty singles, seventy-two doubles, and twenty-eight multiples, and a grand central arena for large team play. This is central control." The Chakacat stopped in front of a room without a viewer and tapped a keypad with one claw tip. The panel opened to reveal a room filled with monitors and controls, much the same as the one at Mercy House.

"Do you people do anything on this planet that is not watched by another?" I grumbled as I walked in.

"I take it you don't think highly of spectators," a man said as he came out from behind one of the consoles. He did not rise out of his seat but tapped the controls on one arm and made it glide across the floor toward me.

This Terran male's upper torso bulged with heavy muscles, but he couldn't leave his chair. Space yawned where his lower limbs should have been. Other parts of him were missing as well.

"See anything you like?" he asked.

"I can see that you have one arm and no legs," I said, annoyed by his self-effacing taunt. "Why are you in that chair? Were you not properly fitted with prosthetics?"

"I forgot how direct healers can be." He sounded more amused than offended. "As it happens, I do have prosthetics, but they are uncomfortable, and I prefer the chair. It's faster."

"Artificial limbs are not only for your personal benefit," I pointed out. "They improve your appearance and how others perceive you. How uncomfortable are they? Perhaps they were not fitted correctly."

"Oh, they fit. Only too well." He rested a hand on his thigh, which ended where a knee should have been. "The discomfort is, shall we say, more spiritual."

I had dealt with amputees on Akkabarr, and after an engineering accident on the *Sunlace* during our jaunt to Joren. Loss of mobility and body function often inflicted more pain than the actual injuries. Sympathy, however, rarely helped alleviate the victim's suffering.

"I see," I said briskly. "So you wallow in that chair and your self-pity, and insure that everyone around you does the same. Not how I would wish to live, but you must do as you will."

"We any of us rarely do as we will, Doctor." He offered his hand in Terran fashion. "James Drefan, Games Master. You have many names, according to the bounty particulars, but I believe that you are called Cherijo."

"Yes." I turned to Keel. "Where is Reever?"

The Chakacat was standing between me and the only exit, like a guard. "He will join us shortly."

"While we wait, Doctor, would you be so kind as to remove your weapons and put them there?" Drefan gestured to a nearby table.

I was not eager to give up my blades. "Why do you want them?"

"No one is permitted to carry real weapons inside the dome for safety reasons." He smiled a little. "There are, shall we say, too many temptations to use them."

"I am feeling one right now." I reached under my tunic and removed my blade harness, dropping it onto the table.

Drefan eyed it. "We did scan you for weapons before you entered the dome, Doctor."

Reluctantly I bent down and removed the sheaths strapped to my calves, and added them to the others.

"Thank you. Are you hungry? I can dial up a meal for you." The Terran looked over my shoulder at Keel, who took my blades and departed. "Davidov's blockade has reduced us to living on synthetics, but they're edible."

"I thank you, no." I sensed I was being analyzed, measured, or otherwise toyed with, and my patience stretched thin. "Where is my husband?"

Drefan consulted one of the monitors. "At the moment, it appears that he's crawling through one of the simulator power conduits."

"What? Why?"

"Your husband is determined to escape my custody." He turned the screen so that I could see the image of Reever inching his way through an alarmingly narrow passage. A panel opened, and he was pulled out. "Ah, there. Keel has arrived with some drones to retrieve him."

I watched the screen as the feed switched to another area, where my husband was fighting a domestic drone. The Chakacat stood by and held a weapon trained on Reever.

"What have you done to him?"

"Nothing, except refuse to allow him to leave the dome," Drefan assured me. "This would be his third attempt to escape since my salvage drones brought him in. Apparently he's not interested in accepting our hospitality."

I gasped as two more drones joined the fight. "Tell him to stop."

"I've tried, several times. He won't listen to me, and I'm running out of drones." Drefan looked at me full-face for the first time, revealing a smooth socket where his right eye should have been. "Perhaps you'd care to save my equipment and relay a few words of reassurance to him."

I leaned over the console and enabled the audio. "Duncan, I am here with Drefan. Stop fighting them. Let the feline bring you to me."

Reever shoved the one drone that he hadn't yet disabled out of his way, and came to the vid screen. "How did you get here?"

"I grew tired of waiting for you to come for me." I touched the screen with my fingertips. "I am all right, Duncan. Go with the cat. It will bring you to me."

He nodded and turned to the Chakacat. "Take me to her now."

Drefan reached over and shut off the vid. "You're very devoted to each other, I take it."

"Take it however you like." I watched my husband and the feline retreat out of sight. "It's a mistake to come between us."

"Admirable." Drefan moved his chair around me to access another screen. "But on Trellus, that sort of bond could be rather dangerous."

"To anyone who threatens us, yes." I faced him. "Why did that Tingalean attack me? Is it sick? Has it gone mad? Is that why Davidov has quarantined the colony?"

"I wish I had the answers you desire, Doctor, but I am as mystified by these events as you." He input some data on the console, his one hand moving back and forth along the keys with considerable speed. "What is your connection with Davidov?"

"None. I met him only yesterday."

"And your husband?" He looked up as the Chakacat and Reever came in. "Reever, how kind of you to join us."

I saw the blood on my husband's tunic and in his hair a moment before I embraced him. "What did they do to you?"

"Nothing yet." He looked over my head at the crippled Terran. "Why is she here? What do you want from us?"

"Your wife owes me nothing. Her debt belongs to Mercy, and I believe they've amicably settled the terms of repayment." Drefan studied us for a moment. "She can pay your debt to me, if she is willing."

Reever's mouth flattened. "You will not use her in your games."

"I confess, I am intrigued by the idea of forcing a surgeon to do battle, especially one who cannot be killed," Drefan said, "but no, I do not want her for the games. I merely ask that she perform the same services that she promised to Mercy. Full medical examinations for every member of my staff."

His request surprised me as much as Mercy's had. There had to be more to this than the fact that Trellus had no physician on colony. They were worried about something specific, a serious health issue, and they wanted me to find it or confirm it.

"If the colonists are suffering from some sort of illness," I said, "I will be glad to treat them. But I have to know what is happening here."

"There is no plague for you to cure this time, Doctor," Drefan said. "Only the most common of injuries and sickness. Before Davidov came, we would send them off colony for treatment. Now we do what we can for each other, but I would feel better having a professional check out my people."

Reever looked at me and shook his head slightly.

"My wife will examine your staff," he said to Drefan. "That will satisfy my debt to you?"

"For the salvage, yes," the games master said. "You will soon need protection from Posbret and some of the other colonists, which I can also offer."

"We can deal with them ourselves," I told him before Reever replied.

"If that is your wish. There's only one more thing." The crippled Terran changed the image on the viewer to that of the surface, where *Moonfire* had crashed. "If you intend to leave Trellus, you will need viable transportation. That appears to be a problem."

"If you want the ship for salvage," Reever said, "take it."

"On the contrary. I have sent my engineers out to examine the damage to your scout, and they tell me that we have the parts and resources required to fix it." Drefan gestured toward a screen that showed the *Renko* in orbit. "We might even be able to distract Davidov long enough to allow you to launch and escape before he notices."

He had given it some thought, I noted. "You expect us to take you along?"

Drefan smiled at me. "No. I'm staying here. Once you're out of range of Davidov's signal jammers, you can transmit our relays to the quadrant authorities, and they will send the militia to deal with him."

I knew we couldn't leave Trellus unless the Jorenians sent a rescue party, or *Moonfire* could be repaired. At the same time, I didn't trust Drefan and his eagerness to help us. He didn't know us, and he wasn't being truthful with us.

"Why haven't you repaired your own ships?" Reever asked.

"After the last attempt to escape the colony, Davidov destroyed them all," Drefan said. "You can see the wreckage on the south side of the colony complex, where our main transport facility used to be. Be grateful that your ship is still viable."

"You have specific data on these repairs that I can review?" Reever asked, and the other man nodded. "Assuming what you say is true, and your plan can be carried out, what is your price?"

"I want you," Drefan said to my husband, "to fight in my games."

Reever paled.

"No." I knew how much Duncan had suffered during the years he spent as a slave. His Hsktskt owner had forced him to fight in the arenas, where he had no choice but to kill or be killed. "My husband cannot fight."

"He had no difficulty routing my drones," Drefan told me. "But if he doesn't care for bloodsport, I will make it a single match—one with an opponent worthy of his skills."

"I will accept," Reever said quietly, before I could repeat a refusal, "under two conditions. I will not fight to the death."

"Agreed," Drefan said. "And the other?"

Reever gripped my hand tightly. "I want to first see this worthy opponent fight."

The games master turned to Keel. "Have Tya brought to the melee room."

We followed Drefan's glidechair out of the control room and down to what he called the hover view.

"Our customers became bored with the old stationary observation decks," he told Reever as we stepped into a large, round, flat-bottomed area furnished with seats. "This allows them to change positions above the simulation, to get the best vantage point. Important when you're running large programs, and the fighting can become confusing from the ground level."

"Your assistant told me that the people I saw fighting were colonists and simulations," I said. "But they all looked real."

"Our simulators are not based on League or Jorenian technology," Drefan said. "We trade with a supplier who has collected some interesting artifacts from distant worlds. I'll wager that what we use here is not like anything you've seen."

The hover view launched down a short tunnel

into a spacious, empty simulation grid. We floated silently above it, and then Drefan brought the craft down to what he called the optimum observation level.

"The grids are modified versions of League standard holoprojectors," Drefan said as he worked on the console in front of him. "Each simulation is stocked with an appropriate quantity of holographite, which is charged with light energy and converts itself into whatever we wish: weapons, landscapes, climate conditions, terrain, and of course, opponents."

Optic emitters flickered as the simulation program initiated, and the yellow and black grid disappeared, replaced by a seething alien jungle and red-brown skies.

"Itan Odaras," Reever murmured.

"You recognize the place." Drefan sounded pleased. "It's one of our most frequently programmed simulations."

"It is the wrong color." My husband did not seem pleased at all. "The ground should be soaked with the blood of the three point seven million beings that were slaughtered during the ten years of fighting there."

"Our customers want the illusion, my friend," Drefan said. "Not the reality."

Reever met his gaze. "I am not your friend, Games Master."

I kept my hand in his, but my attention was drawn down to five figures that entered the grid.

Four of them were large crossbreed marauders, dressed out in full raiding gear, with long swords and clubs. The fifth, a drednoc in combat armor, carried huge double-edged battle-axes in both spiked gauntlets. I recognized the drone as the same one that had driven the Tingalean away from me on the surface.

"Your drednoc is very unusual," I said. "Why did you choose to . . . ?" My voice trailed off as a sixth and final combatant entered the grid. This one was as tall and almost as broad as the machine giant, but wore a metallic thermal garment and a clear ice-stone slave collar around its scaled throat. "Your simulations are quite convincing."

Reever stood, equally riveted. "That is not a simulation."

"Your husband is correct," Drefan said. "The raiders are generated holographite constructs, but the drednoc and my Hsktskt gladiator are real."

"Gladiatrix," I said, identifying the combatant as a female from her brow scales and pelvic notches. "Was she marooned here when Davidov came?"

"No. I own her."

Reever made a harsh sound. "That's not possible. No Hsktskt has ever been successfully enslaved. If they are captured, they commit suicide at the first opportunity."

"True, unless the Hsktskt is under a life-debt to you," Drefan said, rubbing a finger across his chin. "As this one is to me."

"*You* saved the life of a Hsktskt," Reever said.

"I bought the life-debt she owed to another." The games master smiled at my husband. "I've shocked you. Surely you know that you can buy anyone or anything if you have the right price."

Reever looked disgusted now. "Hsktskt do not sell themselves."

I watched the female Hsktskt take her position facing all five of her opponents. She waited in place, unmoving, as the marauders called out insults and the drednoc's halo deepened to a dark purple. She seemed unaffected by the noise or the number of combatants she would fight.

"Tya." Drefan spoke over an audio com that could clearly be heard down on the grid floor, and waited until the Hsktskt looked up at him. "I want you to give our visitors a proper demonstration of what you can do." He input something on the hover view's console.

The female Hsktskt regarded the games master steadily as a sword and shield materialized at her feet. She made no move to touch the weapons.

"Pick them up, Tya, and use them this time." Drefan waited, but the Hsktskt remained unarmed. He sighed. "She can be very stubborn." He pressed another button, and a lyrical chime shimmered through the air.

The sound galvanized the four marauders, who charged the Hsktskt, roaring promises of death and dismemberment as they ran. Tya waited until the first pair nearly reached her before she dropped and knocked them off their feet with a sweep of her tail.

A third heaved his hammer down on her skull, but she rolled out of the way and leaped to her feet. She ripped the skull-basher's arm from his body and bludgeoned him with it before thrusting her talons into the hearts of the two on the ground. The fourth staggered as his armless comrade fell into him, and she brought two limbs together to decapitate both of them simultaneously.

I couldn't breathe, but I could shout. "Behind you—the drednoc."

An ax flashed, but Tya heard my warning and moved in time to avoid a fierce, killing blow from the mechanical giant. The second ax might have buried itself in her abdomen, but she seemed to anticipate the movement, bowed her back, and caught the shaft as it swept past with one of her lower limbs. A wrench should have knocked it from the drone's grip, but it countered the move and spun away. She followed, watching the drednoc's moves. She did not seem afraid or worried, only focused.

I gripped the edge of the hover view, the alloy rim bruising my palms. I had never seen anyone but Reever fight with such speed or dispassion.

At last the drednoc attacked, and raked its spiked gauntlet across Tya's face, trying to damage her large, vulnerable eyes. She grunted as she dropped and drove her shoulder into the drednoc's chest plate. I heard the sound of armor denting before Tya knocked the drone back and dropped to the ground to grab the weapons she had ignored since the battle began.

"Whoever programmed your drednoc," Reever said to Drefan, "has never fought in the arena."

"Indeed." Drefan eyed the mechanical giant. "Perhaps you can give me some input later."

The drednoc reeled back a few steps, and then brought its second ax down with a hook toward Tya's triangular jaw. She met the curved blade with her shield, and sparks flew as the metals clanged and ground together. The ropy muscles in her arms bulged as she countered the force and strength of the drone, and the weapons quivered between them.

"That's enough," I said, afraid to see another Hsktskt die before my eyes. I had watched too much of that on Vtaga. "Stop this now."

"Have you seen enough?" Drefan asked Reever, who nodded. He tapped the console and the simulation vanished, leaving only the Hsktskt and the drednoc facing each other. At the same time, Drefan lowered the hover view to floor level and exited the craft, his glidechair soundless as it moved across the grid. "Disarm, Tya."

Tya dropped the sword and shield before Drefan's chair.

"Very good." Drefan turned to Reever. "Now that you've seen her fight, will you accept my terms?"

"No," I said at once. "He cannot fight her. She is too strong. She will kill him."

"It is only an exhibition match, Doctor, and Tya will do as she's told," Drefan informed me. He gave the Hsktskt a thoughtful look. "Won't you, my dear?"

The Hsktskt female studied me and then Reever, but I saw no emotion or concern in her saucer-sized yellow eyes. She seemed less animated than the simulations she had fought. Slowly she tilted her head back, baring her throat in a gesture of submission.

"Very good," Drefan said.

I could not believe a Hsktskt female warrior had just capitulated to a warm-blooded cripple whose neck she could snap with one flick of her wrist. Not after watching her fight the way she had. "Is everyone on this planet insane?"

Instead of taking offense, the games master grinned like a boy. "Probably."

Tya straightened and went to exit the grid. She paused after passing the drednoc, turned, and looped one of her arms around its head. With a wrench she tore the sensor case off the chassis and tossed it at Drefan. The drone's head landed in his lap. She looked at Reever again before she departed.

"Well." Drefan picked up the drone's head and regarded it ruefully. "I did instruct her to give you a proper demonstration."

Drefan insisted we share a meal with him, and I agreed to, but not because I was hungry. I needed time to think of something I could offer him in return for repairing *Moonfire* that would not require Reever to fight that Hsktskt.

I didn't care what Drefan claimed she would or would not do. The image of her tearing the head off the battle drone would not get out of my head.

We went to Drefan's quarters, where Keel was waiting. The games master ordered the Chakacat to prepare a Terran meal, and then moved his glidechair over to a cabinet, from which he removed a container of spicewine. Although he had only one arm, he deftly poured it into three servers.

"Why do you want my husband to fight Tya?" I asked. "Why not a simulation? They can be programmed to assure that he is not harmed."

"There is no sport in that, Doctor," Drefan said as he handed us each one of the servers. "I know of only one other Terran to whom a Hsktskt owed a life-debt. I never thought he would crash on Trellus and become indebted to me. Can you blame me for wishing to recreate such an event?"

"I did not fight a Hsktskt on the sands to earn the life-debt," my husband said. "I stopped the assassination of an important Faction member."

"It's said that you did that by dragging the assassin into the arena," Drefan tacked on, "and cutting him to pieces."

My husband gave him a bland look. "Such stories become overblown legends that barely resemble the actual events."

Drefan lifted his server in a silent toast. "Yet you were adopted by TssVar and made a member of the Faction for what you did that day. It must have been quite impressive, seeing as TssVar also adopted you as a blood brother."

"I would like to know where you have gotten your information," my husband said casually.

"Here and there. Rumors abound in my business." Drefan regarded his server. "The last of my spicewine. I have another three bottles, and then I will have to make do with synthale until we rid ourselves of Davidov."

Reever didn't touch his server. "How did you acquire Tya's life-debt?"

"Davidov sold it to me." Drefan smiled as I gaped. "It was the last transaction he made before he shut down the colony, in fact. I suspect it was to punish her, or us, but I could not pass up the bargain."

"Hsktskt do not allow themselves to be treated like commodities," Reever told him. "They consider it beneath them, like most warm-blooded behaviors. Did Davidov tell you any details about how he acquired her life-debt?"

"He told me that she held the rank of centuron during the war. He met her just after her superiors had apprehended her for deserting her post, or something like that." Drefan shrugged. "I presume you know what the Faction does to military deserters? Davidov refused to give me any of the specifics, and Tya never speaks of it."

"They're hung upside down in public, and then they're beaten to death. Slowly. It takes some weeks for them to die." Reever regarded the other man closely. "Davidov spent many years freeing Hsktskt slaves. I find it unlikely that he would rescue a member of the Faction."

The smooth brow over the crater that had once been Drefan's eye lifted. "You know Davidov well, then."

"We have shared some causes in the past." Reever's expression remained impassive. "Why do you wish me to fight her in front of an audience? Is this some creative form of execution?"

"Her kind have enslaved and slaughtered millions of members of humanoid species, including the founders of this colony," Drefan said. "If anyone should be executed, it should be her."

"I will not fight to the death," my husband reminded him. "No matter what she or any of the Hsktskt have done to you."

Keel interrupted the conversation to announce that the meal was ready, and then silently left Drefan's quarters. I would have been happy to wait until the men finished eating before I started my meal, as I didn't recognize the unappetizing-looking stew Keel had dialed up, but Reever touched my arm and linked with me.

Eat with us, he said. *It is Terran custom, and Drefan responds better to you than me.*

What do you wish me to ask him?

Find out how he came to be here on Trellus.

I sampled the stew, which contained cubes of synpro instead of real meat. Despite this, Keel had somehow made it savory with a skilled addition of piquant herbs. I complimented the dish and inquired as to what had been added.

"I believe it's rosemary, thyme, and sage," Drefan said. "My assistant grows Terran herbs for me in one of the agridomes."

"There is nothing like food from one's homeworld." I tried very hard not to remember some of the things I had eaten on Akkabarr. "What made you leave Terra and journey all the way out here?"

"I intended to stay on the homeworld and increase my family's holdings." He wheeled over to the prep unit and returned with a server of water. "My pursuit of that goal eventually brought me here."

"Were you injured on Terra, or while you were traveling?"

"I lost my limbs in a mining accident." Drefan glanced down at his leg stumps. "I wanted to die after it happened. A friend convinced me that my life was not over." He said *life* as if it meant *punishment*.

"So now you indulge bloodthirsty game players and rescue rogue Hsktskt cowards."

He chuckled. "I suppose I do."

"You must have paid Davidov a great deal for her life-debt," Reever said.

"Twenty thousand stan credits," Drefan replied. "Hardly a blip compared to what I could make if I gave your wife to Davidov." He glanced at me. "I don't think Tya is a coward. If she were, she would never fight as she does."

He gave nothing away in his tone, but I sensed that he actually cared about the Hsktskt female. "Has she ever said why she deserted her post?"

"Davidov told me that she botched a raid, and she didn't want to face the consequences. Excuse me for a moment." Drefan moved his chair over to the console, where he summoned Keel.

"I understand that a Hsktskt raid wiped out the original colony on Trellus," I said when Drefan returned to the table. "Surely Mercy and the others who survived cannot be pleased by Tya's presence on Trellus."

"No one outside my staff knows Tya exists," Drefan said. "Nor will they, until I broadcast Reever's match with her throughout the domes. It should be quite entertaining." He turned to my husband. "That is, if you agree to fight her."

Reever put his hand over mine. *He is not telling the whole truth, but unless he helps us repair* Moonfire, *we cannot leave Trellus.*

I didn't want him to go anywhere near that Hsktskt, but he was right. Davidov had left us no choice. *I trust your judgment.*

To Drefan, Reever said, "I will fight her."

Eight

Drefan would not allow Reever to leave Omega Dome until I performed the exams on his staff, which I calculated would take several days. I had an obligation to return to Mercy House to do the same there. I suggested contacting her and making arrangements to share my time between the two domes, but Drefan refused to let me signal the brothel owner.

"I have to tell her about the Tingalean," I said. "Her drednocs were destroyed, defending me." Hopefully we would not be expected to pay for them as well as the salvage, or Reever and I would never get off this world.

Reever caught my arm and swung me around to face him. "You were attacked?"

I'd forgotten that he didn't know about the skirmish with the Tingalean. "It happened when I came here from Mercy House. I wasn't hurt."

"You two have a great deal to discuss," Drefan

said. "You will stay here tonight with Reever, Doctor. I will signal Mercy and make arrangements with her on how best to share your services until the exams are completed." But if either of you tell Mercy or anyone outside Omega Dome about Tya, I will void the repayment agreement."

"The next time we go sojourning," I told Duncan as we followed the games master out of his quarters, "we are bringing an entire cargo hold of credits with us."

Drefan escorted me and Reever to our rooms, and bid us good night. I expected him to lock us in, but the door panel controls were enabled inside.

"He is very trusting," I said as I secured the entrance.

"The entire facility is under constant monitor," my husband said as he walked around and inspected the place. "That is why I was not able to come to you. He will also be watching our every move." He pointed to several areas. "Tell me what happened with the Tingalean."

I recounted how I had been escorted by drednocs from Mercy House, and described the Tingalean's vicious attack. "It used a mining laser on them. They never had a chance to defend themselves."

"Drones are mechanized constructs, Jarn," Reever said. "Not people."

"It still wasn't fair." I went to the external viewer, which showed the remains of the old ore-processing towers. "Do you sense how afraid they are?"

"Colonists who are isolated like this often develop suspicious natures," Reever said. "Davidov's blockade has not helped."

"I think it is more than that." There was only one substance I knew that could invoke the worst fears of an entire population: Odnallak bone dust, which an old enemy of Cherijo's had used to infect the Hsktskt on their homeworld. The plague on Vtaga had brought out primal fears invoked by the memories of an ancient, extinct threat. "SrrokVar could not have infected this planet. He never had the chance to send PyrsVar offplanet with the bone dust." A thought occurred to me. "Could someone else have taken it from Vtaga?"

"TssVar saw to it that the entire supply was destroyed. However, all that is needed to create it are the bones of an Odnallak." Reever came to stand behind me. "Do you believe the colonists' paranoia to be that excessive?"

"I don't know. Perhaps my own fears are magnifying things. I will scan them for dust contamination when I begin the medical exams." Once more I saw the Tingalean's blood-rimmed eyes in my mind, which puzzled me. "Can you retrieve some specifics about the Tingalean species on the room terminal?"

Reever went over to the console and input an inquiry. "The colonial database offers only general information."

I looked at the screen. "There." I pointed to one submenu header on species anatomy. "I need to see this section." Reever pulled up the data, and I studied the text and diagram that appeared. "Magnify the optic structures." As the screen filled with the Tingalean's cranial case, I noted the muscle encircling the being's orbital socket membrane. "As I thought. There are no blood vessels."

Reever looked. "I don't understand what you mean."

"In the Tingalean's eye sockets, there are no blood vessels. The eye structure is protected by a mucusoid layer surrounding it and the optic nerve bundle." I gnawed at my bottom lip. "I know that I saw blood in its eyes, all around the rims."

"If it had a head injury, the blood might have run into the eyes," Reever said.

I concentrated, recalling the blur of the Tingalean's features. "It was not injured or bleeding. There were no penetrating wounds to its face or skull. The only way to cause that much bleeding in this species would be to pull its eyes from the sockets, sever the optic nerves, and then push them back in place. But doing that would blind it, and this one could see perfectly."

"It may have attacked someone before you," Reever said. "The blood of its victim may have gotten into its eyes."

I shook my head. "The blood was Tingalean in color."

"I will check to see how many of its kind are on Trellus." Reever switched the screen to the colonial census database, and input a population inquiry. "There is only one Tingalean listed as residing on colony."

"So the blood didn't come from another Tingalean." I frowned. "Is there a death record listed for a second?" When he shook his head, I exhaled in frustration. "How many people are on Trellus?"

"According to colonial census, two thousand, four hundred and eight have permanent residence status," my husband read from the screen. "Eighty-two visitors have arrived but not departed."

Something occurred to me. "What was the population count seven days ago?"

He changed the date of the inquiry. "Two thousand, four hundred and eleven." Before I could ask, he added, "There were no deaths recorded during the last week."

If the three missing colonists had died, the information should have been immediately put into the database. That was standard procedure, even among independent outposts and secluded societies.

A vague dread settled over me. "What was the population count thirty days ago?"

"Two thousand, four hundred and twenty-three." He paused. "No deaths recorded for any of them, either."

Twelve had disappeared in the last thirty days. "And the week just before Davidov began the blockade?"

He made another inquiry, and pulled up a different figure. "Two thousand, six hundred and twelve residents. Ninety-four visitors." He looked up at me. "There have been no deaths recorded for the missing, or anyone on the colony over the past year."

It was too large a number to be an accounting error. "Duncan, two hundred and sixteen people do not simply disappear. If they're not dead, they must have escaped. But how are they getting off the planet?"

"Drefan told me that no one has left Trellus since Alek began the blockade," Reever said. "It is possible that they are dead and the records are incomplete."

"Almost ten percent of the population is gone," I pointed out. "If they died of natural causes or misadventure, that would mean this colony's mortality rate is five times greater than any other settled world in this quadrant." I thought for a moment. "Who is responsible for the census?"

"It is compiled by drone monitor," my husband said. "Someone may have tampered with the program to conceal the true status of the missing."

"Perhaps. But what if they are really gone, and no one knows about it but the drone monitors? If they can't leave, and there are no bodies, where could they be?" Pain spiked through my head, sudden and sharp, and I pressed my fingers to my temples as images began boiling in my mind. "That slave depot. Catopsa. Something like this happened there."

"Jarn." Reever drew me away from the console. "It is better that you not try to remember it."

"The memories are yours, not mine," I reminded

him, grimacing as the pain spiked. "The guards. Hsktskt . . ." I could not create order out of the chaotic images. My forearm started to feel peculiar, almost as if it were hot. "Why does it hurt to remember that? I was not there."

"Cherijo was." He put his arms around me and pulled me against his rigid frame. "I should not have inflicted you with a past you never lived."

I pressed my cheek against his shoulder. "Tell me what happened on Catopsa. What did the guards do with the missing slaves? All I remember are angry centurons, heat, and humanoid body parts. And my arm hurts."

"The body parts were all we were able to recover," Reever said. "Some of the guards were using the missing slaves as food." He waited before he added, "Cherijo was branded with a slave identification code. It kept healing over, so the Hsktskt kept branding her." He touched my forearm where I felt the pain. "Here."

"It didn't happen to me." I pushed the hurtful memories away. "Do you think the colonists are practicing cannibalism?"

Reever shrugged. "It would not be the first time an isolated group of starving individuals resorted to such desperate measures."

I thought of the stew Drefan had served us, and my stomach clenched as I reached for my scanner and passed it over the front of me. My stomach contents showed on the display as partially digested synpro. "If they are, they didn't feed anyone to us tonight."

"I do not see that kind of desperation, and Alek claimed that he was making regular supply drops." Reever tipped my chin and looked into my eyes. "You are exhausted. Come and rest with me. We will have time in the morning to inquire about those who are missing."

I recalled the ultimatum Davidov had delivered after *Moonfire* had crashed. We had only thirty days to find and kill the Odnallak.

Time was not our ally.

Despite the strange sleeping platform and unfamiliar surroundings, I fell asleep quickly, safe in Reever's arms. I did not wake until I felt his warmth moving away from me, replaced by cold alloy, fiery breath, and an angry voice.

They ordered us not to kill you, but said we could use you as often as we wished.

The alien male from my dream had returned. This time I felt more aware of my body, and how it had been manacled and chained. My limbs felt heavy and dull, and my mind clouded, as if I had been drugged.

The cabin in which we were slowly revolved around us, items tumbling out of containers, equipment smashing against the interior walls.

My brother has no taste for your kind. The claws that had been choking me only a few moments before caressed my cheek. *But I wondered. I wondered how you might be.*

I wanted to look through the view port and see how close we were to the surface. *Oforon, there is still time to send a distress signal.*

I've tried. No one will respond. The Toskald are blocking all transmissions. Black eyes squeezed shut as he held on to my chains, the only thing keeping him and me from tumbling about the cabin. *The League would not come even if they received it. We were always expendable, my brother and I.*

The wind buffeting the transport began to howl outside the hull, a petulant child frustrated with a toy it could not break. *My husband and daughter care about me.*

You think they still search for you? Oforon uttered a sound of sour amusement. *You're a fool. They believed Shropana's ruse, just as everyone else did. They think you long dead.*

I had felt dead, until this moment. I wasn't Jorenian, but at last I understood why they left behind messages for their kin. I couldn't go into the embrace of the stars without speaking one last time to the ones I loved.

Please, I begged. *Release me. Let me send one signal. Only one, I promise. I must say good-bye to my family.*

No. His grip on the chains tightened as the ship spun faster. *If the signal is intercepted by others, they will relay it to Shropana in hopes of collecting the reward for you. He will use it as an excuse to invalidate our contract. My family will get nothing.*

I was so cold I couldn't feel my hands or feet, and the darkness crowded in around me, swallowing Oforon and the spinning ship. Something else lay waiting in the shadows, something predatory, watching me with eyes afire.

Wait. I'm sorry. Don't leave me, Oforon. I don't want to die alone.

You're not alone. The thing in the shadows inched closer. *I'm here. I'm like you. Left for dead. Alone.*

"Jarn."

Reever's voice pulled me out of the dream so suddenly that I sat up with a jerk and a cry.

"I am here." He pulled me into his arms. "You were calling out in your sleep."

I rubbed my eyes and nestled against him. "I was having a nightmare." As the distressing images from the dream faded away, my heartbeat returned to its normal rhythm. "I didn't mean to wake you."

"I have been up for some time." He pulled back, putting space between us. "Who is Oforon?"

To hear the name said aloud made fear and sweat crawl all over on my skin. I forced myself to think calmly. "It is the name of the male in my dream. We were on a ship together. I think I was his prisoner." I grimaced to hear myself speaking as if it had been real. "It was only a bad dream."

"Perhaps." Reever watched me closely. "Tell me what you remember about the male from the dream, and where you were."

"He was not Terran. Hair covered his face." I gestured over my own. "I was in chains and very cold.

The ship we were on was spinning, out of control."
I grimaced as pain lanced through my thoughts.
"You should have warned me how much your
memories of Cherijo would hurt my head."

"I did not give you that memory," Reever said
quietly. "I have never heard this until now." He hesitated before adding, "It must have happened when
they were transporting you to Akkabarr. The ship
you were on crashed on the surface."

"That can't be," I said. "You were not with her
then. How could I recall something you did
not . . . ?" A flood of realization and anguish si-
lenced me.

The dream, not a dream but a memory. One of
Cherijo's.

Reever cupped my face between his hands.
"Don't be afraid, beloved. Whatever comes back to
you, it will not change who you are. Cherijo died on
Akkabarr."

"As you say, Husband." I thrust myself away
from him and grabbed my garments. "I will make a
meal for us. I wish we were at Mercy House. She has
idleberry tea."

I dressed and went out to the food prep unit,
where I dialed up tea. I knew Reever wanted to talk
about what had happened, but I had had enough of
Cherijo and the past for one morning.

The door panel chimed, and Reever rose and
went to answer it. Drefan's Chakacat came in with a
tray of bread that had been twisted into fancy
shapes.

"Drefan sends these with his compliments." It set the bread down on the table. "After you have had your meal, the games master requests that Reever join him in the drone bay."

I exchanged a look with my husband. "For what purpose?"

"Yesterday your husband observed that Tya's drednoc opponent lacked proper arena programming," the Chakacat said. "Drefan wishes to review the current battle algorithms with your husband and learn how they can be improved."

Reever nodded. "I will look at them."

I felt impatient. "Maybe we should charge him a consultation fee."

Keel remained behind after Reever left. At first I thought it meant to clear up the remnants of our meal, as it had the night before, until it spoke. "Doctor, Drefan wishes me to ask if you will look at some remains that were found outside the dome last night."

"You recovered a body?"

"Not exactly." Keel coughed, and for a moment looked as if it might regurgitate something. "The drone found only some skin."

It could be from another victim of the Tingalean, or a trace of one of the missing colonists. All I could do with tissue was run some DNA and pathogenic scans, if Drefan had the proper equipment for the tests, but at least that would be a start. "What sort of skin? How much did it find?"

Keel's whiskers twitched. "From the scales, it appears to be Tingalean. From the amount we recovered, I think it must be all of its skin."

My appetite faded. "Someone skinned it? That would be fatal. Where is the rest of the body?"

"I cannot say." Keel avoided my gaze. "I think that is what Drefan wishes to learn. If you can tell that from the condition of what remains, that is."

I retrieved my medical case. "Take me to it."

Keel led me through the labyrinth of corridors to an area guarded by several drones like those that had pursued Reever yesterday. Both the Chakacat and I were scanned before we were permitted access to the room where the skin had been taken.

"Does Drefan believe someone will steal the remains?" I asked as we walked into a large, well-equipped laboratory.

"No." Keel did not expand on that reply, but brought me to a low-temperature storage unit. Inside sat a large sealed disposal container with a clear plas lid.

I peered in and studied the mound of derma, which was blackened and partially liquefied. I thought it might have been burned, until I scanned the container. "This can't belong to the Tingalean that attacked me yesterday. The decomposition is too far advanced. Unless . . ." I glanced over my shoulder. "Can you quarantine this room?"

"Drefan had a containment generator installed last night." Keel pointed to one of the consoles. "The center work table can be isolated within an energy shroud."

I lifted the container, which weighed more than I expected. "After I move this over there, initialize the field."

The Chakacat did as I asked. Once the bioelectric curtain buzzed into place around me, preventing any microorganisms from entering or leaving the space, I pulled on a mask and gloves and opened the container. Sickening odor instantly filled the contained area.

"Next time, genius," I muttered to myself, blinking away reflex tears, "wear a breather."

I slowly tipped the container over to place the contents on the table. Despite my care, the derma slid out and landed with a plop, spattering the front of my garments with greenish black fluid. I first scanned for cellular defects, but found no evidence of disease or contagion. I took a probe from my case and began lifting and smoothing out the crumpled skin.

"The derma looks to be intact." I walked around the table to work on the other side.

"Does that have some significance?" Keel asked.

"It means that it was not removed from the victim in sections, but all at once." I measured the hide's thickness and carefully rolled it over and flattened it to inspect the underside. "I cannot find any blade, pulse, sonic, or other weapon marks to indicate precisely what was used for the removal."

"Could a form of radiation have done this?"

"Doubtful. The skin would be burned, and it would slough off the victim in flakes and peels." I pulled down an emitter arm and peered closely at the holes. "I cannot see any puckers or stretch marks. It is not inside out. It was not fieldstripped."

Keel came to stand by the curtain. "How am I to define 'fieldstripped' to Drefan?"

"Watch." I turned and held up one of my hands. "Imagine my glove is derma, my hand the body it covers, and the opening at my wrist a mouth or eye." I took hold of the edge of my glove and peeled it backward, removing it from my hand until it hung, inside out, from my other fingers. "Large carcasses with thicker skin require more effort, of course."

Keel gave me a strange look. "That is all it takes to skin a body?"

"If the game's skin is thin and flexible enough, it can be done immediately after a kill," I said, putting on a fresh pair of gloves. "Otherwise, the carcass is parboiled first, to loosen the hide, and then stripped." I saw the Chakacat's throat move, and belatedly realized that I had been too candid. "I should not have described it so graphically. I beg your pardon, Keel."

It looked from me to the remains and back again. "How do you know of such things?"

"We had to hunt our food on my homeworld. I know most ensleg societies do not," I added quickly. "Akkabarr is an ice world, upon which nothing grows. The Iisleg were left to die there, and had to become hunters or starve."

It nodded at the table. "Do you think something ate the insides of that?"

I saw no tooth or claw marks, or other signs that the skin had been ripped away from the flesh by something feeding. Rather than offering such details, which would upset the feline again, I merely said, "It does not seem likely."

I performed several other scans before completing my examination. "The only other thing I can tell you at this point is that this is not the Tingalean who attacked me. This individual died four to seven days ago."

"Could it have molted?"

"This is not simply a shed layer of hide. This is all of this person's skin." I made a circling gesture over the remains. "All three layers are here. I know of no species that molts to such an extreme degree."

After I replaced the remains in the container and sealed it, Keel shut down the field and allowed me to cleanse. I took advantage of the Chakacat's distressed state to help myself to some of the medical supplies, which I quickly concealed under my garments.

"I would like to begin the medical exams as soon as possible," I told Keel as we left the lab.

"I will speak to Drefan about it," the Chakacat said.

I followed the feline back to the rooms the games master had given us, and found them empty. It promised that Reever would join me shortly and left me there.

I used the next hour on the room terminal, pulling up all the dermatological information the colonial database had available on the Tingaleans and skimming through it, looking for a medical condition to explain the state of the remains. I found no accidental injury, illness, or disease that correlated with my autopsy findings.

"Something had to remove the hide perfectly, in one piece." I searched in one of the console bins and found a datapad, which I used to create a chart and an autopsy report. I had just finished transferring the data from my scanner to the pad when Reever walked in. The filthy condition of his clothes, face, and hands made me drop what I was doing and hurry over to him.

"You did not fight that Hsktskt, did you?" I demanded as I searched for blood and other signs of injury.

"Not yet," he said, catching my hands to stop me. "I'm fine. I took apart one of the drednocs that were disabled by the Tingalean, to see if I could retrieve its sensor recordings. Unfortunately, the laser melted the command core where they are stored."

I needed to pass some things to him without Drefan seeing it on his monitors. There was only one place in the room where I could do that.

"You and your garments need a wash," I said, giving his arm a playful tug. "Come and I'll do both."

When I tried to pull him into the cleanser full-clothed, Reever resisted, until I looked past him at one of the monitors and then into the cleanser. He understood and followed me inside the small chamber.

"Drefan could not put a recording drone in here," I said as I produced one of the slim utility knives I had taken from the lab. "The sonics would disrupt the feed. So we can do as we please, with no one watching."

Reever nodded. "What did you have in mind?"

"Many things." I inserted the tip of the blade under the edge of his tunic. "You are wearing too many clothes." With one smooth incision, I sliced open the front of his tunic.

My husband's eyes darkened as he braced his hands against the unit's walls. "And after you remove my garments? What will you do?"

"Something will come to mind, I'm sure." I slit both sleeves from wrist to shoulder to show him how sharp the blade was. "Perhaps you have some specific thoughts on the matter."

"I may." He bent his head and put his mouth on mine, initiating a link at the same time. *Why are you playacting like this?*

Drefan's monitors can't watch us in here, but the unit is not soundproof. They can still pick up our voices.

He nodded. *How many blades did you take?*

Five, including this one. As I cut through the waist fastener of his trousers with one hand, I used the other to strip off my tunic. *Two in the right pocket, one in the left. One in my right boot.*

Out loud I said, "I love how you touch me. Your hands are like water, all over me, everywhere."

"I would drown myself in you." Reever smoothed his wet palms over my breasts. *We will both carry two, and hide the spare where we can easily retrieve it. Did you see any pulse weapons?*

I dropped down, cutting his trouser leg open to the knee, and pressing my mouth to his wet thigh. The soft, fair hair on his legs tickled my cheek as I glanced up at him. "Do you like this?" I teased the crease between his leg and hip with my tongue. *No, but Mercy tried to give me one before I came over here. I would try to smuggle one over, but I think Drefan will scan me for weapons every time I leave or enter the dome.*

"I like everything you do to me." His hands tangled in my wet hair, pulling it back from my face. *I don't want you going unarmed anywhere on this colony.* He hissed in a sharp breath as my tongue found other ways to please him. *If I ever let you out of bed again.*

I brought him to the edge with my mouth before I stood, shedding the rest of my clothes as I straightened. The link between us faded as my husband lifted me off my feet and out of the cleansing unit.

"We will get the bed linens wet," I said as he turned and carried me toward the sleeping platform.

"I don't care."

That I could make Duncan do and say such things thrilled and shocked me. Iisleg men never allowed women to have such power over them. My husband claimed not to have emotions, but to watch his self-control shatter made me think differently.

He dropped me on the platform and straddled me. "Why are you smiling like that?"

"I have been here two days and only now am I doing something I like." I wriggled my hips, adjusting myself to fit our bodies together. "This *was* supposed to be our—what did you call it? The sweet time?"

"Honeymoon."

Reever covered my breasts with his palms, gently pinching my nipples between his fingers before he lowered his head to them. What he did with his mouth made my insides feel hot and tight, but it was how he looked at me that made my heart constrict.

"There are no words," he murmured, moving up to kiss my mouth, "for how beautiful you are to me."

I rolled in his arms until we sat facing each other, my thighs bracketing his. "When we leave here," I said, putting my hands on his shoulders and raising myself for his penetration, "I want to spend a week in space. Someplace where no one can find us."

His breath tickled my ear. "And then?"

"We will barricade ourselves in the cabin."

He clamped his hands on my hips. "You can have whatever you want." His eyes darkened as I took the initiative and pushed, taking him inside me. "Especially this."

When he tried to move, I wrapped one of my legs

around his hips. "Hold still. I want to feel you there."

He put his teeth to the side of my throat. "You want to torture me."

I clutched at him, desperately trying to hold on to that first moment, when I felt him completely inside me. It was the completion my body craved, but it was surrounded by a complex tangle of emotions I had never felt with anyone else, even our child.

I cared for many people, and I loved Marel. But Reever had become part of my soul.

"Jarn."

I felt him pulsing deep within my body, and kissed a bead of sweat from his chin. "Now you can move."

He was strong and hard and slow, so slow. He moved in my body in a matter of degrees, so that the friction between us built in the same manner. He was taking revenge for my teasing, I knew, but I didn't care. Duncan was inside me, Duncan was loving me, and I had never felt more alive or more at peace.

Two made one.

He turned me onto my back, propping himself over me without stopping the deep, languid glide of his body into mine. "Jarn," he whispered, going still. "You are crying."

I felt one tear escape and slide down my cheek. "With joy, Husband. With joy."

Nine

Keel came to our quarters the next morning to inform me that Drefan and Mercy were still negotiating on how best to arrange my schedule so that all of their employees could be examined. The Chaka-cat indicated that the negotiations were not going well.

"Mercy is angry that Drefan has kept you here when you are her property." Keel glanced at my husband. "Technically speaking, of course. Drefan feels that Mercy might do something ill-advised if he permitted her to see you, so he refuses to allow her access to the dome. She is now threatening to go to colonial security and file a grievance against Omega Dome for illegal appropriation of lawful salvage."

"While they are bickering over me, I may as well start with the staff here," I said. "It will give me something to do until they work out an agreement." I turned to Reever. "Will you come with me?"

"Drefan wishes me to assist you, Doctor," the

Chakacat said. It didn't look exactly enthusiastic over the prospect. "We have reserved a sparring room for your husband, as well as practice programs he may find valuable."

"That is acceptable," Reever said. To me, he said, "It has been a long time since I've fought an exhibition match. It will help me to practice."

I suppressed a smile. Reever worked out every day; he was always prepared for a fight. However, he intended to use the simulator terminal to gain access to Drefan's database; we had talked through our link about the possibility last night.

Still, I hated being separated from him. "Be careful when you use the practice programs," I said as I picked up my medical case. "I do not need more work."

Keel took me back to the laboratory where I had examined the Tingalean's remains.

"Drefan would like you to begin examining his personal staff," it said as it watched me set up an exam area. "Would you care to start with the domestic servants or the bodyguards?"

"I will start with you," I said. "Remove your garments and sit on the table."

Keel took a step back. "I do not require an examination. I have not . . . There is nothing wrong with me."

I eyed the feline. "You are part of Drefan's personal staff. You will be assisting me. I will not allow you to do that until I have performed a thorough exam to insure that you are not diseased or carrying a contagion. Get on the table."

The Chakacat muttered to itself as it stripped out of its garments and climbed onto the flat alloy surface. "This is ridiculous. I'm in perfect health."

I checked the table's panel and noted the displayed height and weight measurements on my datapad. "You are five kilos underweight, and your nutrient levels are slightly below League standard for your species." I glanced at it. "That is hardly perfect."

"I have no appetite," it said with some indignation. "I despise the taste of synth."

"So do I, but the blockaded cannot be choosey. Lie down." I waited until it stretched out, and slowly passed a scanner over it from head to back paws. "What is your age?"

"I was whelped twenty-nine seasons past."

I mentally converted the seasons into standard solar years. That made it very young, little more than an adolescent. "How long have you served the games master?"

"All of my life. He bought me as a youngling from the Garnotan breeder who owned my parent." It closed its eyes. "My species is hermaphroditic."

"I know." I switched the scanner over to check its blood chemistry, and took a sample. "Your hormone levels are somewhat elevated. When are you planning to breed?"

"Never."

"You should consider taking a contraceptive

blocker, then, before your glands decide the issue for you." I connected the scanner to my datapad to download the results and set them aside. "I am going to palpate your abdomen. I know most felines dislike being touched around the belly, but I will be careful and not hurt you."

Keel nodded, but its body remained tense as I checked for masses and lumps. "I don't think I've ever been examined by a doctor who treats people. My breeder had a veterinarian give us our inoculations and body checks."

"Well, you are my first Chakacat patient." I pushed back the pile of its pelt to check for parasites. It felt and smelled clean, and appeared bug-free. "The Hsktskt Hanar has ordered that all life-forms enslaved by the Faction are to be freed. When does Drefan plan to comply with this order?"

Keel looked surprised. "Drefan does not own any slaves."

"You just said that he bought you from the Garnotans," I reminded it.

"He did, but he gave me my freedom as soon as I was old enough to take care of myself. I am a paid employee now, free to leave Trellus whenever I wish." Keel's whiskers twitched as I checked the insides of its ears. "I am not recognized as a sentient being, however, so I have chosen to stay here, where I am treated as such."

That sounded very much like a form of slavery to me, but I thought of something else. "The Hsktskt gladiatrix wears an icestone collar fitted with a neural transmitter. I know that is used to control slaves with pain through nerve induction."

"Tya is an exception. We don't know her well enough yet to trust her. When we do, Drefan will remove the collar and nullify her life-debt." Keel propped itself up on its elbows to observe as I checked the mobility of the four joints in each of its arms and legs. "At least, I hope he will. We cannot keep her here on Trellus. She is nothing but an incitement to riot."

It might talk tough, but I could hear the worry under the words. "Not even for the use of the bloodsport gamers?"

Its whiskers bristled. "That is the worst of it. She is useless to us as a combatant. She will fight only simulations or drones. Against living beings, she will only defend herself. I told Drefan she was not worth the credits, but he had to have her. He's been acting oddly ever since the skin games started."

"What do you mean, 'skin games'?"

Keel flinched. "I misspoke. I meant ever since Davidov started playing these games with us. That is all."

It was, as Mercy would say, a lousy liar. I set down my penlight. "Keel, I cannot help Drefan or Mercy or anyone if I don't know what is wrong here."

"There is nothing—"

"Then why won't Davidov let anyone leave? Why do Mercy and Drefan want their staff checked by me? What do they think I will find?" I waited for it to respond, but it only stared at me, its eyes hard. "You said skin games. Were you referring to the Tingalean's remains? Was it killed and skinned in one of the games played here? Is that what you fear?"

Keel shook its head. "Drefan would never allow anyone to be murdered under his dome."

"Who would?"

Its eyes shifted toward the external viewer, and the dark, lifeless surface outside reflected on its slitted pupils and colorless irises.

"Keel, tell me. I promise you, I can help."

"It was killed by the shifter. The one taking the skins."

"There have been other victims?" When it nodded, I thought of the missing colonists. "How many?"

"We find two or three every week." It climbed off the table and began dressing. "The first time it happened was a year ago, when a Beleset free trader came to Trellus. The day after the trader came, we found his skin in an empty shop. We thought the shop merchant had murdered him, as she had disappeared. Then we found her skin a few days later."

"Why does this . . . shifter . . . take the skin?"

"To disguise itself. That's why we don't know what it is or what it looks like." Keel strapped on its blade harness. "The skin it steals begins to decay, so it lasts only a few days before it must discard it and take another. That is how it shifts from body to body." It looked at me. "They say it is an Odnallak.

That this is the secret of how they change form. By stealing and wearing the skins of other beings."

I had learned a great deal about the Odnallak during the plague of memory on Vtaga. Like the Lok-teel, they were true shape-shifters, able to alter their forms to mimic those of other beings. Unlike the helpful little mask-makers, the Odnallak were not so benign. They often used telepathy to draw on the deepest fears of those around them, and shaped themselves accordingly. Given their terrifying ability, they certainly didn't need to disguise themselves with the skin of another being.

I wanted to tell Keel this, but I considered what the effect would be on it and the other colonists. These people were already suffering from fear-induced paranoia. Suggesting that something other than the Odnallak was responsible for the killings might push them past the point of self-control and reason.

Had Davidov made the same, erroneous assumption? Was that why he had stranded us here? To catch an Odnallak he had assumed was murdering others for their skins?

"What is being done to find this creature?" I asked the Chakacat.

"We scan everyone who enters or leaves the dome," Keel said. "Not only for weapons, but for DNA as well. But we have never caught the shifter. It uses other means to move from one dome to another."

"Where do you find the discarded skins?"

"On the surface, in the air ducts, behind consoles, everywhere. It leaves them wherever it finds its next victim." Keel gestured toward the access way where I had been attacked. "One of the sanitation crew cleaning up the mess Mercy's drednocs made disappeared yesterday. He was last seen near the control hatch in which the shifter left the Tingalean's hide."

I walked around the lab as I thought. "Where are the bodies? Have you stored them? I need to perform autopsies on them."

"There are never any bodies," Keel told me. "Posbret says it eats them."

I wished for a moment that Mercy had shot the raider instead of negotiating with him. "Posbret is wrong. The killer could eat the soft tissue of one body in several days, perhaps. But it is very unlikely that it could consume two or three a week. Very few sentient species can eat bones and cartilage. Why would you give weight to the opinion of a stranded offworlder?"

Keel looked uncomfortable. "Posbret wants to find the shifter himself so that he can make a deal with Davidov. He's gone so far as to torture some suspects to get information out of them."

"Or keep them from sharing it?" I suggested. "That sort of behavior would make him my prime suspect." The puzzle of what had happened to the bodies of the missing colonists still bothered me. "Were there disposal units in the vicinities of the skins you recovered?"

"Yes, but we always check them for traces of

DNA from the missing. None has ever been found. We've searched the tunnels and the mine shafts too." Keel looked down as its wristcom bleeped. "Drefan needs me in central control. I should not have related all of this to you. He will be angry with me."

"Then don't tell him about it." I saw the doubt in its eyes and made an exasperated sound. "Anything I discuss with a patient is privileged information, and regarded as completely private, under quadrant medical regulations. I can't tell anyone even if I wished to." Although I intended to pass everything to Reever that I had learned from the Chakacat the moment we had time to link.

"I don't care if he is angry with me," Keel said suddenly. "This is not one of his games. We need you to help us find the shifter, and stop it from killing more people. You promised to help."

I thought of Davidov's ultimatum. "Believe me, I will do everything I can."

Six hours later, I handed an enormous pile of garments to one of Drefan's bodyguards, a Nekawa whom I had to scan standing up, as the exam table would not hold her bulk.

"Well?" she asked, the lacquered curls of her crimson hair barely moving as she worked a divided skirt up over her legs. Each was twice as wide as my torso. "I'm not going to die, right?"

"No one lives forever," I lied.

"You're funny." She pulled on her tunic. "I meant, I'm healthy, aren't I?"

"No, you're not. Your blood pressure is elevated, your esophageal passages are inflamed, and the bones in your legs have a dozen small stress fractures." I picked up her chart. "According to your species standards, which I downloaded from the colonial database, your body mass is four times as dense as it should be for a female of your height and weight."

"My kind are not built like you, Terran." She rolled the twin mountains of her shoulders. "So I'm bigger than most. It serves me well in my job. What of it?"

"You're overweight because you eat too much, not because you're Nekawa," I said. "You spend most of your waking time on your feet, but your frame is not sturdy enough to carry so much extra weight. That and poor nutrition are why your bones are cracking. Your throat is sore because your belly acitoxins are constantly backing up into it. Also from putting too much food in your stomach."

She hmphed. "So?"

"So unless you change your dietary habits, you will die much sooner than you should. Bend down." When she did, I straightened her collar, which she could not see, thanks to her six extra chins. "There. Now, tell me why you're eating so much."

"I'm hungry."

I eyed her.

"It's mine habit," she said, pouting a little.

"It needs to stop being your habit."

"Not mine as in belonging to me, mine as in mining. It's how we were trained to work down there." She pointed to the floor. "When we saw tools, we worked. When the food buckets dropped down to us, we ate. When the drones rolled out the thermal blankets, we slept. If we didn't, we were whipped. So every time I see food, I have to eat. I can't help myself."

I had already made note of the Nekawa's numerous scars, healed fractures, and arutanium burns. Her years working in the StarCore mines had taken a moderate toll on her body, but the conditioned responses from that hellish existence were doing much more damage.

"You are no longer a slave controlled by whips and feeding times," I advised her. "You are free now to make your own choices. If the sight of food causes an involuntary hunger response, I suggest rather than eat that you immediately drink two liters of water chilled to forty degrees."

"Ice water?" She snorted. "What will that do?"

"It will soothe your throat, fill your stomach, and make you feel as full as a large meal would." I tapped her chart. "It will also help reduce the amount of acitoxin your digestive system produces, and—by not eating something with calories you don't need—it will help you lose the extra weight."

She thought over my suggestion. "I could carry a water jugget with me, the way we did below. In truth, I miss the weight on my hip." Her tusks gleamed as her expression lightened. "You give good advice, Healer."

I nodded. "Now follow it."

The Nekawa turned and made a low, lovely sound. "Have you prior claim on that Terran male hovering out there?"

I swiveled around and through the viewer saw Reever standing outside in the corridor. "Oh, yes. That one is mine."

"I would probably squash him on the first mating. Still, I will stop eating so much in hopes that you get tired of him and discard him." The big female bumped her hip against my shoulder in a friendly fashion, and nearly sent me staggering into a supply cabinet. "Enjoy your good fortune, little healer."

After the Nekawa departed, Reever came in. A bruise darkened his left cheekbone, and sweat soaked his hair. "Jarn, are you finished here?"

"For now. That was the last of Drefan's bodyguards. He has fourteen of them, and not one under three hundred pounds. I did not think a crippled man would need so many." I went over and touched his face, gently touching the bruised cheekbone to assure myself there was no damage to the bones and muscles beneath. "Perhaps I can persuade him to lend one to you."

"I reprogrammed some of the sparring simulations," my husband said as he covered my hand with his and initiated a mind link. *I bypassed his system security and isolated the terminal in our quarters.*

We now have access to all the information Drefan possesses.

"You must have set the physical limitation protocol to zero," I said out loud. "Let me put something on that." *What about the recording drones? Drefan will see whatever we do on the terminal.*

I adjusted the lenses and overhead emitters, Reever told me as he sat on the exam table. *He can still monitor what we say and do while we're in the room, but reflected light will make it impossible for him to read what is displayed by the terminal screen.*

Very clever, Husband. I took a cold compress pack out of a cabinet and wrapped it in a bandage. "This will help reduce the swelling," I said as I brought it over and held it to his cheek. "Next time, you should duck faster."

As I fussed over the bruise and told him harmless anecdotes about the bodyguards I had examined, I channeled through our mind link my memories of everything Keel had said about the shifter killing the colonists,

"There," I said when I had finished both tasks. "That should feel better now. Men and their games. I will never understand them." *As long as it needs new skin, this creature will not stop killing for it. We have to find it, Duncan, and put an end to these games.*

"The games they play here are more complicated and serious than they seem," Reever said. "But I have no doubt as to who will prevail in the end."

* * *

The next day I was sent back to Mercy to spend the day examining her staff. Drefan chose to keep Reever at Omega Dome, both to help his engineers begin repairs on the scout and to insure my return the next day.

"You can trust me to come back," I said as I shouldered my medical case. "Mercy told you that she would share my services, and it is not as if I can leave the colony when you are not looking."

"Consider it a gentle incentive," the games master replied. "Mercy feels that she has prior claim over you, and is very unhappy with the current situation. She agreed to my terms, but if she can persuade you to ignore them and remain under her protection, she will."

"I give you my word, I will return tonight," I said. "Whether Mercy likes it or not."

Drefan inclined his head. "Remember, tell her nothing of Tya or what you have seen here." His one eye shifted from me to my husband and back again. "The settlement of your husband's debt depends on your discretion."

Drefan sent me back to Mercy in a heavily reinforced, drone-piloted glidecar that barely fit into the access way. Mercy, Cat, and eight drednocs in battle mode stood at a view panel watching for me at the entrance to her dome. From the anger reddening her face, I guessed that she was not merely unhappy with the situation. She appeared ready to throttle someone.

Hopefully not me, I thought as I climbed out of the

vehicle and squeezed through the narrow gap between it and the access-way wall to get to the first air lock.

"You all right?" Mercy's voice demanded over the com. She didn't look at me, but watched the drone glidecar slip backward away from the air lock.

"I am fine," I said, stepping into the next chamber, where I was thoroughly scanned. "Drefan wouldn't allow me to personally signal you."

"Drefan is a jackass, and don't worry about it." Mercy met me at the door panels and inspected me as if I were crawling with parasites. "Your husband okay?" I nodded, and she took hold of my chin. "What did he do to you while you were over there? Don't lie to me."

"He did nothing to me or Reever." I had expected her to be angry and out of sorts, not furious. "We were treated well by the games master, and he even accepted my offer of services to settle my husband's salvage debt. I began examining some of his staff yesterday." She kept glaring past me and at the access way beyond, and I remembered the attack. "I regret the loss of your drednocs. If I could have saved them—"

"Screw the drones." She put her thumb under my left eye and pulled down the lid. "No blood, but it's not like anyone can tell by looking. He didn't try to use you?"

Her actions and questions perplexed me. "Use me for what?"

"Never mind." She put an arm around my shoulders and guided me out into the corridor. "You're staying here for the duration."

"Until tomorrow," I amended, "and then I have to go back. You agreed."

She laughed. "I would have agreed to bed an Ichthorii to get you out of there, sweetheart. You're not going anywhere."

I stopped, dropping my medical case and resisting when she pulled at my arm. "If I don't go back, Drefan could harm my husband."

She shrugged. "I'll find you another one. We've got plenty of males on colony. Just tell me what size, shape, and color you want."

Cat hopped over to join us. "Look at her, she's fine," he said to Mercy. "Now will you calm the hell down?"

"Who's not calm? I'm calm. She's calm. We're all kinds of calm." Mercy turned to me. "Let's go. I've got my best dreds guarding a nice, secure treatment room for you."

I refused to move. "If you don't intend to honor the agreement you made with Drefan, say so, now, and I will go back to Omega Dome."

"Oh, yeah?" Mercy planted her hands on her hips. "I got eight drednocs right here who say you're not. Try and get through them."

Her mocking sneer made something inside me snap.

I grabbed the front of her tunic and pulled her until her face was an inch away from mine. "Look, *sweetheart,*" I said through my teeth. "I don't know what sort of crybaby whiny-assed paranoid delusions you're experiencing at the moment, but I don't have *time* for this. *You* are going to do whatever the crippled guy wants you to so that Reever doesn't get hurt. *I,* in turn, will not kick your well-used ass all over this dome. Are we clear on this, or do you need a preview?"

Mercy's chin sagged. *"Cherijo?"*

Cherijo, indeed.

"We're clear," Cat said, hopping up to us but making no move to interfere. "You can let her go now, Doc."

"Very well." Carefully I released my grip on her garment and cleared my throat. "You say you have a treatment room prepared? I would like to see it."

Mercy closed her mouth, turned on her heel, and stalked off.

The Omorr picked up my medical case and gestured toward the staff's quarters. "Right this way."

I followed Cat to the treatment room, which had been stocked with a motley assortment of medical supplies and equipment. A dining table had been refitted with weight sensors and extension arms, and several of the plush furnishings from the lobby lined the walls.

"What we didn't have, we appropriated or rigged," the Omorr told me as he set my case on a tiered table. "I know some of it's not standard"—he nodded toward several flexible, snakelike emitters in one corner that were slowly undulating and

casting soft, multicolored light around the room—
"but it should serve. If you find that you need
something more, don't yell at Mercy. Signal me
and I'll take care of it."

My head pounded like a second heart. "I should
not have lost my temper with Mercy like that.
Drefan warned me that she was angry and might attempt to keep me here." I felt as weary as he looked.
"What did she think happened to me?"

"When the dreds went offline yesterday, she was
sure the shifter got you," Cat said. "Then when you
didn't come back from Gamers, she thought Drefan
would use you as bait, to tempt it to try again. She
hasn't eaten or slept since."

And I had threatened and shouted at her. "I
should find her and apologize—"

"Please, don't," Cat told me. "I love Mercy more
than my life, Gods know, but she's a bully. She believes she knows exactly how to run everyone's life.
It's good for her to find out that she can't." Speculation gleamed in his dark eyes. "You know, that's the
first time I've heard you sound like a real Terran.
What brought that on?"

"I cannot say, but it gives me a headache." I took
a syrinpress out of my case, dialed up a mild dose of
analgesic, and injected myself. "I will need a few
minutes to set up, and then you can begin sending
in the girls."

Ten

I spent the next several hours examining Mercy's pleasure-givers, all of whom were by professional necessity familiar with medical exams. None presented any ailments, and although several had minor work-related complaints, I found them all to be in good to excellent physical condition.

"Increase the temperature and mineral content of your cleanser feed," I advised Kohbi, a Munitalp who reported experiencing discomfort with her gluteus minorus after servicing a particularly vigorous regular. "Soak in a hip bath for thirty minutes each night, and advise your trick to handle you with more care."

"That one?" Kohbi blew some air through a skin flap. "His drill speed is permanently set on sonic blast."

"Unless you enjoy sleeping on your belly," I replied, "I would introduce him to the concept of extended, gentle foreplay."

"I'll try. My kind don't sleep in this stage of life, you know." Kohbi tugged on the narrow tube of virulent green silk that served as her only garment.

"Saving it up for your next *lokhgetiti*?" I joked.

"Yes, it should be any sol now." She eyed me. "Few offworlders know our word for the transition time."

I thought for a moment, and found the memory Reever had given me. He had witnessed the phenomena during a year spent among Kohbi's people. Some of those memories were unhappy, so I said, "I must have heard it from another patient."

She grew more interested. "How many other Munitalp have you treated?"

None, I thought as I noted the impending transition on her chart. But apparently Cherijo had seen enough while serving as a trauma physician on Kevarzangia Two to also give me complete knowledge of the species.

"I can't remember," I said truthfully. "Have you informed Mercy that you're due to evolve?"

"Not yet." Kohbi spit out several lengths of silk, the same livid green color as her garment, and wove it between four of her pincers. A few moments later she draped the head end of her torso with the resulting covering. "She has enough on her mind lately."

"I doubt you want her to find you cocooned somewhere and unable to speak because you haven't yet regrown your vocal passages." I switched off the chart. "Your next stage of life will render you mute as well as nonsexual for several weeks."

"Oh, right, it's my silent season. That did slip my mind." The Munitalp absently rubbed her pelvic arch. "I'll talk to Mercy, but I'd appreciate it if you didn't mention my *lokhgetiti* to the others. I know the multimorphs will understand, but the oneforms might overreact to my body shift and do something crazy again."

I looked up. "Crazy such as . . . ?"

"There was this Psyoran." Kohbi's pincers clicked as she rubbed them against each other. "You know how they shed their frills every so often for new growth? Posbret saw the guy drop a neck flap while he was walking through one of the common areas, and decided the Psyo was the one playing the skin games." He voice went soft. "They beat and questioned him for three sols, and then they strung him up outside colonial security. He died dangling from the end of a cord. Just because he was growing some fresh exoskin."

"I see," I said, thinking of a female Psyoran Cherijo had known on Kevarzangia Two. The species were gentle, helpful creatures that often went into the medical and spiritual fields so they could help others in need. The thought of one being lynched simply for its bodily functions outraged me. "I won't pass this information on to the others, but Kohbi, talk to Cat. He will see to it that you're given a secure place to cocoon."

After Kohbi slithered out, I went to find Mercy.

Despite Cat's assurances, I still felt that I should apologize for how I had spoken to her, if not for what I had said. One of the girls directed me to try looking in a place she called "the solitude room."

"Sometimes when Mercy gets angry, she spends a couple of minutes getting some feedback in the 'sizer," the prostitute told me. "It's quiet and helps her work out her frustrations." She bumped her hip against mine. "Ask her if you can have a turn with my mindset. You'll love it."

I didn't understand half of what she told me, but followed her directions to the room. I found it empty. As frustrated as I felt, I could use the benefits of the 'sizer, whatever that was. All I saw in the room was an upholstered chair, privacy screens on the viewers, and several pairs of shades designed for different types and numbers of eyes.

I sat down on the chair and examined the eyeshades made to fit a Terran. Sensors of a type I had never seen before lined the interior frame as well as the lenses. Curious, I slid them on.

I felt something tickling the back of my neck, and smiled as I came fully awake. "You have two months to stop doing that."

Prehensile gildrells slid around my throat and into my hair like a bunch of long, white snakes, while three muscular pink arms tugged me back against an equally hard body.

"In two months, the contract will be signed," Cat said. "You'll be my wife. Then I can do anything to you that I desire."

The idea that we would marry was still something of a shock, and a thrill. Thrilling because I wanted it as much as he did. Shocking because there was no record of an Omorr ever taking a human for a spouse.

That I had once been a professional pleasure-giver, and now was a brothel owner, and that he had been the son of a preacher and now ran my brothel factored in there, as well.

"Hmmm." I wriggled my hips, adjusting to the interesting changes in his lower anatomy. The genitalia of Omorr males remained within a pelvic recess, extruding only when they felt an undeniable need to mate. Cat definitely had some needs. "Where are you taking me for the honeymoon?"

The tip of one gildrell tickled the rim of my ear. "Terra?"

I giggled like a young girl. "Oh yeah, they'd love us."

Two of the delicate membranes on the ends of Cat's arms spread over my breasts, while the third stroked down over my bare belly to slip between my thighs. What he did with those dexterous webs of flesh was the reason more Terran women should get over their alien prejudices, I thought. Because they were really missing out.

"What the *hell* do you think you're doing?" Mercy said as she snatched the eyeshades off my face and checked the inside. "This is my mindset."

Being jolted out of dream and back into my own body so abruptly made me fall off the seat.

"What was that?" I rubbed my hands over my face and looked at my palms; sweat covered them.

"One of the girls sent me here, and I just . . ." I didn't know how to describe the experience.

She put her hands on her hips. "Did you have fun with my boyfriend?"

"Mercy, when I put those shades over my eyes I was you. I was in your body. Thinking your thoughts. Feeling . . . I was . . ." I looked up at her in horror. "Those aren't eyeshades, are they?"

"Uh, no, they're not." She reached down and helped me back onto the seat. "It's okay, Cherijo. You didn't actually do anything with Cat. I did. You watched." She exhaled heavily as she reached over and picked up the now-smashed shades. "This is a mindset." She pointed to the chair. "And this is a fantasizer. The two of them create neurosimulations recorded from actual experiences. We use this room to relax, and for tricks who prefer to have sex by themselves."

"But how do they . . . oh."

"Exactly." She pocketed the broken mindset. "I shouldn't have left the 'sizer on, but I got called away. Your husband is looking for you. Cat routed his signal to the exam room console. Do you know how red your face is?"

As hot as it felt, I could only imagine. "I'm so embarrassed. Please believe me, I would never have touched this equipment if I had known what it does."

"You didn't strike me as the voyeur type." She went to leave and then hesitated and looked back.

"You're still blushing. I didn't think a doctor could do that. So what did you think of Cat?"

"He was, uh . . ." I tried to think of a diplomatic phrase. I settled for the truth. "Amazing."

"That he is." She grinned for a moment. "But if you ever touch him in real life I'll kick *your* uptight little ass all over this dome."

Once she left, I hurried back to the exam room and answered the relay from Reever.

"*Waenara,*" his voice greeted me, but the relay remained blank on my display. "I am out at the crash site with Drefan's engineers. You must adjust your vid feed." He gave me the code for an upload connection, which allowed me to patch into his envirosuit monitors and view what he was seeing. An image of Trellus's rough, rocky surface coalesced onto my screen, and moved up and down slightly as Reever walked.

I didn't see engineers, *Moonfire*, or any of the domes. "What are you doing out there?"

"There is an impact crater several hundred meters from the scout," my husband replied. "I am walking out to have a look at it."

Through the feed I saw the curved rim of the crater. It didn't seem large, but the blackness of its interior area indicated that it might be very deep.

We couldn't link through a machine, so there was no way I could tell if what he had told me was truth or a convenient excuse. "You do not have enough to do with the ship?"

"I thought I saw something."

More reason not to go near it, I thought, but held my tongue as he approached the edge. His gloved hand appeared in the screen, and he directed an emitter into the crater.

"Can you see what it's doing to the light?" Reever asked.

A thousand tiny prisms with jagged bands of purple, blue, and green filled up the screen. I described them to him and added, "Your suit or the channel must be distorting the feed."

"No. I see them, too. They're everywhere." His voice changed, became almost dreamy. "So beautiful."

A dark crater reflected sparkling light, but in the wrong colors. Sudden, nameless panic seized me.

His helmet isn't shielded.

"Duncan, show me *Moonfire*." When he didn't respond, I shouted, "The reflected light is hypnotizing you. Look at the ship. Now."

Slowly the image on my screen changed, and I heard my husband drag in a deep breath. "Cherijo, the crater is filled with black crystal."

"Don't look at it again," I warned. "Walk away from it and go back to *Moonfire*." The image on my screen remain fixed on the scout but began to shake. "You don't have to run. It can't chase you."

"It can't," Reever said, turning his head to show me four surface terrain vehicles barreling toward the scout. "But those STVs can."

Static crackled over the audio as pulse fire shot out from gun turrets on top of the STVs. The beams smashed into the ground all around *Moonfire*, sending the engineers scrambling for cover. The four vehicles split apart, moving to surround the scout as they continued to fire on the helpless engineers.

My screen image turned to a forty degree angle as Reever dove behind a pillar of crumbling basalt and landed on his side.

"We are not armed," he said over an open channel. "Cease fire."

Several Gnilltak dressed in battle gear jumped out of the vehicles and seized one the cringing engineers.

"I claim this ship as my property," a familiar, pleasant voice said. "You will repair it now."

Posbret.

I used my wristcom to send a signal to Cat. "Posbret and his raiders are attacking Reever and some of Drefan's engineers out on the surface. They want our ship, and they're prepared to kill them to take it. Can you send help out to the crash site?"

"Drefan's dome is closer," Cat replied. "I'll relay an alert to him."

I felt helpless as I watched the raiders pull the engineers out from their hiding places while Posbret boarded *Moonfire*. No one had seen Reever yet, but the raiders fanned out around the crash site, obviously searching.

"Duncan, we're alerting Drefan," I told him. "But you have to get out of there."

"There is no place to go," he said, "except the crater."

"No, stay away from it." I saw the red flash of a tracer beam move across the screen. "Incoming."

A pulse rifle fired, and the screen image went wild as Reever rolled to avoid the blast. A second blast sent a slow-moving shower of rock and dust over the screen, and I heard a distinctive hissing sound.

The sound of his air supply, escaping the envirosuit. "Duncan, are you hit? Did they breach your seals?"

"No. I landed on a sharp stone, and it pierced one of the suit seams."

"Don't pull it out."

"I have nothing to patch it." His voice sounded thin, and he panted his next words over a peculiar rumbling. "Something's coming." The images shifted as he sat up, and I saw one of Drefan's massive drednocs coming up fast behind the raiders. "Jarn. Prepare for multiple casualties."

The drednoc's mode halo widened, and then sent a strange arc of purple light sweeping through the crash site. As it passed over the raiders, the power cells on their weapons turned black, as did the emitters on all of their vehicles. The energy wave had almost dissipated by the time it reached Reever, but then the image on the screen vanished, along with the audio.

I ran out of the treatment room and into Cat, who caught me with all three arms, and pinned me against his nearly bare chest.

"Hey, where's the fire?"

For a dreadful moment I thought I would blurt out what had happened in the solitude room. But I had not meant to intrude on his and Mercy's privacy, and I didn't have time to feel embarrassed, anyway.

"I need to get to the crash site," I told him. "I'll need a pulse weapon, the fastest surface vehicle you have, and some spare O_2 tanks."

"It's all right," the Omorr assured me. "Drefan's drednoc stopped the raiders."

"Reever's suit is damaged and leaking oxygen. I have to get to him now or he'll suffocate." I slipped out of his grip and ran in the direction of the exterior air lock.

By the time I reached the suit lockers someone was already coming through the air lock. I saw it was Drefan's battle drone. It carried two limp bodies under each extensor arm. One of them was wearing a raider's gear.

"Duncan? *Duncan.*" I pounded on the plas panels separating us, and then the control panel, but the locks would not release. None of the bodies the drednoc carried moved.

"It won't until the pressure equalizes and the biodecon is complete," Mercy said as she joined me. She studied my face. "Well, at least you've stopped blushing. That's progress."

"Bypass the decontamination cycle." When she hesitated, I added, "Or I will."

Mercy heaved out a breath and began reprogramming the air lock controls. "If I lose my skin because we didn't scan them, I'm going to come back and haunt your scrawny little ass forever."

"Whatever." I shifted my weight from foot to foot until the panels finally opened and I could get inside. I began yanking off helmets until I found Reever, unconscious, his face covered in frozen blood. I felt a sluggish pulse beneath his jaw. I covered his nose and mouth with a portable breather. "Mercy."

"Right behind you." She rolled an enormous, flat-topped cart into the air lock. To the drednoc, she said, "Put them on here."

The drone carefully lowered all four bodies onto the cart, and then gripped the handle as it pushed them into the suit chamber.

"Follow me," I told it, and hurried down the corridor toward the treatment room.

Mercy kept pace with me. "Cat is setting up some beds for them. What else can I do?"

"You can assist me." I glanced back to see if the drednoc was keeping up. "I'll need a clean, empty space that I can isolate and use as an operating room."

"I've got an air lock for cargo deliveries on that side of the house," she said. "You can do ten or twenty surgeries in there, all at the same time, if you want."

I was hoping I wouldn't have to perform any. "In here," I said to the drednoc as I rushed into the treatment room. Cat was waiting, along with

Ekatarana and four of the beds from the pleasure rooms.

At that point I would have put Reever on the floor. "Transfer the men to the beds," I ordered the drednoc. "Carefully, one at a time."

The drone complied, and as soon as the first one was transferred I took out my scanner and began triage.

"Unconscious, mild concussion, vitals are stable," I recited as I read the results displayed. "This one can wait." I moved to the next body, one of Posbret's men. The raider had taken a severe blow to the abdomen, and was slowly hemorrhaging. "This man needs surgery. Mercy, get that cargo air lock ready for me."

The third man was Reever, and I ripped his suit open to find the source of his bleeding. I knew that if his injury was not as severe as the raider with the ruptured spleen, I would have to delay his treatment. If it were equally serious, I would have to choose between them. Among the Iisleg it was a matter of rank: The male most important to the tribe was given preference. Among Terrans, the male judged most likely to survive had priority.

The man I loved, and a man who had tried to kill him. It was not going to be a hard choice to make.

Reever's eyes opened to slits. "Jarn."

"Be still," I told him. "You are bleeding from somewhere." Or he had been, for the blood on his skin was now half dried. Something hard and sharp brushed my hand, and I found a jagged rock lodged in the side seam next to his rib cage. "Here is the culprit." I pulled it out to show him, but he had slipped into unconsciousness again.

I passed my scanner over the area, but it showed no open wound or internal hemorrhaging, and only some minor bruising around the ribs.

I dropped the scanner, tore apart his tunic, and wiped the congealing blood away, looking for the wound I knew had to be there. He had lost at least a pint of blood. Yet all I could find was a pink scar that slashed diagonally through a wide patch of contusions. The sight of it made me step back from the bed.

I knew Reever's body. The scar had not been there this morning.

I passed the scanner over him twice more, but it showed no other injury. Somehow his wound had healed between the crash site and the dome.

Reluctantly I put aside my shock and the rest of my feelings, and moved to the last man. This engineer had several proximity burns on his appendages, but none of them were life threatening. I moved back to the raider with the ruptured spleen.

"This one needs surgery now, but the rest can wait." I grabbed my case, took out a syrinpress, dialed a dosage for painkillers, and handed it to Mercy.

She took it the same way she might a pressure grenade. "Why are you giving me this? I'm no healer."

"You're my new ward nurse. If he wakes up"—I

pointed to the engineer with burns—"give him an injection. Try to rouse the one with the concussion, and keep him awake if you can."

"What about your husband?" she asked.

"He's fine." I looked at Cat, and tried not to remember how he had kissed Mercy/me. "Are you as good with your hands as . . . Mercy says you are?" He nodded. "Come with me. You're my surgical assistant."

Eleven

The cargo air lock proved to be an excellent emergency operating room. I used the biodecon to sterilize the air, me, Cat, and the patient, and then set up a manifest station as an instrument stand. I laid out everything I needed and identified each for Cat so he would know what to hand me when I asked for it. We gloved and put on two of the disposable surgical shrouds from my case, and I injected the raider with a powerful sedative that would have to serve as general anesthesia.

"What if I drop something?" Cat asked.

"I stop operating and stab you in the chest." Why did Cherijo's words burst out of me whenever I was operating? I glanced at him. "I apologize. I'm kidding."

He eyed the instrument stand. "I hope so."

I had no blood with which to transfuse the raider, so I rigged a syrinpress and some tubing to both provide suction and autoinfuse the patient with his own blood.

"What is making him bleed like that?" Cat asked as I enabled a lascalpel and made the necessary incision to get under the patient's ribs.

"He took a hard blow to the belly," I said as I used the rib spreader to open up the cavity, and several sponges to soak up the blood oozing out of the spleen. "Drefan's drednoc must have hit him. The blow made a tear here, see?" I pushed aside part of the stomach loop to expose the rupture in the spleen. "In humanoids, this organ filters out old blood cells and produces lymphocytes, which make antibodies. It's always filled with blood, and bleeds badly when damaged, so I have to seal the tear or it will kill him."

"He tried to kill your husband," Cat reminded me. "Maybe you should return the favor."

"Doctors take an oath to do no harm," I said. "It applies to all patients, not simply allies or the ones we like."

Cat squinted at the raider's insides. "Do I have one of those?"

I glanced sideways at him. "Omorr have two, as it happens. One on either side of your body." I remembered how much of Cat's body I/Mercy had seen and touched, and quickly turned back to the patient.

"Your face is turning a strange color," Cat said. "Should I adjust the air temperature in here?"

It took two hours for me to repair the damage to

the raider's spleen, which thankfully proved much more resilient than most humanoid species. Cat remained silent and moved only to hand me the instruments I needed, for which I was grateful.

"That's it," I said as I finished closing. "I'll need to keep him on close monitor for the next day, but barring complications he should survive." I pulled down my mask and saw how the Omorr's gildrells poked out from under his. "What is wrong?"

He pulled the bloodied gloves from his membranes and dropped them on the table. "Nothing, except that you just came here, cut open that man, and rearranged his insides like you do it every day."

"During the rebellion, I did at least two or three splenectomies every week. I think I could do them blindfolded." I realized how callous I sounded and gave him a rueful look. "I am sorry. I should have warned you about the nature of field surgery. It can seem quite brutal."

"Brutal? You saved his life. None of us could have done it, even if we'd wanted to. I am beyond impressed." Cat regarded the state of my surgical shroud. "Yours is a messy business, though, Doc."

Now that the raider was no longer in danger of bleeding out, I could go back and deal with the others. I instructed Cat on how to use the drednoc to bring my patient back to the treatment room, and then headed there myself. But as I stepped out of the air lock, I saw my husband, pale-faced but standing on his own, waiting beside the control panel.

"What are you doing here?" I went over to him and found myself in his arms. *"Duncan."*

"I am all right, *Waenara*," he assured me, kissing the top of my head. "It's been a long time since I've watched you being a surgeon."

"I am putting you in restraints the next time you are wounded," I snapped. I turned and tucked my arm carefully around his waist. "Come back to the treatment room. I barely had time to look at you properly. Are you in pain?"

On the way there, Reever said, "I'm not wounded, but I have an interesting new scar across my ribs."

"Yes, I saw it." And now I had to explain to him why. "Duncan, I need to talk you about all the medical tests I've run on you since we left Akkabarr."

He nodded. "You said the results were favorable."

"Not exactly." I groped for the right words and found myself making excuses. "I was going to tell you about this while we were away on this sojourn, but then we crashed here and, well, the right moment never presented itself."

"It's what Joseph Grey Veil did to me after I was stabbed on Terra," he said. "Those cells he put inside me. They've changed me, haven't they?"

Only one other person knew the truth about the chameleon cells. "Did Squilyp tell you this?"

"Cherijo said the cells were responsible for my kidney regenerating. My eyes healed very quickly after the battle during the rebellion. And they prevented me from dying on Vtaga when SrrokVar's drone stabbed me through the chest."

I stopped outside the treatment room. "The chameleon cells Joseph Grey Veil implanted in you have infiltrated every part of your body. Evidently they remain in a dormant state until they're stimulated by sickness or injury. Then they replicate and replace the dying cells. Since they can mimic any cell structure in your body, they can repair any damage done to it."

His hand touched my cheek. "You were afraid to tell me this?"

"What Cherijo's—what my creator did to you was wrong," I said. "He had not tested the cells properly; he used you like a test animal."

He didn't seem concerned. "He did the same to you."

"You don't understand, Duncan. There could still be complications." My voice hardened. "I don't understand how she could let him experiment on you."

"I was dying, Jarn. As much as I despised Cherijo's father, he saved my life. He may have greatly increased my life span as well, is that not so?"

"If there are no complications, and the cells continue functioning as benevolent symbiotes," I said, "your wounds will heal, you will not be susceptible to disease, and you will not age."

"Whatever happens"—he took my hands in his—"you are not to blame for what was done in the past."

The tension eased from my chest. "You're taking this very well." So well that I wondered if I should risk telling him about my experience in the solitude room.

"All you must do now is replicate the process Joseph used to create the cells," Reever said. "You have plenty of time before Marel reaches maturity and needs them."

I felt bewildered. "Why would I put chameleon cells in our daughter? She is in perfect health."

"We conceived her before Joseph Grey Veil implanted the cells in me," Reever said. "If Marel has not inherited the gift of your genes, her life span will only be that of an average Terran."

"As it should be," I said, very carefully. "Duncan, you and I are no longer Terran. I doubt we could even be classified as human. I cannot recreate the chameleon cells, and I am certainly not infecting Marel or anyone else with them."

He stepped back. "So you would have us outlive our own daughter, when we could share our gift with her?"

"Our *gift*?" Anger made my hands clench. "Have you forgotten all that has happened since Cherijo escaped her creator and fled Terra? She has been hunted, tortured, imprisoned—*enslaved*—all because she cannot die. How many others have died trying to obtain the secret of her immortality for themselves, or to protect Cherijo from those who would take it? Duncan, this *gift* has been like a curse upon her soul. It terrifies me to think that Joseph inflicted it on you. And now you would have me do the same thing to our daughter? The three of us will never be safe again."

"No." Reever took hold of my shoulders. "You are wrong. No one knows about Marel. We will not let anything happen to her."

My heart felt like a stone in my chest. "No, we will not, because I will never replicate the process. If you cannot accept that our daughter will live a normal life span, then we should give her to the Torin. With them, she can live her life among other mortals, and you will not have to watch her die."

"I told you after the rebellion," Reever said, very softly, "the only way you will separate me from our daughter is to kill me." He touched his side. "I think that will be rather more difficult now."

Mercy came out of the treatment room and looked at both of us. "I hate to interrupt this tender moment or whatever you two are having, but the painkiller is wearing off the guy with the burns, and the one with the headache keeps trying to nap. Cat will be here in a minute with that raider you should have let die, too."

"I will signal Drefan and tell him what is happening with his men." Reever turned and walked away.

I stayed in the treatment room through the night so I could monitor the raider I had operated on. Reever never returned, but Mercy came in the morning to tell me that Drefan had signaled, insisting his men be returned to Omega Dome at once.

I expressed my opinion of his request in candid terms.

"Yeah, I think he's an utter jackass, too." Mercy shrugged. "But if we don't take them back, he's sending more of his drednocs to get them. Much as I'd like to blow up the access way between us, I really don't need an interdome battle right now." She sighed. "He wants you over there, too."

I considered telling her about Tya, and then thought better of it. "Very well. I will prepare the men for transport." I brushed some hair out of my face. "Have you seen Reever?"

"Not since he walked out of here yesterday. Did you tell him about your little spin in the fantasizer? Maybe he's sulking." When I shook my head, Mercy went to the console and signaled Cat. "Where is Reever?"

The Omorr replied, "He took two of our drones and returned to Gamers."

"I want the drones back." Mercy terminated the relay and caught my expression. "Trouble in paradise?"

Words of resentment welled up inside me, but Iisleg women did not complain about their husbands. "We had a disagreement about our child."

"You know, when Cat and I get into it, I lose my temper, and yell, and say things I don't really mean." Mercy grimaced. "He knows how I am, and stays away from me until I settle down. I'm thinking Reever does the same thing."

I shook my head. "Reever just tells me that if I want my way, I have to kill him."

Mercy whistled. "Whoa. He doesn't compromise very well, does he?"

"He doesn't compromise at all." I gave her an exasperated look. "Why are you being so sympathetic? I thought you were angry with me."

"I thought you were a naive, clueless kid." She gestured toward the engineers and the raider being prepped for transport. "Way you handled them? I should have you protecting me."

"I would make a terrible bodyguard," I advised her, "but I thank you for the compliment." I looked down as she handed me a wristcom. "I already have one of my own."

"This one's been modified with a one-touch emergency autorelay and locator beacon." Mercy showed me the recessed slide switch. "It works off a pair of binary command crystals, which Drefan can't monitor or jam." She showed me a duplicate of the device around her own wrist. "I've got the other one."

I knew of the crystals, which were perfectly tuned twins that responded only to each other. They were so rare as to be very nearly priceless. "Mercy, you should not have done this."

"Too late." She smiled. "Don't worry, I got the crystals from an old friend who can't use them. If you're in trouble over at Gamers, turn it around your wrist twice to activate the beacon, and sit tight until Cat and I come and get you."

I accompanied the patients back to Omega Dome, where they were taken to a simulator room programmed to serve as a hospital ward. Drefan glided in as I was making them comfortable.

"How are the men?"

"Stable, no thanks to your impatience." I kept my back to him as I changed the abdominal dressings on my spleen patient. "Where is Reever?"

"He is presently beating the algorithms out of my Hsktskt combat program in a sparring chamber." Drefan maneuvered his chair in between the berths and peered at the surgical site. "What is that very interesting-looking poultice made of?"

"A form of ambulatory mold." I picked up the Lok-teel, which had cleaned the impurities and bacteria out of the patient's wound, and allowed it to slide under the edge of my sleeve. "It feeds on refuse and waste, and exudes a sterile astringent."

Drefan watched the bulge of the mold move under my sleeve. "Is it the same mold you used to change your facial features when Posbret came looking for you at Mercy House?"

I kept my face blank. "I don't know what you mean."

"Don't you, *Ana*?" His one eye shifted down to a light that began blinking on the arm of his glidechair. He tapped it and said, "What is it, Keel?"

"Posbret and his entire crew are here in main control," the Chakacat replied, its voice tight. "I don't know how they got in, but they want you to turn the Terrans over to them. They say if they're not here in one minute, they're going to start shooting everything that moves."

"We'll be right there." Drefan terminated the relay and looked up at me. "I don't think a mask is going to fool him this time. Shall we try the truth?"

Posbret had brought at least fifty men with him this time, I saw as I followed Drefan into the control room. Keel stood in the center of the raiders, dangling from Posbret's pudgy fist, which held the back of its harness.

Their sweat soaked their orange and brown fur as well as the air, creating a cloud of fear and fury.

I had not bothered with the Lok-teel mask, and as soon as the raider leader saw me he produced a brilliant, satisfied smile.

"You're smart to bring the shifter to me, Games Master," he told Drefan. "I'll see to it that she pays for what she's done."

"I am not the killer that you seek, Posbret," I said. "Think about it. My ship crashed here three days ago. The skin thief has been attacking your colony for the last year." I pulled down my lower eyelid. "You see? No blood around my corneas." I tugged at my forearm. "My skin is my own."

Some of the raiders began shifting and muttering under their breath.

"You didn't look like this at Mercy House," Posbret said, gesturing at my face. "The only way you could change your face and hair is if you're a shifter."

I considered showing him the Lok-teel under my tunic, and then thought better of it. "I didn't think a lot of face paint and hair dye would convince you, but Mercy is quite talented with enhancing a woman's appearance."

Posbret's serene brow furrowed. "You're lying. You could have faked that crash to gain more access to us. You could be more shifters, come to help kill us. You'll tell me the truth when I put you on the rack." He motioned to three of his men.

Before the trio could take hold of me, I held out a medical scanner. "Here is your truth, raider. Pass it over me. It will show you that I am who I say I am."

"You could have programmed it to give false readings," Posbret argued. "To protect yourself."

When Reever and I escaped this world, I was going to find a cure for paranoia. "Pass it over yourself first and see."

Keel fell from Posbret's fist and landed on all fours as the raider leader snatched the scanner out of my hand. He switched it on and passed it over himself and then two of his men standing nearby.

"All right, so we read normal." He turned it toward me. "Let's see what's inside you."

I stood motionless under the scanner's beam and waited without comment for Posbret to study the results.

He frowned. "You're Terran." He looked up, his liquid brown eyes perplexed. "Maybe it's the other one."

The door panel to the control room opened, and

Reever came in, his arm supporting my spleen patient.

"I am as Terran as my wife is," Reever said, helping the raider cross the room. "But feel free to scan me as well."

"Jhgat," Posbret said, astonished. "I thought you were dead."

"You left me out there to die," the raider said, his voice harsh. "Drefan's battle drone brought me in with the other wounded. I was busted up bad inside." His tired eyes shifted toward me. "She's a patcher. She opened me up and fixed me."

"Why would she do that?" one of the other men demanded, raising a pistol and aiming it at my patient. "She put something inside you?"

I stepped into the line of fire and let Cherijo take over. "I didn't save this man's life so that you could shoot him, you neurotic moron. Put down the weapon. *Put it down.*"

The raider slowly lowered the pistol.

I turned to Posbret and gestured toward my patient. "Are you satisfied now, or do you want to scan him, too?"

The Gnilltak's leader shoved past his men and came to stand over me. "Why did Davidov offer four million for you?"

"The bounty has been withdrawn," Drefan said before I could answer. "We received the signal from the *Renko* last night."

"I saw the relay," Posbret said. "Why did he offer it in the first place?"

A very good question, I thought, trying to formulate a reasonable response.

"Davidov blockaded Trellus to keep the killer from escaping," Reever said. "He used the bounty to find us, lured us here, and deliberately stranded us. He believes that we can find your killer, and stop it."

"We've been looking for the fucking thing for a year," Posbret snarled. "What does he think you can do?"

"I don't know," Reever admitted. "My wife has successfully solved many crises on other worlds. Maybe Davidov believes she can do the same here. His motives are not our concern. We'll do whatever we can to help you."

"Then you're a fool, Terran." The raider leader's perfect lips formed a ghastly grin. "Because the only thing you're going to do down here is die."

Twelve

Once the raiders left the dome, Drefan sent a maintenance crew to repair and reinforce the air lock they had blasted out, and had two of his drones escort my spleen patient back to the simward. The games master suggested that I continue with my exams of his staff.

Reever, I saw, had disappeared again. "Would you ask my husband to signal me when he has finished in the sparring room?" I asked Keel, who nodded. I turned to Drefan. "You can come with me."

His brows arched. "For what reason?"

"You're the first one I'm going to examine."

Instead of protesting, Drefan silently accompanied me to the room I had been using for exams, and deftly hoisted his body out of the chair and onto the table.

"I should tell you before we begin," he said, "that I'm not as pleasant to look at as the Gnilltak."

"I'm not interested in your personal beauty," I

advised him. "Can you undress without assistance?"

"It was the first skill I taught myself after losing my limbs." He released the fasteners on his tunic, baring a wide, heavily muscled chest with a row of crude-looking dark blue symbols forming a circular pattern over his heart.

I didn't recognize the symbols. "Is that tattoo decorative, or does it mean something?"

"This part says 'one-one-six-nine-four-seven-one,'" he told me, pointing to the upper portion of the symbols. "Slaves are not permitted the privilege of names. The two side rows are my original owner's identification and contact code. I didn't bring much at auction, so he didn't bother with a locator implant."

He spoke of his enslavement as if it meant nothing to me. "And the bottom row?"

He ran a thumb over the symbols. "Certification that my second owner set me free."

I passed a scanner over him while I surveyed the condition of his arm and leg stumps. "Were your amputated limbs severed, diseased, or damaged?"

"They were crushed," he told me. "An unbalanced load of raw ore fell on top of me."

My scanner showed an elevated level of arutanium in his blood, and hundreds of minute fragments of the alloy embedded in his shoulder and hips. I also found traces of it in his bones, teeth, and hair. "You should be dead, Games Master."

He chuckled. "You're reading the metal inside me, I take it."

"Yes, and there is enough inside you to build a few drones." I had never examined a living being with such levels of the poisonous alloy. "Your accident could not have caused it to leech into your bones."

"That happened before I was flattened." His blue eye gleamed. "I became immune to arutanium while I worked in the mines. Breathing in the dust all day does that to you, if it doesn't kill you first."

To build up that kind of resistance would have required an extended exposure under extreme working conditions, perhaps for years. "How often were you exposed to the ore dust?"

"For the entire length of my enslavement in the mines." He closed his eye. "Or, to be more precise, five standard years, eight months, fourteen days, ten hours, and six minutes."

I set my scanner aside and use my penlight to examine the crater where his other eye should have been. There were odd calluses around the edge of the smooth socket. I found more just like them on his temples and the bridge of his nose. "Do you wear something over your face on a frequent basis?"

"I use a welding shield when I work on the drednocs." His eye shifted as he studied my face. "Your eyes are dark blue. I had thought they were black, like your hair."

I rolled him onto his side, and immediately

wished that I hadn't. So many healed lash marks crisscrossed his back that it appeared corrugated. A dozen small craters dotted the vicious scars indicated where chunks of his flesh had been torn out. Here and there were raised, shiny stripes that appeared to be healed burns.

He had been beaten, repeatedly, almost to death. I had never seen anything like it.

I tried three times to speak before the words came out of my mouth. "How was this done to you?"

"The mine guards favored pulse-spike whips," Drefan said. "They're ten feet long, made of flexible alloy cable, and barbed with four-pronged metal orbs. They can be programmed to deliver an adjustable charge through the length of the cable, if a slave deserves extra punishment." He moved his shoulders. "I usually did."

I blinked the tears out of my eyes and began to scan the length of his spine for nerve, tissue, and bone damage. "I thank you for explaining it to me."

"I warned you that I wasn't pretty," Drefan said as I sniffed and checked the alignment of his cervical vertebrae. "Don't cry, Cherijo."

"I am not crying. I am only a little congested." I rested a hand on his shoulder as I tried to control my emotions. "I was a field surgeon during a war. I have seen the violence that men can inflict on each other, but this . . ." I stopped and took in a shuddering breath. "Did they punish the ones responsible for abusing the miners?"

His voice went soft and flat. "Not enough."

*   *   *

A week later I had finished the examinations at Mercy House, and had only one more to perform at Gamers. I had found no trace of the Odnallak or the skin thief among those I examined, and the days I spent working passed without incident. Cat told me that they had never gone so long without a colonist disappearing or a skin being found, something that was rapidly improving the mood around the domes.

"I've received dozens of signals requesting appointments to see you," he added as he escorted me to the air lock on my way to Gamers one evening. "People think you're doing something to keep the shifter from taking more skins."

"If only I could take credit for that." I took my case from him and shouldered it. "I hope you are correcting their assumptions."

"I've tried." He glanced at the drednoc waiting to take me across the access way. "I haven't seen Reever since the raiders tried to grab your ship."

I had been sharing my time between the two domes equally, but Drefan insisted I spend my nights at Gamers. Reever remained there to supervise repairs to the scout and practice in the sparring simulator, but despite the nights and days I spent there, we barely saw each other.

Reever was avoiding me.

My husband rose and left our rooms before I woke, and rarely returned until I fell asleep at night. I waited up for him, several times, hoping to talk and settle the argument over the chameleon cells and Marel. Reever simply left as soon as he saw that I was awake.

Now I offered Cat the same excuses I had been telling myself. "He has been busy working on the ship and practicing for the fight."

Cat's dark eyes narrowed. "What fight?"

"A simulation. It is something Drefan wishes him to do." I wished I could confide in Cat. Still, Reever's debt to Drefan was nearly settled. I would not jeopardize that. "I must go. I will return in the morning."

The drednoc accompanied me through the access way to Gamers and left me at the air lock. I thought it was odd that the battle drone never used the same entrance as I did, but perhaps Drefan had it go to where he kept his other drones.

"Good evening, Cherijo," Keel said as I came out of biodecon. The Chakacat had made a habit of meeting me whenever I returned from Mercy House. "Drefan wondered if you were able to finish the exams of Mercy's staff."

"I was." I took out my datapad. "All I have left is Tya." I looked up. "I have time to perform one more exam. You can send her to my lab now."

"Now." Keel looked uneasy. "That could be a problem."

"Keel, Drefan wished me to examine his entire staff. Yet he continues to stall me when I ask to see Tya. If he does not wish me to check her, just say so."

"It's not that." The Chakacat looked around before lowering its voice. "We keep her in a secured area, and Drefan doesn't like to let her out often."

"I can examine her there, if you wish," I offered, mimicking its tone. "Only tell me first why we are whispering about her."

"Drefan," it said, as if that explained everything.

More of his games, no doubt. "Take me to her, Keel."

The secured area turned out to be a modified detention unit, hidden in the back of one unused section of a storage area. Keel held me back as it opened the door panels.

"Inhibitor webbing," it said, pointing to the energized mesh filling the entry. "Tya, I'm bringing the healer in to see you."

No reply came from the dark room.

"I will need some lights," I told the Chakacat as it deactivated the webbing and pulled it aside. Cool air washed over me as I entered and Keel enabled the cell's overhead emitters.

The Hsktskt lay on two berths that had been welded together to accommodate her ten-foot-long body. She wore a thin white tunic and a modified skirt that covered her lower limbs and tail. Alloy restraints held down her other limbs. She appeared to be asleep.

"Stay here." Keel moved a little closer. "Tya, the healer has come to check you."

Two lids retracted from a yellow eye as big as my

face. "It is not time to fight," she said, her voice scraping out of her throat.

I saw the dryness of her skin and the dark depressions under her eyes and around her nostrils. "Why is she so thin and dehydrated?"

"I don't know. She has food and water." Keel gestured to a prep unit that had been installed in the cell. "Although, to be honest, I've never seen her using it."

I went over to check the unit. "She's not using it." My skin shivered with delicious pleasure as frigid air poured down on me from an overhead vent. Such low temperatures could be lethal to Hsktskt. "This cell is too cold for her."

"They think it controls me," Tya said, and ripped the restraints from one arm, and then the other. With a few more jerks she was able to free herself and roll off the berth. I watched her rise and touch the back of her neck. "Like the straps. And the food." She bent, shaking, and braced herself against one wall.

Her frame appeared very thin for a Hsktskt.

"Keel, get her some water. Now." I put my medical case on the berth. "Sit down before you fall down, Centuron."

Tya did so, and the berth creaked. "I have no rank, warm-blood. Did the cripple not tell you so?"

"The cripple does not talk a great deal about you." I took out a scanner and passed it in front of her chest. She was at least seventy-five kilos lighter than she should have been, and her stomach and digestive system were completely empty, explaining the gauntness of her form. "Why are you starving yourself?"

Tya opened her mouth and displayed triple rows of sharp, serrated-edged teeth. "I don't want that food."

"I suppose I can install a feeding tube in your gullet." I took a syrinpress, dialed up a massive dose of reptilian nutrients, and infused her with them. I looked over at Keel. "Have you programmed that unit for a Hsktskt diet?"

The Chakacat brought a server of water to me. "Yes. That's all that's on the menu."

I offered Tya the server. When she didn't move to take it, I said, "I can also start an IV, if you like."

She took the server, drank the contents in one swallow, and handed it back to me. "Leave me."

"I must examine you." I glanced at Keel. "Would you wait outside, please?"

Agitation made the Chakacat's whiskers twitch. "Healer, I do not think that is advisable."

"If she intends to harm me," I pointed out, "she will do it whether you are here or not."

Tya lay back on the berth and closed her eyes. "The warm-blood is safe with me, little cat."

"I'll be just outside here if you need me, Healer." Keel left with great reluctance.

As I scanned Tya, I studied her outward appearance. Even the Hsktskt rogues on Vtaga, who rarely had enough to eat, had not been so emaciated.

"Why do you not eat?" I asked her. Before she answered, I added, "If you will not tell me the truth, I will recommend to Drefan that we put you on a feeding tube."

She didn't look at me. "The food here is repulsive."

"I agree, but for now there is no alternative to synth." She didn't respond to that. "My knowledge of Hsktskt cuisine is limited, but if you do not care for what is programmed on the prep unit, I can ask Keel to—"

"Vegetables."

I frowned. "What about them?"

"I eat vegetables and fruit," she said gruffly. "Not synpro."

I had never heard of a Hsktskt who did not eat meat. "Did your former owner refuse to feed you protein?" She remained silent. "Very well, I will have Keel program the unit to provide fruits and vegetables."

I continued the exam. Her scale coloration was unlike any I had seen on Vtaga, extremely plain, with none of the distinct shifts and whorls in the color patterns that represented Hsktskt bloodlines. She had far too many white scales as well; almost half of her body had no color at all.

I considered the few causes of such abnormalities. "Have you had dermal pigmentation therapy?"

"No."

I saw no signs of scarring, burns, or skin grafts. Her hide was, in fact, in pristine condition for a female of her age. "Was one of your parents an albino?"

"No."

I took a step back from the berth. "Why is your hide so white?"

Air snorted through her nostrils. "Because if it were black, I would be a Ghint-polyt."

I checked the scanner's display, and found her vitals to be textbook Hsktskt norm. Given her weight loss and dehydration, that seemed unlikely. She was certainly not a Ghint-polyt reptilian, or she would be mostly black and inarticulate.

"Drefan told me that Davidov sold you to him just before he quarantined Trellus," I said. "Did you know of Alek's plans to blockade the planet?"

"*Alek*," she said, snapping her teeth over the name. "The scum that walks and talks like a male." She sat up. "Why do you think he would confide in slave meat like me?"

"I thought perhaps you overheard something while you were on the *Renko*," I said.

"Nothing you would wish to hear." She studied me. "I have seen you before, with that Terran who moves like an arena slave. He is the one I am to fight."

"Fight, yes, but not kill."

She made a contemptuous sound. "If he steps onto the grid, I will make him wish he were dead. He is not like me. He has a choice. He is a fool for accepting the match."

The self-loathing in her words startled me. "You do not want to fight him? Why?"

"Ask the cripple; this is his doing. My desires no longer matter, warm-blood." Tya rolled over onto her side, presenting her back to me.

I wondered if Drefan was using the match between Tya and Reever for some other purpose. "Tya, if Drefan transmits the match between you and my husband to the rest of the colony, will Davidov be able to monitor the signal?" She didn't answer. "He's already monitoring every transmission from the colony. He would have to, in order to jam them."

The Hsktskt said nothing, so I passed my scanner over the back side of her body. The display brought up the image of a foreign body lodged inside the back of her throat, just below her brain stem. "You have an implant in your neck. Is it a locator beacon?"

Tya rolled over to swat at my scanner, her claws missing it only by a fraction of an inch. "Leave me alone."

I glanced down at the image. "It's just under the surface of your hide. I can give you a local anesthetic and remove it now."

"No." Tya pushed herself off the berth and began circling the room. "He modified it with an extraction code that can be entered only from a device he carries."

"I do not need a code to extract it."

She gave me an impatient look. "If you or anyone tries to remove it without deactivating it first from

Davidov's remote, it will release a cache of poison. I will be dead before my body hits the floor."

I didn't have time to respond to this shocking revelation, for a moment later a familiar voice called to me from outside the detention cell.

"Doc, what the hell are you doing in here? I had to practically blast my way into this place to see you." Mercy walked into the cell. "I know you're busy finishing up, but Kohbi finally cocooned. Cat and I were worried that . . ." She stopped speaking and moving, and stared past me.

Keel came in and took hold of the female Terran's arm. "It's not what you think, Mercy."

Wide, disbelieving eyes shifted toward the Chakacat. "Are you telling me that I'm imagining that Hsktskt over there?"

"No, but you don't understand, she's—"

"Mine." Mercy shook off Keel as if it were an annoying insect and started toward the berth.

I stepped between her and Tya. "No, Mercy."

"There is a Hsktskt lying on that berth behind you," she said in a pleasant tone, "and I'm going to kill it. Give me a knife and get out of my way."

"Let her come," Tya said, sounding listless.

"See?" Mercy gestured. "She wants me over there. Step aside, Doc."

"You can't do this." I put a hand against her shoulder. "She's ill."

"All the more reason to let me put her out of her misery." She tried to push past me, glanced down at my hand, and laughed. "Cherijo, you are not seriously thinking of keeping me from slitting her throat. Tell me you're not that dense."

"I would see you try, Terran," Tya said.

"You," I said to the Hsktskt, "shut up." To Mercy I said, "She's not a raider. She had nothing to do with the attack on Trellus. She's too young." When that didn't get through, I added, "She's nothing but a slave."

Tya made a disgusted sound.

"In five seconds, she's not going to be anything but a pile of young, dead slave." Mercy again tried to shove me aside. "Look, I get the whole oath thing. If you don't want to watch, that's fine. Step outside. I'll tell Drefan you weren't even here."

"I would not go far," Tya said to me as she sat up. "Your friend will shortly need your services."

Mercy's lips peeled back from her teeth. "Yeah, I hate mopping up lizard blood by myself."

"I am not going to let you harm her." I tried to think of a reason that Mercy would respond to. "She belongs to Drefan. He paid a great deal for her. She is his property."

"I'll reimburse him for his loss." Mercy's hands knotted. "I really don't want to belt you, Doc, so I'm telling you, for the last time. Get out of my way."

"This is boring." Tya dropped back on the berth and pulled the thermal sheet over herself. "Wake me when someone wishes to fight."

I took the syrinpress out of my tunic pocket and surreptitiously dialed up a dose of sedative. "Come out into the hall and talk with me for a moment, and then I'll let you do as you wish."

"No, you won't. You'll lock me out of here, and call Drefan, and have my ass hauled back to my dome." Rage made her body and voice shake. "You'll save her, just like you saved all the rest of them. Only this time no one is going to start a war, so really, what's the . . ." She looked down as I infused her, and back up at me. Her eyes filled with astonishment. "You conniving bitch."

"I'm sorry." I caught her as she crumpled. "Keel, help me."

Thirteen

Once I had summoned drones to take Mercy back to her dome, I left Keel to reprogram Tya's prep unit and went to central control, where Drefan was monitoring several games in progress.

I did not bother with pleasantries. "Mercy knows about Tya. She came here to see me, and found me in the detention cell with her."

Drefan rotated his glidechair to face me. "Mercy did not react well, I take it."

"I had to sedate her to keep her from killing the Hsktskt." My gaze shifted past him, to a screen showing Keel securing some inhibitor webbing. "But you already know that. Did you watch the entire confrontation?"

"Of course." He glanced back at the monitors. "There is very little that happens under my dome that escapes my attention."

"Then why didn't you stop Mercy before she

found us?" I demanded. "You knew how furious she would be."

"Mercy needs to face her demons," he said. "As does Tya."

"This is not a game, Drefan. These females are not simulations. Stop playing with them." I turned on my heel and walked out.

Reever had been taking his meal intervals elsewhere, so when I arrived at our quarters I prepared a simple dinner for myself and ate while I reviewed the data on Tya that I had not had time to analyze.

"A Hsktskt who would starve rather than eat meat." I sipped some tea from my glass as I considered my own plate of something Reever called "chicken and rice." The chicken part was tolerable, but the rice tasted like bits of soggy gauze.

I had little practical knowledge of other species' food preferences. Jorenians did not eat meat, as they received the protein they needed from the milk of their herd animals, but they were mammalian-based species, not reptilian. Hsktskt needed enormous amounts of protein to help fuel and warm their massive bodies.

I knew the pains of an empty belly. The Toskald had tried to starve us during the rebellion, and many times I had eaten old meat, needle plants, and other things that otherwise I would never have touched. Even if Tya had some unnatural aversion to her dietary requirements, her hunger should have driven her to eat what was available.

I recalled Drefan's Nekawa bodyguard, and how

she had been conditioned in the mines to eat whenever she saw food. Maybe something similar had been done to Tya, to control her behavior. Then there was the implant I had found in her neck; another method of control, to insure she never attempted to escape her enslavement.

Davidov must have hated her beyond reason to treat her with such cruelty. But why? Did he hold Tya responsible for the Faction's crimes against other enslaved beings? Were the implant and the food conditioning some creative form of torture?

Or was it, as I suspected, something more ominous?

I stayed up for several hours, using the console to access the colonial database and pull up what little information they had on Hsktskt. Most of it covered ways to disable and kill the reptilians, not how to treat them for malnourishment and poisonous implants.

When I couldn't find any worthwhile data, I pulled up studies of various forms of depression in reptilian species. Some pompous asses claimed that reptilians did not experience any emotions at all, but after my time on Vtaga I knew better. The Hsktskt might be extremely reserved, and had disciplined themselves not to show emotions, which they considered beneath them. Yet when they let their guard down, they revealed that they experienced the same anger, joy, hate, and love as any warm-blooded species.

Tya, on the other hand, displayed her emotions

openly, as if her blood were as warm as my own. She had committed the ultimate betrayal of her species by deserting her post during time of war, yet seemed not to care that she had been branded a coward and made a slave.

I knew the Hsktskt, and their rigid, unforgiving culture had strict codes of honor and service. They condemned and harshly punished anyone who violated them. They would rather die than be dishonored or enslaved themselves.

Tya's lack of interest in her own well-being and her aversion to meat might be symptoms of a suicidal state. Indeed, when I had checked with Keel, the Chakacat told me that Tya had never once asked for the prep unit to be reprogrammed to her preferences. The only problem with that theory was how she fought in the grid. During the demonstration for me and Reever, Tya had defended herself with intelligence and vigor, and had used considerable skill to defeat her opponents. A depressed, suicidal slave should not be capable of such deeds.

After some hours it became apparent that Reever was not coming back to our quarters at a reasonable hour, so I cleansed and went to bed alone. Although I felt weary, I spent another thirty minutes staring at the ceiling and trying to work out the puzzles involved with the Hsktskt female.

Finally I closed my tired eyes and cleared my thoughts. If I were back on Joren, this would be the time I would go to check on Marel. The familiar ache of missing my child twisted its blade of love and motherhood in my heart. I knew Salo and Darea were taking good care of her, but it was not the same. I was her mother. I should be with her, to protect her. To be the one to whom she gave her smiles and hugs. To kiss her brow as she slept. I had missed too much of her life as it was.

My body became heavy, and sank into the sleeping platform, dragging me into its moving softness. I had slept on the floor for the first months after leaving Akkabarr. This bed was too soft. It rose up around me, thick and formless and smothering. . . .

Snow light touched my face, and I reached for it, clawing my way out of the suffocating bed linens. It drew me up, high into itself, where the kvinka, the storm winds, roared and the world became mountains of ice, blue and white and unforgiving.

I stood on a cliff above a methane field, with ice crystals scouring my naked face. I squinted, bracing myself against the freezing gusts, and spotted two figures facing each other on the ice. I walked toward them, stumbling now and then as my thin-soled boots slid on the crusted snow. The rapid approach of gigantic, black-purple clouds from the south alarmed me. Such killer storms had been known to sweep entire hunting parties off the ice.

"Do you have a shelter?" I shouted over the wind to them, pointing toward the impending blizzard.

Neither one seemed to hear me, intent on each other as they were. The storm ripped their loose robes away, revealing the forms beneath.

The female stood twice as tall as me, and her

body shimmered as if she wore the dimsilk I had once donned to disguise myself on the battlefield. Her long hair was silver, or white, or perhaps purple; it kept changing color, as did the dimsilk. I could not make out her face, and then I saw why. She had no features, only a smooth oval of gray flesh.

Vral.

I had never seen her before, but I knew her. I knew her as I knew myself, as if everything that had happened to me on Akkabarr had happened to her as well. She had been with me, somehow. But why would the vral come to me now? Why in a dream?

The ghostly-looking female raised her long arm and brandished a sword at her opponent, a drednoc as tall and broad as she.

The icy atmosphere of my homeworld had already left its mark on the battle drone. Frost whitened its armor, and blue icicles dripped from its halo. Yet it did not seem affected as it lifted an extensor arm with a sword attached to the end, also ready to attack.

I felt the unpleasant twang of recognition again. Not as strong as I had with the vral, but I knew this creature. It looked like a drone, but it was something else. Someone else . . .

"Put down your weapons." I had to shout to make myself heard over the kvinka. "The war is over."

A shower of bright orange sparks exploded as their blades met, and the female turned, whirling with the storm, coming up behind the drone and driving her sword into the back of its chassis. It cried out, enraged, and staggered forward, turning just in time to meet her third thrust. It locked blades with her and backhanded her across her blank face with the gauntlet on the end of its other arm.

The female went down, and silver-blue blood splashed the snow, freezing instantly. I ran toward her, calling for the drone to halt its attack. The drednoc dropped its sword and assumed a waiting position.

"Are you hurt?" I dropped down on my knees and reached to turn her over onto her back.

Silver-blue blood had frozen over the blank mask of her face. Before I could touch her, she buried her fingers in the center, clawing at the sheet of flesh and tearing it away from her head.

A face appeared, one raw and horrifying to behold. Tears of blood ran from her slanted, orange eyes, and the unprotected muscle tissue began to blacken and fall away in shriveled strips, revealing orange-red skull bones that bulged and shrank as if alive.

Her mouth smiled as the tissue around it shrank back. "You cannot save my skin, Healer."

I lurched to my feet and staggered backward, colliding with an immovable object. Grapplers took hold of me and turned me around.

"Let go of me," I said, struggling in its grasp. "I have to help her."

The shield on the drednoc's sensor case rose, displaying the lower part of a humanoid face. "Save yourself, Cherijo." It bent toward me, its mouth open, its jagged teeth gnashing together.

I screamed, pushing at the armor with frantic hands, and then the alloy became cloth, and the grapplers strong, five-fingered hands.

"Jarn, wake up," my husband's voice called to me.

The snowy winds snatched at me, but I held on, and then I was back in the bed, in my husband's arms, sobbing against his chest.

"Duncan." I groped at him, blinded by tears. I felt as if my heart would break. "Duncan."

"I am here, beloved," he said, his hand stroking my back in a soothing motion.

I wept and held on to him for a long time, and then tried to speak. "Faces. No faces. Killing. Them. Me." I pressed my hand over my mouth.

"No," he said, tugging my shaking fingers away. "I am here. You're safe. Try to tell me what you saw."

I wanted to tell him of the gray vral, and the drednoc with a humanoid face, but the hysteria had me firmly in its grip. "I never . . . they did not . . . why were they . . . she tore off . . . he tried to . . ." I couldn't stop weeping long enough to make myself coherent. I seized his hands and brought them to my face. "Link with me."

His thoughts, cool and steady, joined the chaos inside my mind. *I am here. I will not let anything hurt you.*

I poured my memories of the dream through the link, where I was finally able to stop babbling and communicate coherently. *Do you see them now? Who are they? Where are they? They will kill each other if I do not stop them.*

They are not real, Waenara. Reever moved through the terrifying images and swept them out of my thoughts until only he and I remained. *They are only a manifestation of your fears.*

No, they were real. I felt it. I knew them. I knew them both. I could still smell the female's blood, and my ears rang with the pitiless sound of her voice. *She was vral. She was a real vral.*

The vral are a myth, he reminded me. *Superstition to house the guilt of the Iisleg for trading with the Toskald in the faces of the dead. Don't you see, beloved? The killer here on Trellus is taking skins from its victims; naturally it would remind you of that time in your life.*

I knew he was right, but part of me resisted his explanation. *What of the drednoc?* I tried to think of what it could have meant. *Could one of Drefan's or Mercy's drones be killing the colonists, and putting parts of them inside itself?*

Drednocs would have no use for organic body parts; it could not be one of them.

The Hsktskt responsible for the plague of memory had been such a being. *What of SrrokVar?*

He is dead, Reever thought with flat finality.

I could see his thoughts processing the bizarre images from my dreams. He went through them methodically, comparing them to hundreds of other faces from his own memory. He lingered for the longest time on the vral, and the nightmare visage she had exposed, tearing away the mask of gray flesh.

I did not want to see her like that, so I broke the link between our minds.

"She is not real," he assured me again. "There were no vral like her on Akkabarr."

"She felt real." I knew I sounded ridiculous. "I must wash my face."

When I returned from the lavatory, Reever had straightened the bed and turned down the bed linens, but remained dressed.

"I suppose you will leave now." I regarded the platform with no small amount of dread. "You should ask Drefan to assign you other quarters. I do not think I will sleep again tonight, so there will be no chance for you to sneak in and out."

"I don't wish to fight with you," he informed me, "but I am not sleeping anywhere else."

My temper, which our estrangement had pulled thin, finally snapped.

"Is this what you did with Cherijo?" I threw out my hands. "Stayed away from her until she grew so lonely she could no longer be angry with you?"

"She never grew lonely." His eyes filled with the faraway look that thoughts of my former self always commanded. "She had medicine. It filled her heart, not me."

My anger went as quickly as it had come. "Then

I pity her, for you cannot love a lascalpel, or a pressure dressing, or a bacterial culture." My mouth quirked. "I am rather fond of the medical database on the *Sunlace*. I wonder if it cares for me."

He regarded me warily. "Does this mean you are calm enough now to discuss Marel and the chameleon cells in a rational manner?"

"No, but you could couple with me," I suggested, "until I become pregnant again. Chances are that our second child will live long enough to suit you."

He didn't say anything for a time, and then told me, "You can't become pregnant, Jarn."

I laughed. "Of course I can. It is only a matter of time before . . ." I stopped as I recalled his appalling childhood. "Has no one told you how children are made?"

"I know how to make them," he said, "but we can never conceive another child."

"What?" Shocked, I sat down on the edge of the sleeping platform. "You are barren?"

"As far as I know, we are both still fertile." Reever placed his hand on my left leg and traced a circle around a spot on the inside of my thigh, and then pressed lightly. "Do you feel that?"

Now I did. I stared down at my leg. "What is that?"

"It's a contraceptive implant," he said. "Squilyp implanted it while you were recovering in Medical, after the transition that made you comatose. It releases enough hormone into your bloodstream to prevent you from becoming pregnant."

"How can this be?" Horror made me crawl backward and scramble off the bed. "Why would he do such a perverted thing? Where is my medical case?" I looked around wildly. "Give me a knife."

Reever took my arm to keep me from hurrying out of the room. "Jarn, after we became sexually active again, I insisted on the Omorr installing the implant. You cannot carry a child to term."

"You did this to me? You are keeping me from having our children? *You dare?*" Fury made me blind, but my hand still found his face as I slapped him. "I had Marel. I will have others. As many as I wish."

"We agreed not to have any more children," he said, his voice cold. "You miscarried Marel in your third month, but you had Squilyp harvest the fetus and transplant her to an artificial womb."

I almost slapped him again. "I did not do any of that," I shouted. "*She did.*"

"In this moment, it is impossible not to think of you as you were," he said, and took a deep breath. "While *Cherijo* and I were on Terra, the Omorr tended to Marel until she was large enough to live outside the tank."

Nausea clogged my throat. "He grew her in a machine? Like some experiment? Like Cherijo—like I was?"

"Cherijo and I made her together, with our bodies, in our bed," he said flatly. "When Cherijo miscarried, she allowed me to believe the baby had died. I did not meet my daughter until she was a year old."

I felt my outrage fade into disgust. "Did she trust you with nothing? Is that why you have become as secretive as she? That you must prevent me from bearing you children, but never tell me why?"

"I never intended to hurt you."

"Truly? Do you know how worried I've been, each time my cycle begins, and I know there will be no child? And you and I coupling every night?" I felt my stomach clench. "Here, all this time, you have been preventing it."

"Joseph bioengineered your immune system to prevent a full-term pregnancy. It will attack and spontaneously abort any child we conceive." He put his hands on my shoulders. "It does not mean the situation is hopeless. When we return to Joren, we can speak to Squilyp about the possibility of using surrogates, if we choose to have more children."

The thought of others having children for us reminded me of the Iisleg custom of taking infants from the ahayag, the tribe's whores, and giving them to barren wives.

"If I cannot carry our babies, then Marel will be enough." I touched the implant in my thigh, and realized how painful it would have been for me to conceive a child, only to lose it. Reever had prevented that. "If you have put anything else in my body, I would know about it. Now."

"The contraceptive is all that was implanted," he

promised, stepping closer. "Are you going to be angry with me over this, too?"

"No." I felt as if I had used up all of my emotions. "I understand why you did it, and I thank you for protecting me. Only *tell* me these things, Duncan. We cannot have secrets between us."

He nodded. "Were you really lonely for me, this past week?"

"Yes, although it has been so long since I have seen you, I am not sure I remember why," I grumbled. "I should be like her and find more patients, perhaps. Fill my heart with them."

"I would rather have my place back." Reever bent his head and kissed the corner of my mouth. "I was just growing accustomed to it."

"If we are going to live forever, we must find better ways to disagree." I wrapped my arms around his waist. "For I cannot do without you, Husband. Not one week. Not one night."

I woke to find Reever gone from our bed, but heard him entering data on the console in the next room. I dressed and went out to find him paging through the various screens of data I had saved on reptilian mood disorders. He was comparing them to another text and frowning at the screen.

I went to the prep unit to make our morning tea. "I examined the Hsktskt female yesterday. They have her locked up like a tithe animal. She has been starving herself."

Reever made a noncommittal sound.

"Mercy also discovered Tya's presence for the first time yesterday. I had to sedate her to keep her from attacking the Hsktskt. Another one of Drefan's games, I think." I brought a steaming server to him and looked at the screen. "Alterforms? What have they to do with a depressed Hsktskt?"

"I thought if she were an alterform, it might explain some of the behaviors you noted in her chart." He picked up my datapad. "I lived among the Hsktskt for many years, but I have never known one to avoid protein."

I related my theory about food conditioning as I pulled up the DNA results of Tya's scans. "She is not an alterform, Duncan. Her body contains no alien DNA. Even the most thorough cellular alterations leave some trace of the original species behind." As it had with PyrsVar, a young Hsktskt whom SrrokVar had alterformed with Jorenian DNA taken from the cadaver of Cherijo's first lover.

"I think Drefan or Davidov are not being truthful about her origins," Reever said thoughtfully. "Tya may have been born into captivity."

I considered the possibility. "Pregnant Hsktskt females are usually not permitted to leave Vtaga."

"Nor would two captive Hsktskt voluntarily mate," Reever said. "Given the chance, they would kill each other first."

"Eggs and sperm could have been harvested from unconscious captives and combined in vitro," I suggested, recalling our conversation from last night. "All they would then need is a surrogate reptilian to bear the brood."

He nodded. "Or a pregnant female may have done as TssVar's mate did, and concealed her pregnancy while away from Vtaga. The maternal instinct to protect is very strong. She might not have committed suicide in captivity to protect the brood."

All this speculation did was create more questions about the female Hsktskt. "If Tya does not eat soon, I will not worry about you fighting her. She will not be able to lift a limb against you, much less a weapon."

He cleared the screen. "If you took a physical sample of Tya's DNA, could you learn more about her than you have with the scanner?"

"At most, I could create a genetic profile, and extrapolate the same for each of her parents." I frowned. "Why would you wish to know that?"

"I don't," he admitted. "What I was hoping was, could you tell from a physical sample if someone has tampered with her DNA?"

"Tampered?"

"Changed it without her knowledge," he explained. "Anything that would explain her more unusual characteristics."

I thought about it. "If such tampering was chemically induced, or molecularly spliced, and I had the proper equipment, likely I could tell you. Those types of procedures create minute flaws in the strands of the helix. They result in sterility and other aberrant reactions." I met his gaze. "What are you thinking, that she has been engineered?"

"I'm not sure yet," he said. "But if you can manage to obtain the samples, I would like you to test Drefan's and Mercy's DNA as well."

Fourteen

Drefan sent a drone to our quarters with a long, flat container and an invitation to join him for the evening meal interval. Reever accepted while I opened the container and took out the garments inside.

"A black jacket and trousers, a white tunic, and a red robe covered over with crystal beads." I showed each piece to my husband before holding the trousers and jacket up against my body. "Too long for me, but I can cut off the ends."

"He sent clothing?"

"Neither of us have more than a single change of garments. Perhaps he is tired of seeing us in the same things." I handed him the robe, which seemed as fine as any rasakt's, except for some missing material at the top. "You are meant to wear the white tunic over the top of this robe, I think."

"The robe is called a 'gown,' and it is made for a female Terran. The trousers, tunic, and jacket are for me." Reever made me switch the garments with him. "On the homeworld, these are called formal wear. You don't wear any other garments over the gown."

"You lie." I held up the skimpy top by the two narrow beaded straps attached to it and measured the fabric with a dismayed eye. "This is indecent. It will barely cover my breasts."

"That is the idea."

"And these?" I removed a pair of spiked red objects from the container. I frowned at the blunt tips of the spikes. "If these are weapons, they need honing."

He took one from me. "They're footgear."

Now I was convinced that he was joking. "They don't even resemble a foot covering."

Reever unfastened one of the straps and insisted I put it on my bare foot. Straps over the toes and heel kept it in place, but when I tried to stand, my leg buckled.

"I cannot walk on these spikes," I said, taking it off. "My ankles will break."

"Very well." He placed the bizarre footgear back in the container. "The skirt of the gown is long. It should cover your boots."

My chin dropped. "I am not wearing that thing."

"Yes, you are," he said firmly.

"On my homeworld," I pointed out, "women do not show their *faces* uncovered, much less half their bodies."

Reever coughed. "Think of it as a way to explore your true planet of origin."

Terra was Cherijo's homeworld, not mine. I didn't care how indecent her people were with their bodies; I could see no reason to wear the gown. Reever seemed equally determined to see me in it. Unless . . .

"If you wish me to couple with Drefan, only say so," I suggested, keeping my expression bland. "I do not need to flaunt my body in such a garment simply to inflame his needs. I can disrobe as soon as I am inside."

Reever took the gown from me. "Jarn, I promise you, I will never ask you to couple with anyone but me."

I could keep pretending I did not understand the mysterious ways of ensleg males, but I had the feeling he knew exactly what I was doing—and on some level, it amused him. "As you say, Husband."

I dressed that evening in the gown. Although the reality of seeing so much of my body exposed did horrify me on several levels, Reever insisted that I looked "charming." He refused to allow me to cover my bared skin with anything, even my unbound hair.

I made as much fuss as I dared.

"I do not like this robe, or gown, or whatever it is," I said as we walked to Drefan's quarters. I had just discovered I had three freckles on my chest, and all of them were showing. "I can feel the air all over the top of me. Garphawayn said I should not let you decide how my hair is worn."

"Squilyp's mate is a militant feminist who thinks all males should be collared and made to serve females," he replied. "Preferably on their knee. But that was a nice try."

Suddenly I wanted to be a militant feminist, too. Whatever that was. "If I were on Akkabarr I would be freezing to death. Females on Terra truly dress like this?"

"Our homeworld has a pleasant climate, so there is no physical reason to wear heavy protective garments," he explained. "The female body is also much admired, so women there display it proudly."

"And they are not attacked, or stolen?" I could not imagine such a culture. "Or whipped to death?"

"You are a doctor," Reever said. "You know there is nothing obscene about the naked body."

"Obscene, no." I tugged at one of the skinny straps, which kept sliding down my shoulder. "Private, yes."

Keel greeted us at the entrance to Drefan's quarters, which contained a great many images of skies on the walls. Not only was Trellus's black, star-specked sky depicted, but those of many other worlds. Reever pointed to one that looked like old ice dotted with snow and told me that it belonged to Terra.

"Of all the deprivations I suffered while I was in the mines," Drefan said as he slowly walked out to greet us, "not being able to see the sky bothered me the most. Doctor, you look beautiful in that dress. Just like a normal Terran woman."

I eyed his prosthetic legs and arm, which he used with a certain amount of awkwardness. "You look more like a normal Terran male with limbs attached."

Drefan laughed. "Point taken." He glanced down and saw the toes of my boots sticking out from under the hem of the gown. "You did not care for the heels I sent?"

"I think they would be valuable if I ever needed to kick a Rilken," I said, "but I cannot walk on the spiked part."

"A sensible attitude." He gestured toward the adjoining room. "Keel has dinner prepared. Please, come in and sit down."

The table in the next room had narrow, burning pillars of different lengths, which Reever identified as small torches called "candles." They were not very effective in lighting the room, but their glow reminded me of the heart of a heat arc, banked for the night. Such things could be pleasant to gaze upon.

Around the candles three places had been set for eating. I did not recognize the tableware, which had gold rims and images of flowers and leaves under a thin transparent glaze. Breast-shaped servers, balanced atop flimsy-looking plas stems, made me cringe a little.

Keel carried in a platter with a respectable-looking haunch of meat surrounded by vegetables cut into unnatural shapes. The Chakacat filled the servers from a plas bottle of dark red liquid and pulled out the chairs.

"That is called merlot, a type of Terran wine," Reever murmured to me as I picked up my server gingerly and studied the beverage. "The meat is roasted beef. Around it are root vegetables called potatoes, carrots, and onions."

"You have only the roots to eat?" I whispered back. "Where is the rest of the plant?"

Reever started to reply, and then said, "I will explain later."

I sniffed the merlot before sampling a tiny sip. It smelled and tasted strongly of alcohol, old fruit, and wood. I squelched a desire to ask for water and attended my meal, which Keel had begun heaping on my plate.

Reever also tested his wine and food, and looked at the games master in surprise. "This is real, not synth."

"I have been saving the last of my stores from the homeworld for a special occasion," Drefan told him. He turned to me. "How do you like the wine, Doctor?"

Obviously it was precious to him, or he would not have hoarded it. I tried to think of something to say that would not offend him, and noticed how the candlelight illuminated the deep color of the wine. "It is very pretty." Eager to change the subject, I glanced down at my plate. "Did you kill this roasted beef yourself?"

Drefan smiled. "Alas, I did not. On Terra, beef is domesticated. We breed and raise it."

I tried to work out his meaning. "Like . . . Keel?"

"No, not like me," the Chakacat said. "My kind are bred to be pets, companions, and servants. Terran beef is bred to serve as food."

I nibbled at the inside of my bottom lip. "They cannot just go out and kill something on the homeworld?"

Drefan laughed. "I'm afraid not, Doctor. Hunting for food on Terra is no longer necessary or permitted. Those who wish to kill their food must pretend to do so with simulated hunts."

"Maybe that is why Terrans are so hostile," I said to my husband. "They have no purposeful outlet like hunting for their aggressions." To the games master I said, "But the roasted beef is very nice. Much like the ptar we snared on my homeworld. Except that it does not have a beak or claws."

"I'm glad that you're enjoying it. Do you plan to ever take your wife back to Terra?" Drefan asked Reever.

"Only if I wish to start a riot," my husband replied. "Or a cult that subjugates and abuses females."

I was about to tell him that I had never subjugated or abused anyone, when something exploded outside Drefan's quarters. A waft of smoke came into the dining area, accompanied by Mercy, dressed in battle gear modified to fit her small frame.

"Sorry to interrupt your meal," she said, tucking a pistol under her belt, "but we have a situation."

"You mean, besides the door panel controls that you just blasted?" Drefan asked.

Mercy tossed a datapad across the table at him, which he caught with his real hand. "Cat picked up the signal; we've been monitoring the *Renko*. It's encrypted. Guess where it came from, and where is the Hsktskt?"

"I did not signal Davidov, and neither did Tya." Drefan skimmed the display. "Cat only traced it back to Omega Dome?"

"He would have pinpointed the location of the transceiver, but the signal lasted only fifteen seconds." Mercy tapped her fingers against the insides of her upper arms. "I repeat, where is the Hsktskt? I want to introduce her to Posbret and his boys."

"I can't let you do that, Mercy." Drefan put down the datapad. "Tya did not send this signal. She has neither the means nor the opportunity to do so."

"No problem, I know how to find her. I'll just follow the stink of death." She swiveled around and stalked out of the room.

Drefan rose and braced himself against the table. "Keel, get my chair and help me out of these prosthetics. Duncan, would you be so kind as to stop my friend from killing my Hsktskt?"

I got up from my seat. "I am going with you." Before my husband could reply, I added, "She likes me. She may listen to me."

Reever nodded. "Drefan, where exactly is Tya now?"

"She is using one of the hand-to-hand simulators," Keel said, and gave us directions and the code to bypass the drone keeping watch over the Hsktskt while she practiced. "I will signal Cat. He can help talk some sense into her. Go."

We hurried out into the corridor, and Reever took my arm. "I will try not to hurt her, but she is very angry. I will probably have to knock her out."

"I had to sedate her yesterday," I said, wishing I had brought my case with me.

We ran to the game simulator where Tya was practicing. On the way we had to avoid several inert drones that Mercy had apparently disabled. The bottom folds of the gown kept tangling around my legs, until I finally stopped and pulled out my knife.

"If females on Terra do wear such garments, our species should be extinct." I slashed at the cloth, quickly cutting most of it away from my legs before continuing on.

We caught up with Mercy outside the game simulator. She shot the drone guarding the entrance before turning her pistol toward us and firing over our heads.

"You're not pumping me full of drugs this time." She backed into the open panels and shut them before we could follow her in.

Reever checked the wall panel. "She's locked out the controls." He took a small device from inside his tunic and attached it to the panel.

"Do I want to know what that is?" I asked.

"No." He keyed in a code, waited for a moment, and then pulled off the plas panel covering the internal locking mechanism. Quickly he rerouted a circuit before replacing the plas and inputting another code.

The doors slid open.

Inside the simulator an arena program was running. A crowd of Hsktskt roared from the stands as Tya sparred with three Jorenian warriors. They were fighting with claws, not weapons, and green blood stained the ugly brown sands.

"End program," Mercy shouted, and the simulation vanished, leaving Tya standing alone in the center of the grid. Mercy held her pistol trained on Tya's head as she moved forward. "Hello, lizard. What did you use to send the signal to Davidov?"

I would have gone after her, but Reever held me back.

"Wait," he said in a low voice, never taking his eyes from Mercy.

"You're that noisy runt who came to kill me yesterday," Tya said, lowering her green-stained claws. "I don't fight children. Go back to your parent."

Mercy fired at the wall next to Tya's shoulder. "For your information, I'm all grown up, and your fucking species slaughtered both of my parents. How did you send the signal?"

Tya folded her arms and said nothing. My husband took a step forward.

"I am going to kill her," Mercy said. "Don't move,

Reever. I can pull the trigger before you can reach me."

My husband stopped in his tracks.

"Tya, did you send a signal to the *Renko*?" I asked.

Large yellow eyes shifted to gaze upon me. "The other nosy midget. Is this place overrun with your kind?"

"It's not going to be overrun with yours," Mercy assured her.

"So you think." Tya bared her teeth. "Did you learn nothing from the last time we came, little one?"

Mercy fired, but Tya moved at the last second, so quickly that her body blurred. The shot ricocheted off the grid beams and burned a hole through the floor.

Reever grabbed Mercy from behind, knocking the weapon out of her grasp and pinning her arms under his. She fought him wildly, kicking and shrieking.

A second energy beam cut across the room, striking Mercy on the shoulder. Her body and head sagged. I turned to see Cat standing behind me and holding a stun emitter. He pocketed it and went over to Reever, taking Mercy in his three arms and lifting her against his chest.

Drefan's glidechair rolled into the simulator, and the games master surveyed the scene. "Is anyone hurt?"

"Yes," Cat said, walking up to him with the unconscious Mercy. "I had to stun her. Something that I'm not looking forward to explaining when she wakes up."

The games master looked at Mercy's slack face with something like regret. "I am sorry, Cataced. She will not listen to reason."

"I don't know why you're hiding a Hsktskt here, James," Cat said. "But when the stun wears off, Mercy will see to it that everyone hears about her. I suggest you do something with it before the colonists start breaking through your air locks."

The Omorr hopped out.

As I had no more examinations to perform, and tensions between Gamers and Mercy House had escalated, I thought it best to go with Reever to check on the progress the engineers were making on *Moonfire*. I also wanted to have a look at the crater of black crystal near the crash site.

"I've added optic shielding to our helmets," I told Reever as we put on envirosuits the next morning for the trip. "That should protect us from the effects of reflected light."

Drefan allowed us to borrow one of his STVs to make the trip out to the scout, and Reever piloted it over the rough surface terrain with admirable skill.

"Why do you want to survey the crater?" my husband asked as we climbed out and enabled our suit weights.

"Black crystal has caused much sickness on other worlds. Cherijo wrote about it extensively in her journals." I glanced back at the cluster of silver-white domes. "If it has somehow infiltrated the water supply system or food synthesizers, it could be poisoning the colonists."

"It never seems to have the same effect on those exposed," Reever said. "It made the Taercal become religious zealots, and the Oenrallian stop aging. How will you tell if it is affecting the colonists here?"

"I did not find any trace of it in the people I've examined," I admitted. "But the crystal has many properties, I think, that we are not aware of yet."

Drefan's engineers greeted us and were happy to show Reever the repairs they had made to the hull, engines, and navigational controls. The little maintenance drone, it seemed, had been a great help to them, as it was able to access areas of the ship that the engineers could not reach themselves without disassembling more equipment.

While the men discussed the work in progress, I went to our quarters in the back of the ship, and found the image Reever had taken of Marel on Joren, just before we left. My heart twisted as I looked at her small, grinning face.

"Soon, baby," I murmured, touching the surface of the image with my gloved fingers. "Soon we will be together again."

I tucked the portrait in one of my utility pouches and surveyed the rest of the chamber. Neither Reever nor I had many possessions, and both Drefan and Mercy had given us enough garments to wear. I unearthed a container of Jorenian tea from a jumbled pile and checked the seal; it was still usable. I also found one of the Omorr blades Squilyp had given me.

It was not much, and not enough to solve the mystery of what was happening on Trellus, or prevent Davidov from keeping his vow to destroy the colony.

Tea and knives. Do you really think that's the answer?

Pain hammered into the sides of my head, making me clutch at my helmet. I knew the voice. It belonged to an entity that had promised to leave me alone.

Wrong. I said I'd stop imprinting you. You're making the connection this time, kiddo.

The interior of our quarters on *Moonfire* vanished, as did my envirosuit. I found myself sitting on black, pebbly soil, looking out at an endless stretch of rust-colored water. It rushed at me in huge, curling waves, collapsing and churning up fountains of orange foam.

A red-haired, nearly naked Terran woman appeared beside me. Two inadequate strips of cloth covered her breasts and loins; dark miniature optic shields concealed her eyes. Under her buttocks lay a colorful rectangle of cloth depicting flat red flowers.

"It's a beach towel," she said, glancing at me as she poured a thick white liquid from a container onto her palm. "Take off your clothes; you could use a little sun."

I looked up at the blue giant star blazing overhead. It made streaks of purple and green in the yellow sky. "I thank you, no. I thought you had merged with the rest of the Jxin, Maggie."

"I did, I am, and I will." Cherijo's surrogate mother seemed unconcerned as she rubbed the lotion into her freckled skin. "You're not doing what we talked about, but it's not like that's a surprise. How's your head?"

The question made the pain intensify. "It hurts."

"Get used to it." She reclined, flattening her body onto the beach towel. "You're stuck with it until you reconcile. Which I would do before you get off this fun-house ride of a planet. There's serious business in your immediate future."

As before, her instructions and predictions made little sense. "Are you aware of what has happened to Reever and me?"

"Aware?" She laughed. "The way you've been broadcasting, the entire merge wants to sever their connections. They can't wait for the day when your life gets boring."

"Then you know there is a crater lined with black crystal near the ship," I said, ignoring her sarcasm. "The same black crystal that you claimed was infecting the galaxy. Is it responsible for the problems here on Trellus?"

"Black crystal does nothing but cause problems," she told me, yawning and stretching her arms out before folding them over the slight curve of her belly. "But it doesn't get all the blame this time. There's only so much crystal can screw with." She turned her head toward me. "Which means yes, maybe, sort of, it's part of the problem, and no, I can't be more specific than that."

"You are supposed to help me."

"Monitor you," she corrected. "Occasionally pop into your brain and set you straight. Which I have done so often the merge is ready to kick me into permanent oblivion."

I could sympathize with the merge, whatever that was. At the moment I was tempted to drag her down to the rusty water and drown her in it. "Is the crystal in the water or the food?"

"This time, neither." She held up a finger with a glossy red nail. "That's all I'm saying. You have to find out the rest on your own."

"Why?" I demanded.

"Free will. It cannot be circumvented, influenced, or otherwise fucked with." She sighed and looked down at her front. "I miss having a body. I really loved shopping for clothes. Remember all the trips we made to the retail centers when you weren't this doormat you've become?"

"Cherijo went with you, not me." My head felt as if it were going to fly apart. "How do I end this connection?"

Maggie rolled onto her side. "You could ask me nicely. Say pretty, pretty please with sugar on top."

I repeated her words, but I was not returned to the *Moonfire*. She was maintaining the link between us now; I could feel it. "What more do you want me to do, Maggie?"

"You could stop fighting yourself." She brushed some black sand grains off her thigh. "It's counterproductive, and I need you whole before the crystal awakens and everything goes straight to hell."

I remembered the vicious argument I had had with her on Vtaga. I had pinned her to a wall by the throat. Then she had mentioned that the crystal was dormant, and that when it woke, it would devour worlds. "I said I will do as you wish."

Maggie's red curls bounced as she shook her head. "No can do, sweetie. I need you both."

"Reever will help." I could barely speak through the pain. "Please, Maggie. My head wants to explode."

"So does mine," she said without a shred of sympathy. "All right, Jarn, have it your way. We'll talk again. In the meantime, watch your step."

Maggie and the alien shoreline melted away, puddling around my feet. The colors darkened and then rose, forming themselves into *Moonfire*'s walls and deck. A white blur solidified into Reever in an envirosuit.

He caught me as I stumbled toward him. "I could feel her all the way on the other side of the ship. What did she want from you?"

"I don't know. When she speaks, I can hardly make out her meaning." I looked through my face shield and saw the hatred and fear in his eyes. "She claimed that I summoned her this time. That I made the connection myself. But Duncan, I didn't try. I wasn't even thinking of her."

"We're too close to the black crystal; that always seems to precipitate encounters with Maggie." He sounded grim. "We'll return to the dome."

"No." I almost shouted the word, and jumped at the vehemence in my own voice. I clamped down on the panic his suggestion made me feel. "Not yet. I need to go to the crater, to see it for myself. I can't tell you why, I don't know why, but it's important. I promised Maggie on Vtaga that I would fight the crystal, Duncan. This"—I gestured toward the view port, and the colony beyond—"is part of it."

"How can you fight something that destroyed her and her entire species?" he demanded. "What does the crystal have to do with Trellus?"

"I don't know, but it starts here." I put my glove on the arm of his suit. "Please. Trust me."

Reever went over to one of the cabinets and pulled out a coil of cord. "I'm going to tether us together before we go near that crater."

"Our weights will keep us grounded."

"There are mine shaft openings all around here. I don't want you falling down one of them." He clipped one end of the tether to his suit and the other to mine. "Come on. I want to be done with this."

We walked from the scout toward the old mining processors. I saw carbon marks from the weapons Posbret and his raiders had fired at Reever and the engineers during my husband's first trip out to the wreck. They reminded me of Cat's threat. I didn't think Mercy would turn the raiders against Drefan, but I had only known her a short time. Her hatred for the Hsktskt seemed unyielding and absolute; she might now regard Drefan as a traitor to the colony.

The crater commanded my attention as soon as we drew within three hundred yards of its edge. It stretched out, a bowl of glittering black, for nearly half a kilometer. From the shape and size I guessed it to be very old.

"I would attempt to take samples," Reever said, "but given the nature of the crystal, I think conducting a visual survey first would be more prudent."

I looked beyond the crater toward another dark depression, near the base of one of the ore processors. "There is another one over there." I took out the geological scanner I had borrowed from Drefan and adjusted the beam to the widest possible field. I passed it over the crater near us first, which showed as a blank oval spot on the display. As I continued to turn, the beam picked up more blank ovals: two, six, ten, fifteen . . .

I stopped scanning when the display showed more than thirty blank spots. "There are more craters like this out there. They surround the old mines and the domes."

He took the scanner from me and studied the display. "Drefan said the craters were caused by ancient meteor impacts." He adjusted the scanner's output. "There is a network of subsurface tunnels that connect all of the craters."

I looked at the web of passages on the display.

"Why would the colonists want to connect the craters from underneath?"

Reever gazed out at the ore processors. "No reason, unless they are mining it."

"Maggie said that the crystal was part of the problem with Trellus." The thought of someone collecting the destructive mineral disturbed me. "We may need to collect a small sample, Duncan."

My husband didn't like that, but nodded.

I held on to the clip of our tether as I slowly approached the crater's rim. Up to the very brink, large, seven-sided crystals sprang out, jutting like shining black teeth.

"The crystals appear to be atypical prisms," he said. "Each has seven geometrically equivalent faces, all parallel to the same axis. That may explain why they reflect light as oddly as they do."

I knelt down and peered at one specimen growing from the very edge. "These were not left behind like this by the meteor."

"No, they appear to have grown after the impact." Reever began scanning the crater. "Mineral crystals can flourish in many different environments, but most need a hydrothermal source. On Terra, quartz typically grows from a mixture of silica and hot ground water."

I shifted my weight, and for a moment I thought something moved inside the crystal. I realized it was light reflected from my face shield, illuminating a flaw. "This one appears to have a bubble of air inside it."

Reever came to stand beside me and directed the scanner at the specimen I was studying. "Not air," he told me. "It's an inclusion of fluid."

"It has water inside?"

"The faces of a single crystal can grow at different speeds and rates, which creates tiny pits or flaws in the interior. As the crystal continues to grow, its subsequent layers can seal the flaws and trap liquid inside." He broke off and adjusted something on the scanner.

"These crystals grew here, on Trellus, after the meteor impact," I said. "Is that not so?" He nodded absently. "Then from where did the liquid come?"

He gestured at the ground. "Likely a water source beneath the surface."

"We need to take a sample of the crystal." I carefully wrapped my glove around the flawed specimen and wiggled it, trying to break it free. It could not be moved even a millimeter.

"I need something to knock it loose." An unpleasant sensation spread through my hand, one I thought I was imagining until I saw a black stain spreading over my glove. "What the . . . ?"

Reever jerked me to my feet by the back of my suit and held my stained glove away from my body and him. "Hold still."

He took from his utility pocket a clump of something stiff and motionless and slapped it over my blackening glove. The frozen Lok-teel rippled once, twice, and then billowed outward, sinking down to cover my glove. After twitching several times, it shrank back to its original size and went motionless.

The black stain had vanished from my glove.

"They did the same thing on Catopsa when the black crystal attacked me there," I said, returning the helpful mold to Reever.

He turned my glove over to look at the back side. "You never told me about that."

I felt the ground tremble under our feet. "Duncan."

That was all I had time to say before the rocky surface heaved and pitched both of us headfirst into the crater.

Fifteen

The glittering maw swallowed us whole.

I could not see Reever. My body collided with falling crystals and rock as the sides of the crater fell away on top of me. I know I called to my husband, but the roar of the surface collapsing all around us drowned out my voice.

An image of Drefan's tortured body came back to me. His limbs had been crushed by falling ore. The same was about to happen to us, as soon as we hit the bottom of this abyss. Our envirosuits were not designed to withstand such battering.

My body never landed, but fell endlessly until something closed around me. At first I thought it was our sleeping platform, and I was about to awaken from a very bad dream. I prayed it would be so.

But our bed was not pink.

The tether jerked me into something much harder that smashed through the shield of my helmet, and that was all I knew before my air was gone and my lungs flattened. Cold bit into my flesh, sinking into it, turning my blood to slush and my bones to ice.

They will never find us, I thought as the cold receded and a soft, lovely warmth replaced it. Even if they could, the black crystal would prevent any sort of rescue. *We will spend eternity together, buried alive.*

Just the three of us, together for all time? an amused, mellow voice asked. *I find that a very intriguing proposition. An eternal ménage à trois. Keats was too much of a romantic, I think, and Byron far too intense and possessive. But Shelley, now I think he would have approved.*

I didn't know this voice or the names it mentioned, but Cherijo's surrogate mother liked to play tricks. *Maggie? Maggie, can you help us?*

No, I am not your friend Maggie. But please, allow me to assist you, my dear.

From there I went alone into the dark, still warm and held close to something, still clutching the tether in my glove. There I stayed, and my last coherent thought was of Reever and, if we died, how soon we would find each other in this next place.

Voices summoned me back from the abyss, although they were muted, as if speaking underwater.

"There are no signs of exposure."

That sounded like Tya, I thought, content to lie where I was and listen to it.

"The suits were breached, I tell you."

And that voice, that was Keel. A very worried Keel.

"After they were retrieved, perhaps," Tya said. "What were they doing out there?"

"Checking their ship."

I heard metal, cloth, and a scanner being activated. Beneath my shoulders I felt a flat, cold surface. Seals opened, and seams ripped. Someone was removing my suit.

Keel made a disgusted sound. "Why put all this gunk in their suits?"

As a sharp blade sliced through the tough outer fabric of my envirosuit, something oozed against my skin.

"It is not gunk," Tya told the feline. "It appears to be some sort of lubricant."

"Pink lubricant?" Keel asked.

"I did not choose the color."

I opened my eyes and squinted through the bright light. Something sticky covered my eyelids and lashes, and I had to spit out a mouthful of fluid to speak. "Keel?"

"Close your eyes, Cherijo. I must wipe your face." A damp cloth did just that. "There." The cloth was held loosely over the end of my nose. "Blow."

I blew, and as soon as I cleared the fluid from my nostrils, the odor hit me. It was as if every rotten, decaying thing I had ever smelled had been piled around me. "*Dævena Yepa.*"

"I know, it's awful," Keel said. "But hold still. I'm going to clean out your ear canals now."

A gentle suction removed the fluid in my ears, but I was too busy trying not to vomit to notice it immediately. The light was adjusted so that it did not shine into my eyes, and a strong, scaly limb eased me up into a sitting position. My right wrist throbbed, as did my back, arms, and legs, but only distantly.

"How bad?" I asked, gagging on the taste in my mouth.

"You have a concussion, some cuts and bruises, and a sprained wrist," Tya informed me as she lifted me off the table. "Your mate appears to be in much the same condition."

"What are you doing?" I asked as she carried me across the room.

"As you can tell, you smell worse than an overflowing waste unit," she told me. "I am putting you in the cleanser before we all puke."

Once inside the unit she had to help me stand, my legs shook so much. My head cleared as soon as the jets came on, and I saw what appeared to be several inches of solid pink gelatinous fluid covering my body.

"What is this stuff?" I stared down at myself.

"We don't know," Tya said, and handed me a scrubber. "But please, wash it off."

I applied a liberal amount of cleanser and scrubbed hard, although after a moment it became apparent that I didn't need to. The fluid didn't dilute or stick to the scrubber, but quickly slid in pink streams down my skin and into the drain.

When I was clean, I stepped out so Tya could cleanse. Keel handed me linen to dry off with, and a robe to cover myself.

"What happened to you out there?" the Chakacat asked.

"The last thing I remember, there was a surface tremor, and the crater near the crash site collapsed." And Reever and I had been thrown into it. "I don't know how I got here, or what covered us in that . . ." I wasn't sure what to call it.

"Tya thinks it is lubricant," Keel advised me. "I am currently reserving my opinion. We found you and your husband in one of the air locks. You were both unconscious, and your envirosuits were filled with this pink gunk. Which I've never seen before, I should mention."

We should be at the bottom of the crater, under tons of crystal and rock. "Who brought us to the air lock? The engineers from *Moonfire*? A drednoc?"

Keel shook its head. "The engineers evacuated the crash site as soon as the tremor hit. There were no dreds out on the surface. We thought you had come back on your own."

"We did not walk back here," I assured it. "Did Drefan have the air lock on monitor?" I had to know what had saved us.

"He did," Keel said, "but the screen went black for two minutes. When the feed came back up, you and Reever were lying there."

Tya emerged from the cleanser, stopped, and pointed to the floor around the exam table. "Look."

I turned and saw that the puddles of the pink fluid that had dripped from the table were spreading and becoming transparent. The unbearable odor disappeared just as unexpectedly.

I knelt down and touched a finger to the now-clear liquid, and brought a drop of it up to my nose.

"If you put that in your mouth," Tya said, "I vow, I will regurgitate my last meal."

"It has no more odor to it." I grabbed a scanner and passed it over the puddle. "Hydrogen and oxygen." I looked up at the Hsktskt. "It's turned into water."

I stood and went over to the table where Reever lay. They had not yet opened his suit, and when I released the seals the only fluid that ran out was more odorless, colorless water. He rolled onto his side and coughed out more of the same.

"He had the same pink substance in his suit?" I asked Keel, who nodded. "Let's get the suit off."

Water soaked my husband's garments, as well as a few spots of blood from some minor lacerations, but I found no trace of the pink fluid.

I checked his eyes, ears, and nose, which were damp but also clear. "What do you remember?" I asked him, hoping it was more than I had.

"Something enveloped us," Reever said. "It came through the tears in my suit and broke through my face shield." His dark gray eyes met mine. "Did the crystal produce it?"

I adjusted the scanner and passed it over him and then my own torso. Both displays showed no trace of black crystal in our bodies. I used it to check the outside of Reever's envirosuit and my own, both of which were also free of the contaminant.

"If it did, it does not exhibit the same properties as the crystal." I glanced down at the wet floor beneath my bare feet. "I would test it, but it's all gone now. All that's left of it is water."

"You are alive," Tya said, her voice harsh. "Be grateful that it saved you."

I turned to her. "Do you know what it was?"

She went to the view panel and looked out at the surface. "It wasn't water."

I performed a thorough exam of my husband, whose scrapes and bruises were already disappearing.

"What is wrong with your wrist?" he asked as I used my left hand.

"I sprained it." I moved my hand and winced. "I will fashion a splint for it."

"Wait." Reever took my hand and turned it up so he could examine the palm. "Your skin looks burned."

"There was nothing to burn me out there." I peered at the swollen redness and closed my fingers over it. "Likely I hit something with my palm during the fall."

"Then why is it shaped like the crystal you touched?" he asked.

I had no answer. "It could not have penetrated my glove so quickly. The Lok-teel cleansed it away almost immediately." I frowned. "What happened to it?"

"I thought it attached itself to my arm. When I was falling, I felt something trying to crawl into my collar seal." Reever pulled his wet tunic over his head and turned from side to side. "It's not attached to me."

I checked the remains of our suits and my discarded garments, but the helpful little mold was not hiding among them.

"It must still be in the bottom of the crater." I frowned. "Do you recall hitting the bottom, Duncan?"

"No." He looked at the door and jumped off the exam table, pushing me behind him.

A group of armed raiders came into the room.

"I never knew Terrans to be so hard to kill," Posbret said, stepping to the front and looking around the room. His smile widened as he fixed his gaze on Tya's back. The pleasure in his soft brown eyes made them shine. "Or Mercy to tell the truth. One learns new things all the time."

Reever moved, only to stop as one of the raiders flanked us and pressed a rifle against the back of my head.

"Interfere," the Gnilltak said pleasantly, "and I blow her brains out."

Posbret crossed the room and grabbed Tya by the back of her tunic, wrenching her around. "Have you enjoyed dining on us, lizard? What were you doing with the skins? Sleeping in them?" He drove his fist into her abdomen.

Tya doubled over, wrapping her limbs around her belly. Before she could straighten, the raider leader clouted her over the back of her neck, and sent her crashing to the floor.

"Stop it," I shouted.

"Not this time, Terran." Posbret stepped over Tya, turning and kicking her in the side. I heard bones snap and surged forward, only to be jerked back by my hair. The fist tangled in it belonged to the raider whose spleen I had repaired.

"You can't help her," my former patient warned. "He will kill you, too."

"I'm not going to kill her. Immediately." Posbret walked around Tya, taunting her with every kick. "No fight in you now, is there? I always knew your kind were cowards."

Tya did not rise, and made no move to defend herself. The only sounds she made were grunts that came from her throat every time Posbret's boot slammed into some part of her body.

Why wouldn't she defend herself?

"Come, try to take my pelt, lizard," the raider leader demanded. "I would see you try before I grind you into dust beneath my heels."

Raiders scattered as Drefan's massive battle drone pushed into the room, its halo shooting a focused purple pulse toward Posbret. The raider tried to raise a weapon, but the stun burst sent him to his knees beside Tya.

The drednoc lumbered over, picked up the raider leader by the collar, and addressed the rest of the men. "You are ordered to leave the premises. Comply at once or you will be shot."

There was no arguing or negotiating with a machine, and the raiders knew it. They began backing out of the room.

Posbret lifted his head and spat on Tya. "It is fitting, I suppose, that he owns you. A beast to serve a monster. Enjoy your last hours, Hsktskt, for I will be back for you. And when next we meet, I will bathe in your blood as I skin you alive."

I sent Reever to find Drefan and, with the help of Keel and some staff drones it summoned, moved Tya from the floor to an exam table.

"I thought Drefan had reinforced security," I said as I used a cloth to wipe the blood from Tya's muzzle. "How did they get in here again so easily?"

"There are different ways into the domes," the Chakacat said. "Some of them are below the surface. Mercy knows those tunnels better than anyone on the colony."

I pushed aside my anger with Mercy and focused on Tya. Posbret had battered the Hsktskt female, whose body had already been weakened by starvation and dehydration. Wherever his boot had landed, her flesh had split. A quick scan revealed several massive contusions, but none of the broken bones I had expected.

"The implant," Tya muttered through teeth stained with her own blood.

I remembered Posbret's brutal blow to the back of

her neck and made another pass with the scanner. "It appears to be intact, and I am not reading any traces of poison."

Keel heard the last of what I said as it came to stand beside me. "Why did you scan her for poison?"

"It is nothing," Tya said before I could answer.

From the way she was behaving, I had to assume that Keel and Drefan didn't know about the implant. "It is a routine procedure," I lied.

Keel looked troubled. "She will recover soon?"

"Why?" I infused the Hsktskt with a local anesthetic and began suturing up a deep gash. "Will Drefan punish her if she is not able to fight Reever?"

"Drefan doesn't abuse his people."

"But she's not a person, is she? She's a slave." I saw the distress in Keel's eyes and realized I was taking out my temper on the wrong person. "If she has time to rest and eat, she should heal in a few days. If we can keep the raiders, Mercy, and the rest of the colony from assaulting her, that is," I tacked on.

Keel helped apply cold packs to the worst of the impact injuries while I dealt with the muscle tears.

"Drefan is nowhere to be found," Reever told me as he walked in. "How is she?"

One of Tya's swollen eyes opened to a slit. "Well enough to fight you, Terran."

"You are not fighting anyone," I told her as I bandaged the sutured cut and moved on to the next.

Tya's eye blinked. "You do not own me."

"I do until you heal." I applied another infusion of painkiller to deaden the next wound and adjusted the beam on the suture laser. I leaned down and whispered, "Do not tempt me to put another implant inside you."

The Hsktskt female muttered something and closed her eyes.

"Posbret must have heard about the Hsktskt female from Mercy," my husband said to Keel. "I had assumed that she and Drefan were friends."

"It's more complicated than that." The Chakacat braced its paws against the table and looked down. "Mercy bought Drefan after he lost his legs and arm in the mines."

I almost dropped my suture laser. "She wished him to serve in her brothel?"

"They knew each other long before his enslavement," Keel said, and began to say more, then fell silent.

"I pulled some interesting facts from the database last night," my husband said. "It seems that Drefan owned StarCore."

The Chakacat hissed in a breath. "Those files are locked."

"They were," my husband said, "until last night."

"Drefan owned the arutanium mines," I said, to be sure. "Here, on Trellus."

"Here and on several other worlds," my husband replied. "According to the files, he inherited them from his parents. Evidently his family has been operating mines on Terra and other worlds for several generations."

"They only owned them and collected the profits," Keel said in a defensive tone. "The Drefan family never left the homeworld or saw any of the mines."

"If that is the case," I said, "then who ran them?"

"Alien overseers," my husband told me. "When Drefan took over the mining company, he decided to offer to pay his overseers profit shares instead of the flat fees his parents and their parents had always paid them."

Keel shook its head. "You don't understand. He thought it would motivate them to be more productive. He wanted them to care about the business. The shares were only meant to be an incentive."

Reever appeared unmoved. "It worked."

I looked from the Chakacat to my husband. "I cannot follow your meaning when you speak in circles and innuendo like this."

"Tell her," my husband said.

"To increase and secure their profit shares, the overseers began using slave labor in the mines." Keel gave me a pleading look. "It was not Drefan's fault. They never informed him of their actions."

"Drefan should have known," Reever said harshly. "It was his business. His responsibility. The atrocities the overseers committed were to protect his profit."

"Drefan never knew," Keel insisted. "He is not capable of such cruelty."

I noticed how intently Tya was listening. "How was Mercy involved in this?"

"Mercy discovered what the overseers were doing to the slaves in the StarCore mines here," Keel told me. "She had the mines shut down by reporting the use of slave labor to the quadrant authorities. They extradited Drefan from Terra and detained him while all of his mining ventures were subjected to inspection."

"Obviously they found the slaves," I guessed, "and set them free."

"Unfortunately, that was not the case. In an attempt to cover their crimes, the overseers killed most of the slaves before the quadrant investigators arrived," Keel said. "A few escaped into the far reaches of the tunnels and survived. As for the rest, the overseers pitched the bodies into the slag furnaces in order to destroy them, but they forgot about the records of sales from various slavers to StarCore."

"Quadrant seized the records," Reever said, "and used them to identify those who had been murdered."

"What did they do to Drefan?" I asked.

"At the time Drefan could afford the best legal representation, and he did cooperate with quadrant," Keel said. "He was stripped of all assets, exiled from Terra for life, and sentenced to ten years on a League penal colony."

"That doesn't explain how he ended up working in the mines," I said.

"Drefan was abducted from League custody just after the trial," Reever said. "It seems quadrant authorities did not have him under adequate safeguard. Everyone assumed he had arranged his own escape."

"He was sold to slavers and put to work in an arutanium mine on a non-League world," Keel said. "He was kept below the surface for five years."

Keel told us how Drefan had been crippled, saving some other miners from falling ore, only to lose his own limbs. Rendered useless to his owner, Drefan was sold for a pittance at a public auction.

"That was when Mercy bought him."

Keel nodded. "She freed him, nursed him back to health, and had him fitted with prosthetics. She also lent him the credits he needed to set up Gamers. But Mercy has never forgiven him for what happened to the StarCore slaves. Neither has Posbret. He was one of the few survivors who escaped execution at the hands of Drefan's overseers."

Tya got up from the exam table and pushed past me, trudging out of the room. Keel followed, but Reever caught my arm as I went to go after them.

"Let the Chakacat look after her. You are exhausted."

I was, and the terrible story Keel had told us made me feel out of sorts. Until now I had admired James Drefan for surviving a terrible accident and flourishing despite his disabilities. Now a part of me thought he might deserve them.

"Do you think Drefan was ignorant of what was

happening to the slaves in his mines?" I asked my husband.

"If he did not know," Reever said, "he found out firsthand."

Despite the disturbing ordeals and revelations of the day, I was exhausted, and sleep came easily to me that night. As soon as Reever pressed my head to his shoulder, I closed my eyes and let myself dissolve into blissful unconsciousness.

When the dream came, I resisted it. My weary soul desperately needed peace, and for a time I struggled to remain in the nameless, shapeless darkness.

Until she came, and held out her bloody hands, and looked upon me with her face of smooth gray skin. The lady of sorrows, some of the oldest Iisleg called her. Regret made flesh.

Come, Jarn. Her voice caressed my ears. *Come and walk with me.*

I could not deny her.

We crossed the ice, walking as the skela did, testing each snow bridge with our notched staffs to be sure they would hold our weight. The sky wallowed in its winds, consumed and consuming them, painting itself with the colors of the light split by prisms of frost. On the horizon, ptar glided, restlessly searching for a careless hunter.

Under my outfurs, my dimsilk robes felt stiff. The weight of my field pack dragged at my shoulders, tugging at muscles knotted with fatigue. I had been born on this world, and I had left it, gladly, to find a better place for myself and my child among the ensleg. But where the vral walked, there I would go. I had worn her face. I knew her heart.

Do you? She turned, swords in both hands, her dimsilk flowing against the bitter wind with soft, almost liquid grace. *What of your heart, skela?*

On her blank face I saw shadows form a likeness of a young Iisleg child. Enafa, the novice skela who had been killed simply for touching me. The shadows changed and became my daughter, her sweet lips forming her name for me.

Mama. Mama.

I have tried to be worthy of their sacrifice, I told the vral. *I have done the work. I have served the Iisleg and the ensleg. I have never asked for forgiveness.*

So it is with me, the vral said, raising her weapons.

I thought she meant to attack me, until a glowing purple shadow stretched over my head and fell between us. I tried to turn, to look upon the machine thing that had come to kill, but the vral's robes wrapped around me and flung me into the sky. There I floated above them, a prisoner of the wind and the dream, helpless, made to watch, made to do nothing as their blades clashed and their bodies strained.

The vral's blades spun like wheels, deflecting the energy beams from the battle drone's halo. She thrust at him, the tip of her sword finding seams in his armor, and he bellowed like a man, his own blade slicing at her robes, cutting them and the flesh beneath them to shreds.

Black blood poured from their wounds and puddled on the ice, but it did not freeze. It spread out around them, growing and deepening until it became a lake of darkness.

I fought the invisible hands holding me back, and at last they released me. I fell into the black water, thrashing as it closed over my head.

A thousand voices began speaking to me, all Maggie's voice, echoing in my head as I writhed and fought to make my way to the surface.

It's traveling now.

Infiltrating planet after planet.

It's indestructible.

Only dormant.

It will wake.

Hunger beyond hunger.

Worlds destroyed.

Stars devoured.

The end of this dream called time.

We need you to stay alive.

CHERIJO

Something reached in and yanked me out, tossing me away to fall into a deep snowdrift. I spit out ice and pushed myself backward until I could again stand on my feet.

Beyond me, the two dream warriors stood with their swords poised at each other's throats.

My blood stains your hands, the vral told the drednoc.

As mine does yours, the drone replied.

I held my breath, expecting them to finish each other in the next moment. Instead they stood as statues, each staring down the steel, motionless and silent.

The lake of black water froze over and began to form crystals that grew into a forest of death all around the vral and the drednoc. It embraced them and crawled up their bodies, encasing them inch by inch, and still neither one moved or tried to resist.

Fight it, I screamed. *You must fight it.*

Just before the crystal covered her head, the vral turned to look at me, and orange eyes burned through the blank flesh of her face. *Help us, child of my heart. Save us.*

I woke up screaming.

Sixteen

"There are no gray-skinned, orange-eyed visitors listed in the colony's database," Reever said after several minutes at the console.

I sat, hunched and shivering, under a blanket, a server of lukewarm tea between my palms. I wanted to drink it, but my hands shook too badly for me to raise it to my lips. "What of the colonists?"

"I am checking now."

Few men woken out of a sound sleep by a screaming wife would have abandoned their rest to make hot drinks and check records for life-forms that existed only in dreams. But Reever was no ordinary man, and I sensed that he felt as afraid for me as I did for the vral and drednoc in my nightmares.

Reever came over to sit with me, and helped me raise the server to my lips. "What is it about these dreams that frightens you?"

The tea tasted too sweet, but I drank some to ease

my dry throat. "I don't know. The vral . . ." My teeth began to chatter, and I shook my head.

His arm came around my shoulders. "You are in no state to deal with this now. Come back to bed."

"It's only reaction." I drank down the last of the tea and forced myself to straighten. "What about the colonists?"

"I can find none whose appearance matches your description of the vral," he admitted, adjusting the blanket around me. "I have discovered something else, however, that may explain why the surface is unstable and the crater collapsed."

Black crystal, devouring the drednoc and the vral. "Show me."

I went over to the console with him, and sat down while he stood behind me. The screen displayed a list of names, all of whom lived in one of the smaller domes, and their current residential status. Each lived alone, and had no notations of spouses, progeny, or other kin. None had species names listed, either—only numbers.

"Who are these people?" I asked him. "What are these numbers?"

"They are not completely people." He pulled up one of the colonist's identification images, which showed an artificial face on top of a machine body. "Each number was assigned to a cybernetic being. It had an organic brain and spinal tissue, recovered from a dead or dying Terran, encased in a drone body."

"Reconstructs," I said. "Like SrrokVar."

Reever's hand stroked my shoulder. "Originally the tissue was harvested from newly dead Terrans and placed in drone frames to create laborers for places like StarCore's mines. No one realized that the harvested brains would retain memories, personality, and intelligence, but they began to resurface. The reconstructs organized, applied for, and were granted sentient status a few years ago."

I studied the image of one such colonist. "They don't resemble the drednoc in my dream."

"I think they may be the ones tunneling under the craters," Reever said. "They can go without food, water, oxygen, and warmth for long periods of time. They were designed to be as strong as drones, and are the only living beings on Trellus who could work without wearing special suits outside the domes and survive the freezing vacuum."

I considered the possibility. "With those machine bodies, they might also be immune to the effects of the black crystal. It only affects living beings."

"The reconstructs already know how to mine." Reever brought up a topographical map of the surface. "We lost your scanner in the crater, but I recall seeing tunnels here, here, and here." He traced lines around the crash site back to the colony. "They lead to these three domes. All are located near one of the ore processors."

I saw that the reconstruct colonists occupied one of the three domes in question. "Why would they be mining the black crystal? It is a toxin, but it takes years to infect the inhabitants of a planet. Even then, reactions vary from species to species."

"It kept the Oenrallians from dying," Reever reminded me. "There are always the sort of fools who would believe it would do the same for them. If it were added to an enemy's water or food source, the effects could manifest more rapidly."

"We have to first prove that the crystal is being mined," I said. "Can we gain access to the tunnels under the impact craters?"

"I will find out in the morning." Reever switched off the console.

I checked the time display. "It is almost dawn now. I should go and check on Tya."

"When you were working on her last night, you said something about an implant," my husband said. "Was she fitted with a contraceptive?"

"No." I related what Tya had told me about the implant in her neck. "She said that any attempt to remove it would trigger the release of the poison. It reminded me of that Jorenian patient with the grenade in her belly, but the Tos never used poison."

"No." Reever had been very still while I had told him about the implant, but now he reached up and touched the front of his tunic in a strange fashion. "Blade dancers are fitted with cardiac implants filled with poison before they are sold."

"This one she has was placed in her neck, not her heart." I went to make a new pot of tea and prepare a meal for us. "Why would Davidov do such a thing to her if he intended to sell her?"

"Control." Reever rubbed a hand over his face. "As long as the implant stays in Tya's neck, Alek can locate her, or kill her, whenever he likes. Unless he gave Drefan the tracking trigger."

"I don't think so," I said. "Tya didn't want Keel to know about the implant."

"Davidov could be using it to force her to spy for him," he suggested. "That would give her reason to conceal it from Drefan. Alek may have gone through the pretense of selling her simply to get her on the colony."

I dialed up two bowls of unsweetened, unflavored oatmeal. The Terran grain, one of the few Terran foods Reever and I cared to eat, would warm my stomach and settle my nerves.

"If that is so, then Mercy was right, and Tya did signal the *Renko*," I said. "But what reason would Davidov have for sending an enslaved Hsktskt spy to Trellus? What could she be reporting to him?"

"I cannot say. Alek is greatly changed from the man I once knew." Reever helped me bring the servers to the table. "Have you been able to collect physical samples of DNA from Drefan, Mercy, and Tya yet?"

"No, but there is plenty of Tya's blood all over the lab," I told him. "I scanned her DNA thoroughly, Duncan. She's Hsktskt on the cellular level."

"But she does not behave like one," he said. "She aided Keel in giving us medical treatment, but then she did not defend herself against Posbret. Hsktskt would consider caring for a warm-blood beneath them. They would never voluntarily take a beating like that from one."

"Tya might have been too afraid to fight the raider." I saw the look he gave me. "It's not the same as facing a simulation that you can turn off at any time. It could also have been a suicide attempt. She's very depressed."

Reever shook his head. "That is another indication something is not right with her. Hsktskt do not become depressed."

I thought otherwise, but my husband had very set ideas about the Hsktskt. "Do you want me to take a sample and begin working up a genetic profile on her?"

"We don't need a profile," he said, picking up his spoon and tasting the oatmeal. "We need to find out who she is. Can you freeze Tya's blood, then thaw it and analyze the DNA?"

"Of course." His instructions puzzled me. "But unless I cryo-prep the cells first, freezing the sample will only kill them."

"When a shape-shifter dies, it's said that its body reverts to its original form," Reever told me. "If Tya is not Hsktskt, the DNA from her sample should do the same thing."

"I'd better collect the sample from her instead of the floor of the lab." I went to the console and signaled central control. "Keel, would you bring Tya to the exam room?"

Drefan's face appeared on the screen. "Why do you want to see Tya?"

"Posbret attacked her last night," I told him. "I need to check the status of her injuries. Where have you been?"

"I was unavoidably detained," Drefan said. He sounded tired. "For now, your examination will have to wait."

"Drefan—"

"Tya is missing, and I have other problems I must—"

The signal terminated as the console shut down without warning, and the light emitters all around the room went dark. As I stood and turned, Mercy entered with Cat. Both of them carried pulse rifles, which they pointed at me and Reever. Behind them in the corridor stood several drednocs.

"You two," she said, "are coming with me."

No one attempted to stop Mercy and Cat, who marched us through the empty corridors of Gamers and into the access way back to their dome. The rifles at our back kept me from resisting, although my husband had a few things to say to Mercy.

"My wife has done nothing but help you." He glanced over his shoulder at her set features. "Why are you treating her like this?"

"Shut up," Mercy replied, "or I'll shoot you."

I knew from his expression that Cat was not entirely happy with abducting me and Reever. One side of his face looked badly bruised, and several of the gildrells below the contusion hung limp and unmoving. I resolved to enlist his aid as soon as we were at Mercy House.

Once we reached the primary air lock, Mercy stepped in front of us. "That's far enough." She lowered her rifle and ordered her battle drones to stand down. "We need your help."

I stared at her. "You couldn't simply send a signal and ask?"

"No." She shouldered her weapon and produced a handheld monitor. "This is why."

An image appeared on the screen of several males lying in a bloodied heap on the floor of an access way leading to another dome. The men appeared unconscious, perhaps dead. A large humanoid female dressed in a skimpy garment was bent over one, whom she picked up effortlessly and held dangling above the floor. After she looked over his slack features, she tossed his body aside and reached for another.

"Who is she?" Reever asked.

"Lily, one of my girls," Mercy said. "For whatever reason, she went crazy this morning and strangled her trick. Then she went on a rampage and killed every customer in the house. She broke out of the security grid and moved on to the next dome, and killed all the males she found there. She's between Delta and Gamma Domes now."

Reever studied the image. "You could not find a way to stop or restrain her?"

"We tried, but she's too strong. She knocked me out with one punch." Cat touched the large, dark red bruise mottling the side of his face. "We sent the dreds in after her, but she tore them apart with her bare hands. The other domes have not been able to stop her, either."

"What about your pulse weapons?"

The Omorr uttered a humorless sound. "We shot her a dozen times, on full burn. The wounds they made had no effect on her. She didn't even flinch."

"Why is she killing them and *then* looking at them?" I asked as I watched Lily discard another body.

"Maybe she's admiring her work," Mercy said. "Who cares?" She tossed my medical case at me. "Have you got something in that bag that we can use to knock her out?"

"If she hasn't already taken a counteragent, neuroparalyzer should render her unconscious." I took out a syrinpress and dialed up the strongest dose I dared administer. "I will have to get close enough to infuse her in an artery."

The access way darkened and then lightened as a ship flew over it. I looked up at the belly of the *Renko*, so close I felt as if I could reach up and touch it.

"Davidov, dropping his monthly care package," Mercy said.

"Too early for that," Cat argued. "He's not due for another two weeks."

"I'll make a note to complain later." Mercy frowned at the device in her hand.

I looked, and saw Lily drop the body she was

inspecting and lift her blood-spattered face. She laughed silently and then hurried toward an access hatch.

"Where does that hatch lead?" Reever asked.

Cat swore. "To the drop point."

The four of us donned envirosuits and, along with several battle drones, took an STV out onto the surface.

"So, what do we do first?" Cat asked, his tone heavy with irony. "Sedate Lily to keep her from attacking Davidov's ship, or help her get on board?"

"She can't get at anything but the supplies he drops," Mercy said as she changed the power cell in her rifle. "You know Davidov won't land."

"I could fire a few rounds into his propulsion array," the Omorr said.

"That will not disable Alek's ship," Reever informed him.

Cat gave him a haughty look. "No, but I'll still enjoy doing it."

"Which side of the platform does that hatch open to?" Mercy demanded as she drove up the side of a small incline and stopped, shutting down the engine to survey the landscape.

While she and Cat were debating how best to approach the drop point, I turned to my husband. "If you can distract Lily, I will administer the neuroparalyzer as a mist, through her air supply hose. It should take effect a few seconds after she inhales it."

"You are staying in the STV," he advised me. "I will give her the drug."

"I don't see any sign of her," Mercy said, scanning the area under the ship with a long-range viewer. "Where is she?"

The *Renko* descended until it hovered a short distance from the transport pad, and opened its cargo panel.

"Oh, shit," Mercy whispered, spotting something. She dropped the viewer and shouted, "*Hold on.*"

The transport pad exploded upward, enveloping Davidov's ship in a bloom of dust, energy, and rock fragments. I saw the shock wave heading toward us a second before Reever grabbed me and covered my helmet with his arms.

The STV flew into the air, higher and higher, until I thought we would be catapulted into space. Mercy swore viciously and pounded on the panel until the engine restarted. Something flared, and the surface vehicle turned and fell with languid speed until we crashed into something that crumpled the roof frame and blew out every view panel.

When the dust settled, I used my glove to clear off my helmet shield, and saw that the STV had landed upside down between two rock formations. I saw that the *Renko* had also gone down, a few hundred yards away, its hull partially covered by rubble.

"That was a shaft charge," I heard Mercy say over the suit com. "How the *hell* did she get hold of the explosives? Cat? *Cat.* You'd better not be dead, you stubborn, one-legged son of a toothless Omorr slut, or I'll kill you myself. Wake up. Wake *up.*"

"Mercy," the Omorr said, pressing his gloves to the sides of his helmet. "I survived. I'm conscious. And I'm not deaf. So will you for the love of Jovah *please* stop *shrieking* in my ear?"

"God, I love you," Mercy said, hugging him.

Reever stirred and then came to with a sudden jerk, turning in his harness to reach for me.

"I'm not injured," I told him. "Are your seals intact? Mercy, are you and Cat all right?"

"We're fine," she said.

"*You're* fine," the Omorr snapped. "*I* am in pain. A great deal of pain. I think my head has finally cracked in half."

"So your head hurts. Christ, what did you expect? We just got blown up. You could have . . . " Mercy reached over and slung her arm around his collar to hug him again.

Cat held her and closed his eyes. "What was that about my mother?"

"She was a paragon of virtue. Like you." Mercy straightened and turned her helmet back to regard me and Reever. "Omorr are such crybabies."

Seeing the tears of relief running down her cheeks made me smother a laugh.

Cat sniffed. "You'll speak differently when you have to deliver my eulogy, Adorlee."

"Stuff it, Adoren. Damn it. My harness clip is jammed." Mercy took out a blade and began to saw at the straps holding her to the seat. "Reever, can you and Cherijo get out through the side view panels?"

My husband glanced past me. "Yes. Is the STV transceiver still functioning?"

Mercy stopped cutting and reached out to the panel. "Receiver's trashed, but I think it'll still transmit."

"Contact Drefan and tell him to send help." Reever unfastened my harness, easing me down to the crumpled interior of the roof, and clipped a tether to my belt before releasing his harness clip. "We will need transport for the wounded."

"We're well enough to walk to Beta Dome from here," Mercy argued.

"That charge caused damage to the *Renko*'s weapons array and engines," he informed her. "But the hull is intact."

"There will probably be some casualties," I added, "and the survivors will need to be evacuated."

"I should let them freeze their asses off," Mercy grumbled as she sent the signal.

After we worked our way out of the wreck of the STV, I enabled my suit weights and rechecked my seals before doing the same for Reever. "How many crew members does Davidov have on board?"

"His usual complement is seventy. He may have hired more to help maintain the blockade." Reever had one of Mercy's pulse rifles under his arm. "Stay behind me."

The four of us approached the dust cloud slowly

settling around the *Renko*. Through the haze I saw that the exterior systems and emitters weren't functioning, but the view panels displayed both light and movement inside the ship.

"There is an emergency access air lock below the navigational array on the starboard fuselage," Reever said. "We'll board the ship there."

"What if they decide to shoot us as soon as we're inside?" Mercy wanted to know.

Reever shrugged. "Then they will blow out the air lock and the ship's atmosphere, and we will not have to evacuate anyone."

It took a few minutes for my husband to access the air lock from the exterior control panel, which had been damaged in the crash. He also insisted on going in first, by himself.

"They will probably be armed," I warned him. "Don't get yourself shot."

Mercy fussed over Cat's now-bleeding facial contusion while I watched Gamers. Several STVs emerged from the dome and began moving toward us. A small army of drednocs followed them.

"Once Reever gives us approval to board, I will triage any wounded and prep them for transport," I told Mercy and Cat. "If the survivors are not already wearing envirosuits, keep them busy putting on their gear. Don't provoke any confrontations."

Mercy gave me an innocent look. "You mean, don't kick Davidov's ass into the nearest mine shaft?"

"Especially don't do that."

Reever opened the outer panel and waved us inside. Once the air lock had equalized its atmosphere with the *Renko*'s interior, we removed our helmets and stepped through into a loading dock.

Wounded crew members littered the deck and lined the hull walls. Most appeared ambulatory, but I spotted three unconscious men covered with bloodstained thermal blankets.

A large hand with nine digits landed on my arm, and I looked up into a dark green face with blue eye clusters.

"Can you help my son?" The being pointed to a smaller version of himself under one of the thermal blankets. "He was caught under a cargo pallet."

A female limped over to us. "Are you a healer? I think my knee is broken."

Reever carried another man out of the next cabin and placed him beside the other seriously wounded crew. It was Davidov, who opened his eyes and said something to my husband, and then went limp.

I stripped off my gloves, pulled a scanner from my case, and went to work.

Seventeen

We were able to evacuate the entire crew of the *Renko* by the early-evening hours. Drefan initialized the simward program at Gamers for the wounded, and sent Keel and several other staffers to serve as my nurses.

Mercy took some of the unharmed survivors back to her dome, but the rest stayed at Omega Dome. To keep the colonists busy and away from the crew of the *Renko*, Reever took charge of the ship's cargo and worked with the colonial security to transport and divide among the domes the supplies recovered from the crash.

Drefan supervised the search for Lily, who had disappeared during the crash.

None of the *Renko*'s crew assumed that they were guests of the Trellusans. They were treated with courtesy, but they were also immediately disarmed and put under drone guard. Fortunately none of them chose to challenge the colonists.

Broken bones, internal hemorrhaging, and head wounds comprised most of the serious injuries among the survivors. I arranged with Drefan to use one of his largest air locks as a surgical suite, and with Cat again assisting, I performed surgery on two of the crew to repair their damaged organs.

"Is there anything you can't fix?" the Omorr asked as he watched me close the chest incision I had made on the second patient.

I glanced over the edge of my mask at him. "You are assuming that these patients will survive. Medicine, like doctors, is not perfect. After surgery, there is always the possibility of infection or another complication."

"You mean, go through all this, and then still lose them?" He shook his head. "I couldn't do that."

"Life is precious," I said. "That I perform surgery to preserve it is no different than Drefan sending recovery teams out to the *Renko*, Mercy giving shelter to the survivors, or you ignoring your own injuries to serve as my surgical assistant. We all do our part, Cat."

We transported our patient to the simward, where Keel helped us put him on monitor. Most of the ambulatory patients had been treated, and I saw to Cat before making rounds of the rest. I had nearly finished when Mercy signaled me on my wristcom.

"Cherijo, I need to talk to you. Alone."

I stepped out into the corridor, which was deserted. "I am alone now. What is it?"

"I have a situation over here."

I smothered a yawn. "If you have more wounded, send them to Gamers. It's best we keep them all in one area. If it's another encrypted signal, I can guarantee that there is no one left on the *Renko* to receive it."

"You don't understand," she said, and her voice dropped to a whisper. "I found Lily."

"Don't approach her," I said quickly. "Contact colonial security and tell them where she is."

"I can't."

Her loyalties were going to get her killed. "Mercy, I know you care for her because she worked for you, but she's too dangerous—"

"Cherijo, I found only her skin."

I muted the signal and looked around before responding. "Where?"

"Not far from the drop point," Mercy said. "Near the entrance to the old mine. And that's not all. One of the guys I brought over here from the *Renko* told me that a crew member is missing."

"Who?"

"He doesn't know. They had time to do only a quick head count when they were abandoning ship."

If the colonists found out that the skin killer had become active again, they might panic. With the survivors from the *Renko* on colony, and the possibility that the killer had taken one of them already, things could get very ugly, very fast. "Have you told anyone else about this?"

"No, and I won't," she said. "I'm going to move

Lily's remains over to Alpha Dome for now. An old friend of mine lives there, and he'll watch over them for us. He did ask for one thing in return."

"What?"

"He wants to meet you and Reever."

"Most of the colonists avoid Alpha Dome," Mercy said as she led us through a narrow access way. "Swap can't get around too easily, so he's pretty lonely. I think that's why he wants to meet you."

I looked ahead at the small dome, which had few lights and seemed neglected. "Is Swap elderly or disabled?"

"Not exactly." Mercy stopped at the entrance to Alpha Dome and put down the bag she was carrying to hand us two small nose filters. "This doesn't entirely cancel it out, but it makes it bearable. The only way to completely avoid it is to wear a breather, but I think that's rude." She turned and keyed in an access code.

"Avoid what?" I said, and then choked as a thick, revolting stench rolled out of the opening panels. "Oh, no."

Mercy shoved the filter prongs up my nostrils before fitting her own to her face. The filter did screen out most of the stink. She looked at Reever, who had yet to put on his. "It doesn't get better inside," she said, the filter giving her voice a peculiar resonance as she shouldered her bag again.

My husband reluctantly placed the filter on his nose and followed us inside.

Given the other colonists' obsession with biodecon procedures, I found it odd that we did not have to pass through any air locks or scans. The entry opened up to a curved passage that appeared to be made of polished brown and gray rock from the surface that had been carved in symmetrical ridges.

A closer glance revealed the rippled walls to be constructed entirely from pebbles about the size of my smallest fingernail. All had been cut in different shapes and fitted together so precisely that there were no visible gaps.

"Swap built all this when he was in his rockhound stage," Mercy said as we followed the gentle turns of the passage. "He was crazy for stone for like three years. This is where the offworld stuff starts."

The walls began to change color and texture, becoming conglomerations of blue, green, and black stones. Here and there I spotted subtle patterns that formed geometric shapes. The farther we walked, the more complex the patterns became, until it made my head spin simply to look at them.

My footgear slid on something wet and sticky, and I looked down to see a transparent gelatinous substance coating the floor of the dome.

I pulled Mercy to a stop. "What sort of creature is this Swap?"

She shrugged. "He's never told me, and I've never seen anything like him. But he hasn't shown himself to anyone but me and a couple of the original colony survivors. He's a little shy that way. As far as I know, he's the only colonist who is native to Trellus."

Reever bent and touched the gelatinous ooze. "This has the same texture as the substance that was in our envirosuits, after the crater collapse."

"Swap sheds a lot of it," Mercy said. "He's the one who pulled you two out of that crater and brought you back to Omega Dome."

Now I definitely wanted to meet him. "How much farther?"

She gestured ahead. "We have to go through another part of the collection."

"What does Swap collect?" Reever wanted to know.

"Junk." Mercy smirked. "He calls it art."

The passage widened and divided into five other passages, each transitioning from the rippled walls of stone into structures made of other materials: alloy, plas, wood, and two others I couldn't readily identify. Mercy diverted us through the passage made of alloy, the walls of which were formed at first from hundreds of thousands of hull rivets welded seamlessly together. They expanded into sections of coiled wire, joints, and frames. One segment appeared to be formed out of ten thousand conjoined blades of various lengths, widths, and castings.

"How long did it take your friend to collect all of these objects?" Reever asked Mercy as we passed an enormous starburst made from alloy strips cut from a myriad of view ports, door thresholds, deck seams, and console panels.

"No one knows. Swap originally started his collection underground, in the tunnels where he lived, but moved it up into Alpha Dome after the original colonists built it for him." Mercy ducked to avoid a hanging cluster of gleaming emitter reflectors.

"All of these objects did not come from the colony," I guessed.

"Before the blockade, traders brought them in by the cargo-hold load. Swap always has something someone wants." She smiled back at a wall of alien faces sculpted out of innumerable wheels and gears. "He's become the wealthiest trader in this system."

My husband inspected the faces. "Why does he cement everything together? He cannot use them like this."

"He can't use them anyway, but you'll understand that when you see him. He started making them into walls after the Hsktskt raided." Mercy's grin faded. "It gave us kids something to do, too." She caught my curious look. "Swap took in me and the other kids who survived the raid. He fed us and kept us warm until the free traders showed up."

No wonder she counted him among her friends. "That was very kind of him."

"Personally I think he just wanted the extra hands to help him build this maze," Mercy said. "Once he owns something, he doesn't like giving it up. And he really didn't like it when the Hsktskt helped themselves to his junk."

"They stole my art," a deep, rich voice corrected her. Something boomed as a heavy weight fell, and the floor of the dome bounced. "I couldn't allow that to happen again."

A massive wall of quivering pink slid over the end of the passage, cutting us off. At the same time, it began to ooze into the passage, coming toward us in three solid pink streams of goo.

Reever tugged me behind him.

"Swap," Mercy said, "I know you're impatient to taste them, but at least let me bring them out into the main room."

"Excuse me?" I stared at her. "He wants to *taste* us?"

"Oh, he's not going to eat you." She grimaced as the pink glop rose in a column from the floor and slid against her cheek. "It's sort of like licking, see? It doesn't hurt, and it's the only way he can sense things."

The other streams retreated, as did the third after giving Mercy's chin a lick, and the wall at the end of the passage moved away.

I looked at the sticky residue Swap had left behind on Mercy's face. The smell was so intense it punched through my nose filter. "I begin to understand."

Reever didn't move. "Is this manner of contact entirely necessary?"

"You can take a long, hot cleanse after this," Mercy promised, wiping some of the pink from her face and glancing at her fingers before shaking it off. "I always do."

We walked out of the passage into the main room. Swap had filled his living space with mountains of objects, most neatly sorted by shape, composition, and color. A thick coating of the pink substance seemed to hold them in place, as did a long, winding wall of the same material.

At least, I assumed it was a wall, until it swelled and contracted and began to rise, up and up and up until it loomed over us like a pink mountain.

"Cherijo Grey Veil, Duncan Reever," Mercy said as she gestured toward the tower. "I would like to introduce my friend, Swap."

I could not see a head, eyes, ears, mouth, or sensory organs, or indeed any definition of a body. I couldn't even tell from where his voice came, or how it was produced. The creature seemed to be made of several hundred tons of the sticky liquid, and nothing else. Then I turned my head and measured all of the pink substance I could see, and an idea began to form in my mind.

"I am very pleased to meet you, Swap," I said politely as I took Reever's hand in mine. He linked with me in time to hear my thoughts. *I think it's some sort of colossal snail.*

Or an amoebic life-form, Reever thought back.

Two streams of pink curled around our ankles.

"I am neither a snail nor an amoeba," Swap said, "but I can collect thoughts from what I touch. Rather like you, Duncan Reever."

"Forgive us." I felt embarrassed. "We meant no disrespect."

"I am not offended, Doctor," Swap said kindly. "I understand the need of humanoids to place things in a context so that they may better comprehend their nature. My only regret is that I cannot be so easily quantified. Perhaps it would be best to think of me as a worm. My form is somewhat similar to those you encountered on Akkabarr."

I thought of the tiny ice worms that lay dormant on my homeworld until the blood and body fluids of carrion spilled on the ice. They then lived out a complete life cycle while breaking down the carcass, and their newly hatched young ate the last of the carrion and the dead bodies of their parents before burrowing down in the ice to hibernate until the next awakening.

"You are much, much bigger than they were," I told Swap.

The worm made a sound very much like a laugh. "All things have their proper size and place."

"Mercy tells us that it was you who saved us during the collapse of the crystal crater," my husband said. "You saved our lives. We are very grateful to you."

"Somehow I doubt you and your mate would have died, but considering how you were forced to come here, I thought it best that you not be made to suffer." Swap slowly descended, filling out into a wide hill of pink ooze. "After tasting you, however, I fear I became insatiably curious about you. I would very much like to recite a poem for you both."

"Swap collects songs and verses, too," Mercy said. "I got him hooked on archaic Terran poetry."

"Keats, Byron, and . . . Shelley," I remembered.

"My dear Duncan, you should not worry so much about your wife's memory," Swap said. "Now, I wish to share one of my favorite sonnets with you."

"That's a poem," Mercy said helpfully.

Reever and I listened as Swap recited:

"Eternal Spirit of the chainless Mind!
Brightest in dungeons, Liberty! Thou art,
For there thy habitation is the heart—
The heart which love of thee alone can bind;
And why thy sons to fetters are consign'd—
To fetters, and the damp vault's dayless gloom,
Their county conquers with their martyrdom,
And Freedom's fame finds wings on every wind,
Chillon! thy prison is a holy place,
And thy sad floor an altar—for 'twas trod
Until his very steps have left a trace
Worn, as if thy cold pavement were a sod,
By Bonnivard! May none those marks efface!
For they appeal from tyranny to God."

I was not sure if it was a great poem, as the Iisleg had no poetry. Still, I could appreciate the sentiment behind the lyrical words. My friend, Teulon Jado, had brought freedom and justice out of an undeserved and hellish imprisonment on Akkabarr.

"That is very stirring," I told Swap.

"It is the opening sonnet from 'The Prisoner of Chillon' by Lord Byron," Swap said. "I think it an apt tribute to those who must endure the trials visited upon them without their permission. And Mercy prefers poems that rhyme."

"Poems that don't rhyme sound like just a bunch of words." Mercy set the bag she carried in front of him. "Here's what's left of Lily. I'm sorry I have to involve you in this, but until things calm down, she'll be safer here."

Part of Swap oozed over the bag, and when he slid back, it had vanished.

"Such matters must be handled with delicacy," the worm said. "You can trust me to remain discreet."

"Swap, do you know who is responsible for killing and skinning the colonists?" Reever asked.

"Come on, you know Davidov's Hsktskt is doing it," Mercy said. "Why else would he send her down here?"

"I cannot agree, Mercy. Nor can I put a name to the killer, Duncan. It seems to covet the appearance of others. Oh, dear, I forgot something." Part of Swap moved around us and elongated, taking something wrapped in plas from one of the piles. "This fell from your suit in the crater, Doctor. I did not retrieve it until I could first wrap it in something to protect its surface. My mucus layer is harmless, but it does sometimes leave stains on certain objects."

The sticky plas had been sealed around the image of Marel I had taken from our cabin. That the worm would go to so much trouble to retrieve and preserve it touched me. "I thank you."

"Your offspring is like the heart of a rose," Swap said. "Or the snow, everywhere, carefully descending—e.e. cummings, early-twentieth-century American vanguard poet."

"Do you know who is mining the black crystal, Swap?" my husband asked.

"I am," the worm told him. "I consume it, along with rock, minerals, and other inert materials. It has no negative effect on me, if that is your concern. My physiology is quite unique. Like this creature who is killing my colonist friends and taking their skins."

"We presume that the killer is using the skins to disguise itself," my husband said. "But there are far easier ways to conceal identity that would not require murder. I think its main purpose is to acquire what lies beneath the skin."

"But we haven't found anything *but* the skins," I pointed out. "The killer could be disposing of them by incinerating them or simply throwing them down one of the mine shafts."

"Alas," Swap said, "I can personally attest that no bodies have been left in the passages below the surface."

Mercy made a rude sound. "Of course not. That

Hsktskt is eating them." She turned around. "Is your console chime going off?"

A pseudopod the size of *Moonfire* slid past us to search through one of the ooze-covered piles, from which it retrieved a blinking wristcom. "Would one of you be so kind as to answer this? I fear my form does not allow me to manipulate such minuscule controls."

Mercy took it and answered the signal. One of colonial security's shift supervisors had issued a colony-wide alert, which repeated on an automated loop.

"The mercenary responsible for the blockade, Aleksei Davidov, has escaped protective custody," the supervisor said. "Security will recapture him as soon as possible. Any colonists willing to aid in the search should report to their dome leader. Davidov may be returned dead or alive to central security. The mercenary responsible for the blockade, Aleksei Davidov, has escaped protective—"

"Great." Mercy switched off the audio and returned the wristcom to the appropriate pile. "We need to find Davidov and his Hsktskt before Posbret and his raiders do. Swap, will you help me?"

The pink mass in front of us retreated a few feet. "I am sorry, my sweet one, but no, I will not."

Mercy frowned. "What are you talking about? You just need to sweep the tunnels and make sure they're not down there. I'll check the domes."

"I will not assist you in finding them, or killing them," the worm said gently.

"They're killing our people," she shouted.

"Something is killing your people, but it is not the Terran or the Hsktskt," Swap said. "I will explain my theory."

"I don't need a theory." Mercy turned to me. "Can you find your way back to Gamers?" When I nodded, she stalked into the passage.

"She was just as loud and passionate and determined when she was five years old," Swap said thoughtfully. "Only quite a bit shorter."

"You said that you didn't know who was killing the colonists," Reever said.

"To be accurate, I said I could not put a name to the creature," the worm replied. "Sovant do not take names. Only skins."

"Sovant." I searched my memory for the word, but neither I nor, evidently, Cherijo had heard it. "What is that?"

"A parasitic life-form that invades a host body with its embryonic form," Swap said. "It immediately takes over the victim's mind and begins to eat the body from the inside out. It stretches to fill the spaces it creates, but it cannot replace what it devours. After a few days there is nothing left but the skin covering it."

"When the skin begins decomposing," Reever said, "it discards the skin to infect another host?"

"It cannot survive for long outside a host body. It must capture the new victim, contract to its original size, and pass from the old to the new." The worm sounded disgusted. "There are few signs that it is occupying a body. Unusual strength, ferocity of purpose, and muteness—the Sovant cannot speak."

"Is there bleeding around the orifices?" I asked, seeing again the image of the Tingalean's blood-rimmed eyes.

"In its final days, yes," Swap said.

Reever looked grim. "How do we stop it?"

"The Sovant are drawn to events involving violence and chaos, as they have the potential to wound or weaken those involved," the worm told him. "If there aren't any, it will cause them, as it did with the *Renko*. It will seek out your patients, Doctor. The injured and helpless are its favorite prey, because they do not put up much of a fight."

I thought of all the crew members on the simward and shuddered with revulsion. "We will put guards around the wounded."

"You have two or three solar days before it uses up the body it presently occupies," Swap said. "Duncan, Mercy told me that Drefan has arranged a bout between you and this Hsktşkt female. Perhaps you could adapt that to make a trap for the Sovant."

Reever nodded, but asked, "Why do you think it would come for me or Tya when it could take one of the wounded?"

"Tya is very large, and feeding on her body could sustain it for a week, perhaps more," Swap said. "Your new talent to heal rapidly and replace your own organs might sustain it for months."

I exchanged a look with Reever. "How do you know my husband's physiology?"

"I tasted the altered cells," the worm replied. "Quite a refreshing change from the usual Terran flavor. Quite sophisticated. Rather like pheasant would be, compared to common chicken."

I was fairly certain it was being complimentary. "Thank you."

"My pleasure. I think you should take one of my tunnels back to Gamers now. If you are quick, you can prevent Mercy from shooting the wrong people." Swap slid through his piles toward a large access hatch in the center of his dome. "This way."

Reever and I followed the worm, who showed us a droplift that would take us down to the tunnels.

"The north shaft will take you straight to the air lock at Gamers' maintenance entry," Swap said. "I hope you will use it to come and visit me again. I don't sleep, and no one but Mercy visits, so you are welcome at any hour."

"Thank you," Reever said, stepping into the lift.

Before I followed my husband, I felt a tug on my ankle, and looked down to see a pseudopod gently caressing my leg. I turned back to look at the worm.

"Some of the thoughts I collected from you disturb me," Swap said. "I would offer some unsolicited advice, if I may."

"What thoughts?"

"You worry about the altered cells your husband wishes to give your child," the worm said. "You believe it is a curse. Why?"

"It is a great gift," I replied. "One that countless others wish they could have for themselves. I would not see our daughter hunted or experimented on, as we have been."

"Then perhaps, instead of changing your little girl to be an immortal like her parents," the worm said, "you and Duncan should consider becoming mortal again."

I expected the tunnels below the domes to be cold and dark, but discovered they were just the opposite. A continuous line of small emergency emitters lined the wide rock passage, which had fresh air that seemed only a little cooler than the atmosphere in the domes. I asked Reever why.

"Arutanium mines have to be well ventilated and heated, or the ore taints the air with its poisons," Reever told me. "I would imagine that Swap diverted some of the supply and return from the mine generators to heat his tunnels."

I looked around at the rough interior walls. "So these tunnels are not part of the mine?"

My husband shook his head. "The worm is too big to use any of the colony's passages between the domes. Swap mentioned that he consumes rock and minerals; I imagine his diet is responsible for most of the subsurface tunnels." Reever stopped and pressed two fingers to my mouth. He then pulled me back so that our shoulders touched the wall of the passage.

"Someone is coming," he murmured against my ear.

"I can activate the crisis beacon," Tya's voice said.

"If you have any friends in the vicinity, one of them may come for you."

A male voice laughed. "After you failed, I stranded the only friend I had left here."

Tya and Davidov walked into the intersection of tunnels just beyond me and Reever, and stopped there. Davidov looked pale and hunched, his face wet with perspiration. Tya had one of her arms around him.

"Your ship is down," she told him. "Colonial security has just broadcast an alert for you. These people are very angry. I cannot fight them all, Alek."

"Weren't you counting on them to string me up from the nearest dome strut?" Alek reached up and stroked the back of her neck. "Don't pretend you care what happens to me. We both know why you will jump each time I snap my fingers."

Tya released him and walked a short distance away, keeping her back to Davidov. "Then snap them."

"Go to the colony's main power station," he told her. "Shut down the environmental systems."

She hissed something under her breath. "To which dome?"

"All of them."

I flinched, and felt Reever's muscles coil against my back.

"The entire population will suffocate within an hour," the Hsktskt told him, her tone colorless.

"We can only hope."

She showed him her jagged teeth. "You would kill them all to have your revenge?"

"A great deal can happen within an hour, my dear. If all goes as planned, I'll let you restart the systems." His voice hardened. "Shut them down, or I'll blow the charges I've planted around the domes. Then we'll all die together. One big, unhappy family."

"*I will not kill for you,*" Tya shouted.

Davidov feigned a concerned look. "Oh, my poor, poor girl. You *have* been on your own for far too long. Let me remind you *why* you'll do exactly as you're told."

Tya threw herself at him. Before her claws wrapped around Davidov's neck, she made a peculiar sound and fell to her knees. Instead of showing him her throat, her head drooped forward, and uncontrollable spasms racked her body. Raw, agonized sounds punctuated the grinding of teeth and bones.

Davidov said nothing more, only walking around her as he strode into one of the passages.

Reever held me back until Davidov's footsteps died away, and then hurried with me to the Hsktskt female. Tya had stopped shaking, but her chest worked frantically, and her limbs were locked and rigid.

"Tya?" She didn't respond to my voice. "She's having a seizure. Duncan, help me with her."

We crouched down on either side of her, and between us got her over onto her side. Her eyes had rolled back in her head, and foamy saliva frothed from between her clenched teeth.

I needed to sedate her. "Get my syrinpress from my case."

"No." Tya's slitted pupils reappeared and dilated for a moment before her body relaxed. She swallowed several times before she shoved herself in an upright position. "I am not ill. Leave me now."

"Reever and I heard what Davidov said to you," I told her. "I don't care what he wants. You can't murder the colonists."

She shook her head. "If I do not do as he says, millions will die."

"You don't know that," I said. The wild look in her eyes frightened me. "Tya, what has Davidov done to you?"

"He owns me." Tya looked at me, and the emptiness in her eyes made me catch my breath. "You can try to fight him, but he will prevail. He cannot be stopped. He fears nothing, like the Sovant." Her gaze shifted. "Like your mate."

I glanced at Reever, and missed seeing her reach inside her tunic. My husband darted forward, trying to take something from the Hsktskt, and then a crackling curtain of light fell over me and left me blind, paralyzed, and alone.

The energy blast that Tya had used to incapacitate me and Reever began to wear off after a few minutes. I never lost consciousness, but fought the paralyzing effects until I felt some of my vision, hearing, and body control slowly return.

Reever lay sprawled on the floor of the tunnel, one of his arms flung across my waist. I felt his fingers contract and managed to move my hand to his. When I was able to turn my head, I saw his eyes, wide and unblinking, a few inches from my own.

"Stuh." My tongue resisted speech. "Stuh-un. Stun. *Stunned*."

He blinked once, and one of his fingers twitched against my palm. He could not speak or link with me.

I focused, pushing past the sluggish, nerve-dead inertia imprisoning me in my own body, and reached out to him with my thoughts. I knew Cherijo had been able to initiate a link with Reever several times in the past; she had written about it in her journals. I should be able to do the same.

Instead of bringing myself into Reever's mind, or him into my own, I left my body and drifted into a dark blue cloud spiked with flashing, soundless lightning. Somewhere in the center I felt my husband's presence.

Leave me here, Duncan's voice said. *It will take too long for me to recover. You must go to Drefan and warn him about Tya, and Davidov's plans.*

I was not leaving him stunned and helpless in the tunnels. Not with the Sovant still running loose. *I will signal Drefan.*

The stunner will have disabled your wristcom, he said. *You have to get to a panel or the dome.*

I couldn't leave him, and I had no counteragent that would make the effects of the stunner wear off faster. I could not carry him or drag him far.

So heal him. You know what to do. The Omorr taught us when he healed our hands.

I felt my body reach out, and my palms press against his chest. Something gathered in me, something I had not felt since walking through the bodies of the dead and dying on the battlefields. She had come with me during those endless, bloody days and nights. She had guided my hands.

Who is that inside you? my husband demanded. *Maggie?*

If I can merge our minds, I told him, *I can free your nervous system from the effects of the stunner. Focus on what I am feeling.*

Jarn, you are not a touch healer.

I couldn't explain how I felt, only that I knew I could do this thing. *Focus.*

The connection between us connected more than our thoughts and feelings. The neural pathways in our brains had joined and were as one. That was how Reever was able to control my body when he created a link. He could manipulate my nervous system and even take command of it.

As I did with his now.

I didn't think of what I was doing, or how. I only raced along invisible roads, punching through the crackling curtains of energy blocking my path. As I went through each one, they fell, and the path cleared.

Reever's hands covered mine, and his limbs twitched. The frantic beating of his heart slowed, and his respiration leveled out. I felt his body lift and his arms support me as I smashed through the last of the paralyzing curtains and drew back into my own head, terminating all of the connections.

I opened my eyes to see my husband's, alert and somewhat stunned. He was sitting up and holding me upright. Exhaustion dragged at my own muscles, but I dismissed it and straightened.

"For once Maggie does something useful," he muttered, brushing the hair out of my face. "Are you hurt?"

"Just a little tired." I considered telling him that the one who had guided me was not Maggie and had nothing to do with her, but that conversation would have to keep. We had to stop Davidov. "Please, help me up?"

Reever stood and lifted me onto my feet. My legs felt as if they were filled with Swap's ooze, and for a moment I feared they might buckle. I held on to him until I felt steadier and then tugged him toward the tunnel leading to Gamers.

We made it to the maintenance access hatch a few minutes later and passed through the air lock without encountering anyone. I expected to be met by Keel or Drefan, or even one of the staff drones. The Gamers complex seemed completely deserted.

"They're probably running a game from central control," Reever said as we approached the simward. "I'll go to Drefan. You see to your patients."

I entered the simulator we had set up for the wounded, but the only patients left were the two men I had operated on. I turned around, but the room was empty. "Where are they?"

A small group of Davidov's men came in behind us, all of them carrying weapons.

"We've taken over this dome," one of them told us. "Come with us."

There were too many for Reever to fight, and neither of us had fully recovered from the stun.

"We saved you," I reminded the men, "and this is how you would repay us?"

"Nothing personal, Healer," the man said. "Captain's orders."

Davidov's crew escorted us to one of the melee simulators, where red-brown skies and lush vegetation revealed that the Itan Odaras jungle program was again running. I noted several custom modifications had been made, like the simulated Tingalean guards surrounding Drefan, Keel, and the rest of the staff. A wide pool of ice blue water also took up nearly half of the grid area, although what purpose it served escaped me.

The men followed us in and immediately barricaded the entry. Reever and I were directed to join the Gamers staff. Drefan greeted us with a nod but didn't speak until Davidov's men had left the immediate area.

"They took over the dome shortly after security

issued the alert for Davidov," the games master told us. "They had all of our pass codes and knew exactly where to seize weapons, control rooms, and key personnel. It was all done so quickly and efficiently that I almost think it was rehearsed as a potential scenario."

"Tya," Reever said. "She has been gathering information about the colony for Davidov for months. We heard them talking in the tunnels between here and Swap's dome. He just ordered her to shut down the environmental controls for the entire colony."

"He's controlling her with some sort of implant," I said. "When she refused to cooperate, he did something that made her have a seizure."

One of Davidov's men came over and tossed a wristcom at Drefan. "There is a fool outside demanding admittance. Tell him you are closed."

Drefan turned the wristcom over in his hands. "And if I do not?"

The man raised his rifle and pointed it at Keel's head. "I will kill one of them every minute until you do."

Drefan switched on the wristcom and said, "There will be no games today. The arena is closed until further notice."

"I don't want to play with you, cripple," Posbret said. "I want that Terran scum, Davidov."

"Didn't you hear the security alert?" Drefan asked. "He escaped my custody."

Posbret made a spitting sound. "You Terrans hate

everyone but your own kind. How do I know you aren't hiding him in there?"

"Because he took my Hsktskt with him," Drefan replied. "Maybe you should scan for her life signs. They are quite unique."

Posbret suggested Drefan do something anatomically impossible with his stumps and withdrew into the access way along with his men. Drefan switched off the wristcom and tossed it at Davidov's man. He threw it too hard, however, and it landed in the water with a splash.

"Sorry," the games master said. "My aim was a little off."

"Try that again," the man said, "and I'll burn a hole through your belly."

Once the man retreated to join the other crew members, Drefan turned to me. "What would Davidov want so badly that he would go through the ruse of selling Tya to me?"

I shook my head. "Tya only said something about him wanting revenge."

"He blockaded the colony to keep the Sovant from leaving," Reever said, "and he sent Tya here to hunt it. When she failed to find it, he lured us here and forced us to crash so that we would draw it out of hiding."

Drefan looked fascinated and appalled at the same time. "He offered four million stan credits for you and your wife, when all he intended was to use you as bait?"

"It was a setup," my husband replied. "Drefan

made sure everyone in the colony received the signal broadcasting the bounty. He had no intention of paying it; he only wanted the Sovant to know about our physiologies. The prospect of taking over an immortal body must have seemed irresistible to it. He also knew that if Tya failed, ingesting Jarn's blood, tissue, or bone would poison it."

I stared at him. "You knew this all along, and you said nothing to me?"

"I know what Alek seeks to avenge," my husband corrected. "The rest are logical conclusions."

"Well, this is just great," Mercy said.

We all looked over as she and Cat were forced at gunpoint to join us.

"This is absolutely the last time I break into Omega Dome because I'm worried about some Hsktskt eating Drefan," Mercy told the Omorr. "If I ever mention doing it again in the future, slap me."

"The Hsktskt isn't interested in devouring me," Drefan told her.

"Yeah, well, you're not exactly rolling in skin," she snapped back.

"Tya is going to shut down the environmental systems to all the domes," Reever said to the pair. "We have to find her before she does."

"She'll have to go down into the old mines to get at the support equipment," Cat said. "We relocated it there a few years back to prevent visitors from meddling with the temperature settings."

"I know Tya's scent," Keel said. "I can track her."

"Sounds great," Mercy said. "Now all we have to

do is sneak you three past the seventy guys with all the weapons. Any suggestions?"

While we were quietly discussing how to create a suitable distraction that would allow Reever, Cat, and Keel to slip out of the grid through a maintenance passage hidden behind the vegetation, two of Davidov's men came over.

"That raider is back, and he wants to search the dome," one of them told us. "He's threatening to blast his way in. He's probably got the Sovant with him and doesn't even know it."

"We need the Hsktskt," the other said flatly. "She's the only one who knows how to kill that thing. She can protect us."

"What do you expect us to do?" Drefan asked. "Help you? We're your prisoners."

"You send some of your people to find Tya," the first one said. "Bring her back here."

"Or what?" Mercy demanded.

"Or we start shooting," the second man said, and pointed his weapon at Mercy and Drefan. "Starting with you and him."

At my request, Drefan convinced Davidov's men to allow me out of the melee room so that I could check on my surgical patients. I asked that Mercy be allowed to accompany me.

"I may need some assistance with changing the surgical dressings," I lied. When the man in charge accused me of using the wounded as an excuse to attempt an escape, I shrugged. "Very well, I'll stay here. But if they die of dehydration or infection, their blood will be on your hands."

"Maybe she'll go and kill them so that the captain will blame us for their deaths," another man said.

"She's a doctor. She can't hurt anyone, you dim-wit," Mercy said. "They take an oath to do no harm."

After a short debate the men sent two guards with me and Mercy to the simward. When the guards would have followed us in, I smiled. "I'm delighted to have the extra help. Which one of you would like to empty the bedpans?"

Both guards elected to stay outside.

"So what's the plan, Doc?" Mercy asked the moment the door panels closed.

"I plan"—I looked pointedly at the room monitor, with which the guards outside could watch us—"to check on my patients."

I went over to the first, who was sleeping but had developed a low-grade fever. "This one needs an infusion of antibiotics. There should be a syrinpress in the top of that cart over there. Bring it to me."

"You really take this medical stuff seriously." She brought me the instrument and watched as I dialed up the dosage. "Anything else I can do? Mop the sweat off their faces, or maybe rub their feet?"

"Now look." I grabbed her tunic and used it to pull her close. In a bare whisper, I said, "You can gather up the other instruments from the cart and conceal them in your garments. Pretend you are tidying up the cart. Take anything that has a sharp edge or a power cell."

"You're a genius." Mercy turned her head and kissed my cheek. In a louder voice, she said, "Okay, okay, you don't have to bite my ear off. I'll straighten up things."

I tried not to think about Reever roaming the tunnels in search of Tya as I carefully removed the patient's dressings and inspected the surgical site. I took a moment to change the chest drain and rearrange the tubing to reduce the inflammation before I moved to the next patient.

He woke as soon as I touched his cool brow. "My fourth leg hurts," he complained.

"I'll give you something for the pain, but don't try to move or touch it," I warned as I adjusted the bonesetter attached to the limb. "You had two compound fractures of your front izlac bone, and it needs time to heal."

Once I had him comfortable, I went to the cart to see what Mercy had appropriated. She had done well, taking almost everything that we could use as weapons to defend ourselves. I picked up three more syrinpresses and surreptitiously tucked them under my garments before going to the room panel.

"What are you doing?" Mercy asked, following me.

"Adjusting the bedding." I input the data required to alter the projections, and looked back at the cart. Holograph versions of all of the instruments we had removed materialized onto the cart. "That should help them sleep a little better."

Mercy looked startled, and then grinned. "Oh, yeah, I'm sure it will."

A moment later one of the guards came in. "You two have had enough time," he said, going over to inspect the cart before motioning toward the entry with his weapon. "Let's go."

When we returned to the melee room, Mercy and I silently distributed the instruments to Drefan, Keel, and some of the other staff. I preset the dosage on each of the syrinpresses so that they would deliver a potent but nonfatal dose of neuroparalyzer.

"How much time do you think we have before Tya reaches the envirocontrols?" Mercy asked me as she eyed Davidov's men.

More than an hour had passed since Reever, Cat, and Keel had left. "If the men have not found her yet, not long."

"After she cuts the air and heat, we'll have only an hour." Mercy looked down as Drefan pressed something into her hand, and then immediately pocketed it. "I thought you threw that 'com in the water."

"I threw Cherijo's," Drefan said, making me glance in surprise at my empty wrist. "The one I just gave you still functions."

Mercy kept an eye on the guards. "Who do you want me to signal?"

"If they panic and start to make good on their

threats," Drefan told her, "signal Posbret and tell him how to get in."

Her eyes widened. "You *want* me to let the raiders into the dome."

"Only as a last resort." Drefan turned his glidechair around so that he faced the water. "Hopefully Reever and the others will find Tya soon."

An hour passed, and then another. Sitting and waiting for something to happen made everyone's nerves stretch thin, so we remained quiet but watchful.

Mercy took a pair of eyeshades out of her tunic, smiling as she saw my quick look. "Cat fixed it for me, but don't worry. You can't use it for playback unless you're in the fantasizer." She caressed the device with gentle fingers. "Which is where I'd love to be right now."

I held out my hand and, when she gave me the mindset, studied the inside of the device. The neuron circuitry was more sophisticated than I had imagined. "What happens if you use it on playback without the fantasizer?"

"I don't know." She thought about it. "The fantasizer is the data stream storage and transmission unit. I guess it would play back nothing, or maybe scramble your brains."

"They're not happy," Drefan said, interrupting our conversation. He nodded toward several of Davidov's men, who were arguing in low, ugly voices.

I pocketed the mindset. "What can we do?"

"If things deteriorate, I want you and Mercy to position yourselves behind my chair," he said. "It will shield you from a direct blast."

"James." Mercy caressed his cheek with the back of her hand. "You were the first Terran I ever bedded, the only trick whose credits I ever refunded, and one of the only two males that I've ever loved." She turned her hand around and gave him a small slap. "So quit telling me to use you as a fucking body shield, all right?"

Drefan steepled his fingers and looked over them at me. "If they start shooting, please pull her behind the goddamn chair, Cherijo."

I nodded. "Why did she refund your credits?"

"Maybe *she* doesn't like being talked around like she's invisible," Mercy said. "Ever think of that?"

Drefan gave her a fond look. "I taught her that sex isn't all business."

Something pounded at the door panel, and after consulting with the man in charge and the corridor monitors, the men opened it.

At first I didn't recognize the injured animal that came stumbling in, so much blood covered it. Beside me Drefan said, "Keel?"

The Chakacat dropped at the feet of Davidov's men, who scattered in fear as if it were the Sovant.

I ran to it, bracing myself for the worst. But silvery fur still covered its lean frame, and it looked up at me with one eye. The other eye, along with part of its face, had been clawed away.

"Cherijo." It spat out some blood and a few tooth fragments. "I fear that I lost my first fight."

"We will ask for a rematch." I opened my case to take out what I needed. "Are Reever and Cat with you?"

"No. I picked up the scent of the Hsktskt and went ahead of them." It shivered. "I shouldn't have done that."

"Keel?" Drefan's glidechair stopped beside the Chakacat, and the games master heaved himself down onto the floor. He held the feline's narrow shoulders with his one arm, lifting it gently onto the stumps of his legs. "What happened? Who did this to you?"

Davidov's men opened the door panel, and Cat hopped in. The Omorr appeared unharmed, but my husband was not with him.

"Where is the Terran?" I heard one of our captors demand.

"We were separated in the tunnels," Cat replied. "He should be bringing the Hsktskt here shortly."

That cheered the men, who allowed Cat to come over to us. He swore when he saw Keel's head injuries. "You shouldn't have gone after her, you idiot feline."

Drefan's arm tightened. "Tya did this to you?"

"No, it was a braael." The Chakacat shivered violently, and I tore off my jacket and covered its body. "I cornered the Hsktskt in the processing plant. She didn't try to hurt me, Drefan. When she charged me, I think she was only trying to get away. She didn't use her claws or bite me when I jumped her. I reacted badly, I know, but I have never hunted before this."

I sponged the blood away from the claw marks running down Keel's face. There were only two of them, but they were deep and vicious. The odd thing was that they seemed to have been inflicted backward, as if Tya's claws had caught Keel under the jaw and raked up.

I applied pressure to the side of its face as I used a light to inspect the remains of its eye. It had not been clawed out, but was so badly lacerated that I doubted it could be saved. "Keel, I am going to give you a painkiller. I need to clean and suture these wounds."

It grabbed my wrist. "You have to warn them about the braael. If it comes here, it will go berserk and not stop until everyone is dead."

Cat started to say something, and then shook his head.

"I do not know what a braael is," I said to Keel, humoring it. "What does it look like?"

"It is all black hide and spines, and has fiery eyes. Orange eyes." Keel's voice shook so badly it stopped speaking to gulp in air. "Two curved teeth in the bottom of its jaw. Long, sharp red spines running down its back, and two more at the end of its tail. It has two mouths, one for killing, and one for eating." It rolled away from me and retched.

I held it until it had finished heaving, and then modified the syrinpress to administer an antinausea agent along with the local anesthetic. Keel drifted off into semiconsciousness.

"You should warn the others about this braael," I said to Cat as I gently irrigated one of the gashes. "It sounds like a very dangerous creature."

Cat and Drefan exchanged an odd look.

"I would, Cherijo," the Omorr said, "but there are no braael on Trellus."

I gave him an ironic look. "Obviously there's one."

"What he means is, there can't be a braael on colony," Drefan said. "They are native to Chakara."

I saw something imbedded in the second gash and reached for a probe. "So is Keel."

"Chakacats are not extinct," Drefan said. "The braael are. The species died out a hundred thousand years ago."

I removed the remnants of what appeared to be shrapnel from Keel's face. On closer inspection, I recognized it. "Drefan, did you have Keel implanted with a locator beacon?"

"No. I would never do that to any being."

I took out my scanner and passed it over the small, twisted bit of tech. It matched only one record on the medical database. "This is Tya's implant."

"It was the braael," Keel said, opening its eye and digging its claws into my arms. "It was going to eat my head."

As I calmed the Chakacat and finished treating its injuries, an idea began to form in my mind. I asked

Davidov's men to allow me and Cat to move Keel to the simward.

Once more we were sent there under guard. After I had the feline resting comfortably, I passed a syrin-press to Cat and pointed to a spot on my throat. He nodded and hopped out to where the guards waited.

"Are you finished—" The guard went still as I infused him with neuroparalyzer, and then dropped.

Cat did the same thing with the other guard, and we dragged them into the simward.

"I need to go to the lab," I told the Omorr. "Can you stay here and watch them?"

He nodded. "Be careful."

I hurried through the empty corridors to the lab, where I carefully scanned the remnants of the implant I had removed from Keel's wound. Aside from the Chakacat's blood, there was DNA from a second source. The DNA did not match any other species on record in the database.

I verified that the implant was identical to Tya's before I began dissecting it. It was not, as Tya had told me, a locator beacon. The implant was a modified pain inductor, one commonly used by slavers to control and punish slaves. I found no reservoir of poison or any substance that could have been released into Tya's bloodstream. The modifications seemed very bizarre as well. The implant could still induce a massive amount of pain by generating a small charge that would stimulate the corresponding neural pathways, but it had been designed to suppress certain natural functions and maintain Tya's brain waves in a preprogrammed pattern.

I ran a diagnostic using the information I had gathered from the implant, and the database offered a confusing result. It was as if the implant had been designed to combat a plague that no longer existed.

I went back to the ward and found Cat waiting beside the restrained guards.

"What did you find out?" he asked.

"Someone," I said carefully, "does not want Tya to feel fear."

Eighteen

Cat and I decided to go to central control and use Drefan's battle programs to try to free the other hostages.

"We can generate an entire army of simulations to keep them busy," the Omorr said as he went to the center console and pulled up the different program sequences. "Drefan will know what to do the minute the grid changes."

I had a feeling we had been gone too long, and switched on the room monitor, which confirmed my suspicions. Davidov's men had separated Mercy from the others, and had her on her knees with her hands linked behind her neck. One of the men lifted a rifle and pointed it at the back of her skull.

"Cat," I said, "initiate the program now."

"Damn Drefan for a paranoid fool," the Omorr said. "I can't get into it. The change protocol is pass coded."

"The pass code is five-seven-two-eight-four-three-beta," Drefan's voice said over the audio. "Cat, initiate the Itan Odaras program, submenu nine, armed combatants only. Remove the no-injury safeties."

The Omorr input the codes and I saw the grid waver and change. Three thousand simulated Hskt-skt raiders appeared and rushed at everyone in the room who was holding a weapon.

"Cherijo," Drefan said, shouting to be heard now. "Send a signal to the drednoc storage bay. Use the same code I gave Cat. Order all the dreds to come to the melee room."

I did as he asked, but when I tried to return the signal Drefan didn't answer. I didn't see his glidechair on the monitor, either.

The change to the simulation quickly routed Davidov's men, who were forced back from the hostages by the Hsktskt raiders. The crew of the *Renko* huddled back against the walls, firing uselessly at the simulated reptilians.

Something rumbled outside the control room, and I switched the monitor to view the exterior corridor. Two dozen drednocs in battle mode filled the passage as they headed toward the melee room.

"We have another problem," Cat said.

I turned and saw men pouring in through the air locks. "Posbret's men?"

"Yeah." The Omorr rose and went over to a weapons case, smashing the plas and removing a number of pulse weapons. "They've disabled all of the gun turrets and breached the air locks." He tossed a rifle to me. "I'm going to get Mercy. Wait here."

"The wounded will need my help." I put down the rifle and picked up my case.

"You'll get shot."

"I am no stranger to the battlefield." I met his angry gaze. "I will be careful."

Posbret's men reached the melee room before Cat and I did, and we found them fighting both the crew of the *Renko* and the Hsktskt raiders. Drefan's drednocs, it seemed, had not yet arrived. I slipped inside behind the Omorr, who immediately shoved me behind a tree as pulse fire streamed past our heads.

"The cross fire is too heavy," he said, looking all around. "Do you see Mercy anywhere?"

I saw injured men crawling for cover, and reptilian raiders wrestling Posbret's men. Mercy and the hostages were nowhere in sight, but as I searched the chaos for a sign of them, a stray refraction of light made me look up.

A shimmering figure pulled itself out of an air shaft and secured a rope to one of the ceiling struts before beginning the long climb down. The intruder's dimsilk garments made it impossible to identify who it was, but it was Terran-sized, and moved with inhuman speed and agility that I recognized instantly.

"Up there," I said, pointing. "It's Reever."

"Go and tell him the dreds are on the way. And take this." Cat shoved one of his blades into my hand. "You don't have to kill anyone with it. Just defend yourself, will you?"

I nodded and slipped the blade inside my tunic before I hurried over to intercept my husband as he jumped down the last three feet from the end of the rope. "Duncan."

I flung myself into his arms, holding on to him with tight hands. It wasn't until he bent his head toward me that I smelled his scent, which was all wrong.

I pushed myself out of his embrace. "What are you doing here?"

Davidov pulled the mask of dimsilk away from his face. "Finishing things, Cherijo." He looked down at Cat's dagger, which I had pressed to his chest. "Before you cut my heart out, you might help me catch the Sovant when it comes. It won't be able to resist the fighting."

"The same way it wasn't supposed to resist me?" I asked. "I don't have much faith in your predictions. Where is Reever?"

His fair brows drew together. "Isn't he here with you?"

"He went to stop Tya."

"I'm afraid I can't have that." Davidov moved like water, and suddenly the dagger I held appeared in his hand. "I need her here, with me." He took out a small device and checked its readout. What he saw made him scowl, and he glared at me. "How are you jamming her signal?"

I almost told him that her implant had been destroyed, but I thought it might be useful for him to remain ignorant of that. "I don't know what you're talking about."

A barrage of pulse fire sent us both to the ground. The fighting between Posbret's men, the crew of the *Renko*, and the simulated raiders appeared to be escalating.

"I need Tya here," Davidov said as he pulled me behind a boulder. "Go and find her and bring her back to me."

How did Mercy say it? "In your dreams, stupid."

"Find Tya and bring her here," Davidov said, "or I will detonate the explosives I've planted around the domes. That will end this game once and for all."

"You're bluffing," I said. "You won't blow up anything."

Davidov tapped his wristcom, and an instant later a tremendous explosion rocked the dome. As I ducked and covered my head, bits of the grid ceiling rained down over us.

"That was Epsilon Dome, where all the colony's stores are kept," Davidov informed me pleasantly. "What shall I blow up next? Mercy House? I don't think anyone will really miss the whores. Well, perhaps the cripple." He reached for the keypad.

I grabbed his hand. "Don't. I'll go. I'll find her."

"Excellent." He kissed the back of my hand before I could wrench it away. "You should hurry, Doctor. You have fifteen minutes before I blow the next charge."

I ran out of the melee room and down the corridor to the maintenance hatches where Reever and I had returned from Alpha Dome. I took a few precious minutes to suit up before I left Gamers and descended into the tunnels.

Duncan, Duncan, Duncan.

I didn't know I was chanting his name out loud until my suit com answered me. "Jarn, where are you?"

"Duncan." I stumbled and stopped, bracing myself against one of the rock walls. "I'm in the tunnels, just below where the Gamers maintenance hatch is. Do you have Tya?"

"No, I'm still tracking her."

My heart clenched. "If we don't find her and take her to Davidov within the next fifteen minutes, he's going to start blowing up the domes. He's already destroyed one to prove he can do it."

"Take the first left turn and follow the passage," he told me. "I will meet you at the waste recycling station."

I followed his instructions and waited beside an enormous tangle of pipes and processors until he came out of one of the nearby passages. After giving me a brief, hard hug, he went over to the equipment and began working on one of the consoles.

"What are you doing?" I went to his side. "We have to find the Hsktskt."

"I chased her into one of the dome substations," he said as he pulled up a complex-looking schematic. "She got away from me by crawling into one of the water supply pipes." He pointed toward the screen. "Here."

"You have to be mistaken," I said. "She is too big to fit into a pipe."

"Not anymore," he assured me, studying the schematic. "That line leads to Mercy House's substation. There's a junction I think I can valve off here." He seized my hand. "Come, there's not much time left."

We went to the point where the pipes intersected with another group, and Reever grabbed hold of a wheel, turning it slowly. I heard metal groan and something bang into the side of the pipe. I lifted my scanner and passed the beam over the piping until I found a distinct thermal signature.

"Here," I said. "She's here." I moved as close to the pipe as I could. "Tya, this is Cherijo. Please come out of there. Davidov is threatening to detonate the explosives if you don't go to him now. He's not far. All you have to do is go to the melee room at Gamers."

The signature changed direction and entered another series of pipes. In another moment it was gone.

"Where do these lead?" I asked my husband.

He turned and studied the direction of the pipes. "To Davidov."

Reever and I made our way back to Gamers, running to beat Davidov's time limit. As my breath burned in my tired lungs, and my leg muscles knotted, I tried not to think of Kohbi and the other females who had been kind to me at Mercy House. If Davidov kept his promise and killed them, I would never forgive myself.

Reever stopped outside the melee room and pulled me into a corner by the entry. I removed my helmet—there had not been enough time for us to take off our suits—and watched him do the same.

"I will deal with Alek," he said, taking a pulse pistol out of his utility pocket. "You find Mercy and the others and stay with them."

I nodded. "What about Tya?"

"I don't think we have to worry about her," he said, his eyes so dark a gray they almost looked black.

We entered the melee room, ducking to avoid pulse fire and moving to the nearest cover. The fighting seemed to be nearly over; the crew of the *Renko* was pinned down in one malfunctioning section of the grid, hiding behind the slain bodies of the simulated Hsktskt.

Davidov was nowhere in sight.

As I looked for Drefan and Mercy, I saw something pouring from a supply pipe into the water trap. It was Swap, judging by the pink color of the mass, but when the worm touched the water his body darkened and seemed to expand. Another, smaller form waded into the water and dove under the surface before I had time to see who it was.

"It's Tya," Reever said to me.

We moved closer to the water trap. I peered into

its depths to see if the Hsktskt was trying to attack the giant worm. I saw Tya briefly surface, taking in air through her mouth. Her scaly head seemed to be melting into a mass of gray ooze. A dark pink pseudopod came out of the water, wrapped around her face, and tugged her under.

Men began shouting in victory as the crew of the *Renko* threw their weapons over the wall of Hsktskt bodies and stood with their hands up. Posbret pushed aside his own men to stride up to the wall, where he bent and picked up a rifle. He gave Davidov's men a bloody smile before he began shooting them. When his own raiders shouted out in protest, he swung around and began firing at them.

The largest of Drefan's drednocs stepped into the line of fire, blasting Posbret with a halo pulse. It had no effect on the raider leader, although it did render his weapon useless. He turned it around in his hands and smashed it against the drednoc's sensory case, smashing the outer plas. For a moment the inner shield slid up, revealing a very human face beneath.

"Duncan," I whispered, clutching at his arm.

Now I understood why the largest of the battle drones had been designed so differently from the others. Drefan had built himself a complete chassis to fit around his body and compensate for his amputated limbs. His remaining arm, covered in protective armor and gauntlet, matched the artificial one on the opposite side.

"No wonder he is so awkward with standard

prosthetics," I muttered. "He's been using that thing all this time."

Drefan's reconstruct-styled body appeared to have the same strength and resilience as the other drednocs, but even that did not seem to be giving him an advantage over Posbret. The raider leader wrestled ferociously with him, paying no attention to the damage Drefan's grapplers were inflicting on his arms, shoulders, and head. I didn't understand why until tears of blood began spilling from the raider leader's eyes.

"The Sovant—Duncan, the Sovant has taken over Posbret's body." I tried to imagine what would happen if the skin thief got inside Drefan's drone chassis. It would be unstoppable. "We have to get it away from him."

"You can't," Cat said as he joined us. "Tya is the only one who can kill it."

"Swap has trapped Tya underwater," I said.

"Not trapped." Cat winced as Drefan was knocked over onto his back. "He's helping her. Although he better hurry up. James can't hold it off much longer."

"Tya is the Odnallak," Reever said softly.

The Omorr nodded. "Swap and I had a little chat down in the tunnels. He's going to help her shift into the one thing that monster fears."

Water began to bubble as the dark mass spread across the bottom of the pool, moving closer to the shore. Something like a Hsktskt slowly emerged from the dark stain, its body swelling and changing as the worm's body seemed to pour into it from behind.

"What is Swap doing to her?" I said, appalled.

Reever looked grim. "They're merging."

What was left of the Hsktskt and the enormous mass beneath the water slowly came together into one form. It spread out countless limbs and folds as it moved to the edge of the water, displacing most of it with its bulk. A nightmarish mouth opened at the very top of the grossly swollen body and then slid down the front of it, burrowing into the center and widening. I saw a cavity the size of a mine tunnel open and line itself with hundreds of thousands of pointed teeth, some the size of my head.

I saw all the color drain from my husband's face. "What is it, Duncan?"

Reever looked away from it. "A rogur."

Drefan punched Posbret's face, making it turn toward the water trap. The raider leader went still as it saw the monster lurking at the edge of the water. He scrambled off Drefan's chassis and crawled backward, trying desperately to get his feet under him.

Spine-tipped limbs sprang from the body of the rogur, impaling the simulated bodies of the Hsktskt and dragging them back toward the water. The corpses were flung into the cavernous open maw, which opened and closed in a spiraling motion, swallowing the bodies with compulsive greed.

"When it ruled Vtaga, the rogur was virtually indestructible," Reever said absently. "It swallows its prey whole, and slowly digests them. TssVar said it kept its victims alive in its gullet for months."

"But the rogur is extinct," I said. "Like the braael."

"The Sovant doesn't know that," Cat said. "It has no reasoning. It only kills and eats and breeds."

Posbret managed to escape Tya/Swap's grasp by throwing other bodies at them. For a moment I thought he meant to run out of the melee room, until he abruptly changed direction and came toward us.

Both Duncan and Cat raised weapons and fired at Posbret, but nothing stopped him. When he got close enough for me to see how his skin was rippling, I knew what it meant to do, and whom it would choose.

"Run, Jarn," my husband said as he kept firing until the power cell drained completely.

The pulse beams both Reever and Cat had fired at Posbret had done a great deal of damage to his body, but he seemed unaware of it. Just before he reached us, Cat drained the last of his power cell firing into Posbret's face, which abruptly burst into flames.

I waited until Posbret came within two feet of my husband, and I jumped in front of him. "Don't take him," I told the Sovant. "I'm the one you want."

"Jarn." Reever grabbed my waist between his hands and tried to set me out of the way.

I turned and kissed him, hard, and then jammed the syrinpress against his neck. "I'm sorry."

My husband's eyes widened and he swiped at me with one hand before he dropped to the floor.

I turned to Posbret, who reached up and slapped at the flames on his face until they went out. His fur had been burned off, as had much of the skin beneath it. Fresh blood rimmed his heat-whitened eyes as he regarded me.

Cat dragged Reever out of the way. "What are you doing?"

"Stay back," I said, thumbing the dosage meter on the syrinpress to a lethal dose of neuroparalyzer. To Posbret I said, "I'm the one in the bounty, remember? Cherijo Torin."

Posbret reached for me, but at the last second seized my wrist and bent it until the syrinpress fell out of my hand.

I fought the Sovant's hold wildly, and felt Cat grab one of my arms as he tried to help work me free. Posbret drove his elbow into the Omorr's face, knocking him away from me. He dragged me out of the trees and threw me over his shoulder as he carried me toward the exit.

Nineteen

I didn't know if my body would poison the Sovant, or render it immortal. I only knew that I was not going to let it take me without a fight.

I kicked and struggled, trying to writhe my way out of Posbret's hold. His arm would not budge an inch. I tightened my grip on Cat's dagger and turned, driving it into the base of his skull.

Posbret stopped, reached back, and pulled the blade out of his neck, tossing it away as if it were no more than a toy.

I couldn't reach the other syrinpress I had in my pocket, so I prepared myself for the moment he put me down. I would run in any direction, as long as it was away from him.

Posbret pulled me off his shoulder and held me in front of the scorched ruin of his face. His mouth opened, and he jerked me close as if he meant to kiss me. The stink of his charred flesh made me gag, and then I went still as I saw a bubble of something streaked yellow, red, and green bulge out of his mouth.

It had to be the Sovant embryo, ready to pass from Posbret's body into my own.

I groped in my pocket, hunting for the syrinpress. I found Mercy's mindset instead. I used my thumb to switch it on and jammed it over Posbret's eyes.

He made a guttural, wordless sound and tried to shake off the mindset. When one of his hands released me to claw the unit from his face, I wrenched out of his grip, fell to my feet, and turned to run.

Posbret tackled me before I took three steps and yanked me back up to his face again. The embryo bulged out of his mouth.

I turned my head, clamping my mouth shut and tearing at him with my fingernails, gouging at his eyes and burned flesh. The embryo contracted, hiding itself back in his throat. He seized my head by clapping his hands against my ears, and forced my face to his.

The blows nearly deafened me. I saw a shimmer of dimsilk, and without warning we both collapsed on the floor. I saw Posbret's legs roll away from his body and tried to do the same. The raider leader reached out and clamped his hand around my ankle and began dragging me back to him.

"You can't have her," I heard Davidov say through the roar in my ears, and then saw a sword flash as it came down. The blow severed Posbret's arm from his body, and I kicked free of the dead limb. Davidov anticipated the raider leader reaching out with his remaining arm and severed that one as well.

I crawled away from Posbret, turning over in time to see one of the rogur's spines punch through his torso. As the Sovant embryo began to swell outside the Gnilltak's mouth, Davidov bent down and punched it as if to force it back inside the body. The embryo broke apart and dribbled small versions of itself on Posbret's chest and the floor around his body.

Tya/Swap yanked the limbless torso into the water, where it sank without a sound and was enveloped by the dark mass beneath the surface. The smaller embryos began to roll toward me and some of the crew of the *Renko*, but more pods shot out of the water and speared them, dragging them away from us. The last embryo expanded wildly before it was cast into the maw and swallowed whole.

I shook my head several times, trying to clear the ringing from my ears. I did not hear Reever saying my name until he lifted me from the floor and held me steady.

"I thought I sedated you," I said, frowning at him.

"You did." Anger gleamed for a moment in his dark gray eyes. "The chameleon cells must have neutralized it."

The rogur slid back into the water trap, its body shrinking and separating. A dark pink column of ooze emerged for a moment and shaped itself into a vaguely humanoid form.

"You needn't worry about it now," Swap's voice said. "I have contained all of it inside me, and it cannot free itself."

I stumbled over to the water's edge. "Swap, you must expel it before it takes over your body."

"It cannot control my brain center, Doctor, because I didn't bring it with me," the worm said. "I left it in another part of myself in the tunnels. The Sovant will not eat its way out of me, either. My cells, as it happens, are quite toxic to it."

"Can you digest it?" my husband asked.

Swap made his laughing sound. "Our imitation of the rogur was rather more convincing than I had wished. No, I do not dine on living creatures, even those as destructive as the Sovant."

"You can't keep it inside you forever," I said.

"Its voracious hunger will grow until it eventually consumes itself," the worm said. "That is the ultimate poetic justice."

A part of Swap's dark pink body broke free and moved toward the far edge of the water trap. It became a very tall, gaunt humanoid female with a long mane of silver-white hair and gray flesh who surfaced and began walking up onto the shore.

Tya, now in her Odnallak form.

As she left the water, tiny lights seemed to fly out from her wet hair and circled around her head, spinning down to cover her naked form in a simple tunic the color of new ice. When the garment was complete, they spiraled back up into her mane and became part of her hair again.

"The first time I saw her do that," Davidov murmured to no one in particular, "I understood what beauty was."

Tya's features were not especially beautiful. They looked blunt, soft, hardly more than indentations in the skin covering her face. Then she lifted her heavy eyelids and looked at me directly. Her eyes, two brilliant orange orbs with compound black pupils, seemed to burn with a contained fire.

She walked over to where Drefan still lay, stunned from his fight with Posbret. She seemed to look upon him with regret before her expression blanked and she turned to face Davidov.

"Aleksei," she said in a low, resonant voice utterly unlike the one she had used as the Hsktskt. "You have had your revenge."

"So I have." He looked at her without interest. "And you are no longer under my control."

I caught my breath, I was so sure that the two would attack each other. Then Davidov sheathed the two blades he held and showed her his palms.

Tya turned and walked back to the water trap, diving in and disappearing under the surface.

Swap slid across the grid until part of his form curled around Mercy's bare foot. "Are you well, little one?"

"I have a headache that's bigger than your fossil collection," she snapped, and then reached down to stroke her hand over the ooze. "Other than that, I'm fine."

"Come and see me again soon." Swap licked her

chin, making her laugh, before he slid back under the water and funneled himself into the water supply pipe.

Drefan pushed himself up and came to loom over me. "I will help you with the wounded."

Reever took my hand in his and eyed the games master. "We all will."

We spent the next few hours transferring the surviving crew and raiders to the simward, sorting out who needed treatment first, and patching up innumerable injuries.

Drefan left only long enough to shed his damaged drednoc body and resume using his glidechair, which, when connected to the hover view, worked admirably as a small tractor.

"James," I said after I had seen the last of the wounded. "I am impressed with your version of prosthetics."

"It helped to have a working body again, even if it was mostly drone." He sounded embarrassed.

"I also thought it was very clever of you to program that water trap into the Itan Odaras simulation." I studied his guarded expression. "Although not precisely accurate, considering that there are no lakes, seas, rivers, or other bodies of water on that planet."

He shrugged. "I like water."

"So do Swap and Tya."

"Come here." Drefan led me away from the patients into a quiet corner. "A few days after you and Reever crashed on Trellus, I had a long talk with

Swap about the Sovant," he advised me. "I agreed to help him capture it. The water trap and the rogur were his idea."

"The rogur is extinct," I said. "All of the stories and images of it were destroyed by the Hsktskt during their prehistory. So tell me, how did Swap know how to make himself and Tya look like something no one has actually seen in thousands of years?"

"Swap already knew," he said in a low voice. "He's a larval form of the rogur."

"If you're worried that big, pink, and smelly thing will someday evolve into the gigantic, vicious, mindless, planet-eating bogeyworm of myth, Doc, don't," Mercy told me as she joined us. "It's not going to happen."

"You knew about this, too."

"Some of it." She glared at Drefan. "Some of my so-called friends didn't trust me to keep my head clear. Anyway, Swap can't go to the next stage of his evolution unless he ingests a massive amount of energy. Which he won't."

Energy could be measured in countless ways. "How massive?"

"Take the largest bomb in League inventory," she said. "A couple hundred of those is his idea of a snack."

The power it would take to contain even one blast . . . "What if he doesn't acquire that much energy?"

"Nothing. He sticks to being a sappy, poetry-reading, junk-collecting, overprotective, moveable mountain of pink ooze." She smiled at Drefan. "Which is what we'd all like. More than anything."

It was obvious that Swap had made a difficult choice. Life forever trapped in a body that could do little but could think and reason and love required great sacrifice. But the alternative—becoming an invincible terror that the Hsktskt had described to me as being as voracious and mindless as the Sovant—must have seemed much worse.

"Will Swap die someday?" I asked Mercy.

"If he doesn't evolve, yeah, eventually he will." Something sparkled in her eyes as she glanced behind me. "Don't worry, Doc. Until that day comes, we'll look after him. In the meantime, I think there's someone coming to look after you."

She and Drefan departed as Reever came to me. He didn't touch me, but stared down at me with stony disapproval.

"I'm sorry I drugged you, but I couldn't let it take you," I told him. "I am very attached to your skin."

He inclined his head. "As I am to yours."

"My blood is poisonous," I continued. "Yours is not."

"True." He didn't seem impressed by the fact. "Do you have any other excuses to make?"

"I love you." I smiled up at him. "That is not an excuse. It is why I did what I did. I love you, Duncan, and when it came I was so afraid that it would take you away from me that I couldn't think. I just . . . sedated you." Tears slid into the corners of my mouth. "Okay?"

"No." He swung me up in his arms and carried me out of the simward. "It is not okay."

I tried to look tired and helpless. "What can I do to show you how sorry I am?"

"You can stop trying to look tired and helpless."

A laugh escaped me, and I covered my mouth.

"It is not amusing," he promised me. "For future reference, if you ever again drug me while we are being attacked, and we survive, I will beat you harder than ten Iisleg men."

No, he wouldn't. "Yes, Duncan." I rested my cheek against his heart. "I realized something today."

His eyebrows arched. "You mean, besides the fact that you are extremely reckless and possibly suicidal?"

I nodded. "Swap said something to me after we met him. He said we don't have to make Marel immortal. You and I can choose instead to be mortal."

Reever stopped and put me down on my feet. "Do you know what it would take now to end our lives?"

"We'd have to embrace the stars," I said, referring to the Jorenian term for dying. "Literally."

"Would you sacrifice eternal life for our daughter?"

I thought, fleetingly, of the black crystal. Maggie had said that Cherijo had been created, no, *designed* to stop it from destroying all life in our galaxy. Part of that design was making her immortal. Perhaps someday Maggie might try to force me to do everything she had expected of my former self.

But I was not Cherijo, and that day was not today. "I will live for her," I said. "And you."

Twenty

We should have done something more romantic that night than fall asleep the moment we climbed onto the sleeping platform, but Reever and I were both exhausted. It took every ounce of strength I had left simply to crawl into his arms and close my eyes.

Some ten hours later I woke to find my fully dressed husband placing a tray of tea and morning bread next to the sleeping platform.

"How long have you been up?" I said around a yawn.

"A few hours." He put a hand to my shoulder when I tried to get out of bed. "Keel and Cat are looking after the patients. Drefan and Mercy have Alek in a detention cell, and they are trying to decide what to do about him. They would like to talk to us about his future."

"I hope you aren't going to defend Davidov, or what he did to these people," I said before I took a sip of my tea.

"No, this time Alek is on his own." Reever sat down beside me. "The repairs to the scout are completed. We can leave Trellus as soon as you're ready to go."

"I'll start packing right now." I drained my server and swung my legs over the side of the platform, and then hesitated as I thought of the wounded still needing care. I could leave instructions with Drefan and Mercy on how to deal with them, but that would serve only as a temporary measure. "Duncan, these people need a doctor who can live on colony, or at least visit them regularly. Do you think the Jorenians would be willing to help them?"

He nodded. "There is one more problem we need to discuss. Swap, and Tya. No one can know about them, Jarn."

I didn't think anyone would believe me if I did tell them. "Where is Tya?"

"She disappeared into the water system pipes, and hasn't come back." He gave me a troubled look. "Both Swap and Tya are extraordinary beings. If the Hsktskt knew a larval rogur existed, for example, they would not rest until they destroyed Trellus."

I knew how much the Hsktskt feared their ancient, extinct enemy—even thoughts of the creature could alter the reptilians' brain chemistry. "Agreed. And knowing the League, they would try to steal the worm and use him as a weapon."

"Odnallak are universally feared and despised throughout the galaxy for their abilities," my husband said. "Most are imprisoned or killed."

I gave him a troubled look. "We can't tell anyone what happened here. Not even our friends." He shook his head. "All right, I will say nothing about them."

Reever kissed my forehead. "Thank you."

I pulled back, surprised. "Were you concerned that I would expose them?"

"I know how you feel about lies." He ran his hand over the untidy mass of my hair. "Now eat your breakfast. We have much to do before we leave the colony."

We entered the detention area where Tya had been kept a prisoner for so long. Most of the lights were dimmed, but I could see who now occupied the cell: Alek Davidov.

"Is this more of Swap's poetic justice?" I asked my husband.

"Perhaps." Reever may have had no intentions of defending Davidov, but I could see that he didn't care to see his former friend locked up.

"It's our justice," Mercy said as she and Drefan joined us. "Colonial security has given us their blessing. We can do anything with him that we like." Her voice hardened. "I'm thinking execution."

Davidov came over to stand by the inhibitor webbing. "How do you propose to do it, beautiful?" he said in a perfect imitation of Cat's voice. "Will you make me the happiest man in the galaxy and fuck me to death?"

Mercy turned to Drefan. "If we go with the execution option, I get to be the one who pushes the button."

The games master nodded. "I want the brain and spinal tissue. He can power one of my drednoc chassis for a few decades."

"Isn't there another option?" I asked.

Mercy took out the mindset. "I meant to tell you, Doc, you didn't hit playback on this when you jammed it on Posbret's face. You hit record." She dangled the mindset in front of Davidov's face. "How would you like to spend a few decades in my fantasizer, reliving what it was like for poor old Posbret to be possessed by a Sovant and have his face burned off and his insides eaten alive?"

"Enough of this," Reever said suddenly. "Alek, you have to tell them."

"Duncan. Giving into threats of unbearable torture, so soon?" The Terran's expression grew mockingly pained. "I thought my secrets were safe with you—"

"Tell them about the Sovant," my husband said flatly, "or I will."

Mercy looked murderous. "There had better not be another of those fucking things on my colony, or I will weld this mindset to your head."

"No." The ironic pleasure disappeared from Davidov's face. "That was the last one."

Drefan began to say, "How could you—"

"Because I've killed all the others." Davidov turned his back on us and sat down on the cell's berth. "I had to. You can't tell them apart, and you certainly can't interrogate them. I'll never know which one got onto my ship. I like to think it was this one. It seemed to have a taste for remote places and clueless victims."

"You had a Sovant on your ship?"

Davidov nodded. "It was clever at first, and made the killings look like accidents. An air lock failure. A flash fire in the galley." He took in a deep breath. "And then it took my wife."

As angry as I was with Davidov, I felt a small surge of empathy. "Did you have to kill her?"

His hands dug into the berth's edge. "She was mostly gone by the time I discovered it was inside her. My pilot tried to stop me, of course; the crew thought I had gone mad. The next thing I knew, I was locked up in the cargo hold and that thing had free run of my ship."

"How long did the crew last?" Drefan asked.

"A couple of months. We were on a remote route, and the men really didn't understand what was happening. They thought it was a disease, and signaled for help, and diverted to a trade outpost with a small FreeClinic. By the time we reached it, I was the only one left. The Sovant was saving me for last, I guess. It landed and came for me. I wounded it, but the outpost officials boarded my ship and took it to their medical center."

"Why didn't you tell us this from the beginning?" Drefan demanded. "We would have helped you."

Davidov gave him an ironic look. "I did that at

the outpost. I told them everything, and they thought I was crazy and locked me up again. By the time they stopped squabbling about it, the Sovant had taken the body of a trader and his ship. It was gone."

"So you went after it."

His shoulders moved. "I hired a new crew, bought the *Renko*, and started hunting them. That was ten years ago."

Drefan leaned forward. "Why did you enslave Tya?"

"Enslave her?" Davidov laughed. "I saved her life. She was the Hsktskt's prize arena fighter for years, the one they called TyalasVar."

" 'Soul eater,' " Reever translated for me.

"Tya had been fighting death matches since she was able to walk. One day she threw her weapons down on the sand and refused to fight again. When I found her, her owner was in the process of beating her to death—and I needed a shifter to help me kill the last Sovant."

"She didn't want to help you," I reminded him. "You put an implant in her body that kept her from shifting. You lied to her and told her it would kill her if she didn't do as you said."

He looked unconcerned. "I never said I was perfect. Once I knew I had the last of them cornered here, I needed Tya to stir things up."

"So you made her shift into a Hsktskt and then trapped her in that form." Reever shook his head.

"After everything that happened to us in the arena, how could you?"

"Odnallak use fear to survive. I wasn't asking her to do anything she hadn't done on her own before. It was unfortunate that she despised the Hsktskt so much that she refused to take on the form voluntarily. I didn't have time to persuade her to get over it." He smiled. "I saw the implant as a kindness. Much more humane than beating her the way the lizards did."

"Mercy," Drefan said softly, "give me that trigger."

Davidov looked up and grinned as he touched his chest. "If you think you can bluff me . . ." He felt something, frowned, and tore open his tunic, running his hand over the flesh above his heart. His gaze turned lethal. "What did you put inside me?"

"Nothing new, blade dancer." Mercy took out a small handheld device and showed it to him. "Recognize this? It's the trigger for a cardiac implant. Just like the one I put inside your chest last night, after you ate your last meal. Which was drugged, by the way."

Reever turned to her. "You know what they do to blade dancers."

"Oh, yeah, I've tumbled a few in my day." She ran her thumb around the only switch on the device. "So one push, and no more Alek Davidov."

"Go ahead." Davidov stretched out on the berth. "I'm not afraid of dying."

He fears nothing, Tya had said.

"Mercy," my husband said quietly. "You know Alek only for what he's done here. He was once a good man. He smuggled slaves with me, and returned them to their homeworlds and their families. He saved thousands."

Davidov bared his teeth. "Shut up, Duncan, and let the lady take her revenge."

"After he lost his wife, he lost a great deal of his humanity," my husband continued. "He became obsessed with avenging her death. He loved her very much." He glanced at me. "I don't approve of his methods, but I understand his motivation."

Davidov made a disgusted sound. "Can you believe that he was the most savage, ruthless, unbeatable arena fighter the Hsktskt have ever owned?"

"What do you want me to do, Reever?" Mercy asked, ignoring Davidov's jeer. "Let him walk away?" When my husband nodded, she sighed. "So we go with the backup plan."

Mercy opened the cell door and pulled aside the inhibitor webbing. "We repaired your ship, and put what's left of your crew on it. You have one hour to get off Trellus."

Davidov got to his feet. "You're letting me go?" He sounded uncertain.

"We're throwing you off our colony," Drefan said, his voice cold.

"Remember how you lied to Tya about her implant? That inspired me to do a little tinkering," Mercy told him. "There's a locator beacon in your cardiac implant, along with a pressure-triggered cache of Tingalean venom, for which there is no antidote, by the way. We'll always know where you are, Aleksei. If you try to remove the implant, you'll be dead in ten seconds. And if you ever come back to Trellus again, I'll hit the trigger."

Davidov took a step toward her. "What's to keep me from taking the trigger from you?"

"Nothing. Here, you can have this one." She smiled and tossed the device at him.

"Lights," Drefan said.

The emitters flared to life, illuminating every inch of the detention area. On the walls someone had hung hundreds of brackets. In each bracket sat a trigger identical to the one in Mercy's hand.

"We took the precaution of replicating some spares," Mercy said. "I have some back at my place, and we'll be sending a few offworld to some friends. If anything happens to me or Drefan, they'll be distributed to everyone in the colony. That includes every relative of every colonist the Sovant killed." She cocked her head. "How long do you think it will take before one of them hits the button?"

Davidov inclined his head. "Brilliant *and* beautiful." He took the pack she tossed at him before he turned to me and Reever. "It seems that I'm in your debt again, old friend."

"I no longer count you as a friend."

"That's a shame, because I can be useful." Davidov shouldered the pack. "While I was transmitting my phony bounty around the quadrant, I received several inquiries. One came from a mercenary who was already hunting you. He offered me eight million credits to turn you over to him."

"Who was it?" I asked.

"I don't have a name," Davidov said. "Only a relay code." He recited a series of letters and numbers. "I wouldn't contact him directly, unless you have a death wish. Drefan, I wish you luck." He reached over, grabbing Mercy and jerking her to him for a quick, hard kiss, and dodging her fist. "Enjoy your Omorr, madam."

She clipped him on the jaw with her follow-through punch. "Get off my colony and stay off, you bastard."

And that, I thought as I watched him walk down the corridor and disappear around the corner, was the only thing that I was sure Davidov would do.

As soon as the *Renko* took off from the surface, I suggested we find Tya and let her know that Davidov was done and she was free of him.

"I talked to Swap last night," Mercy said. "He found her and tried to talk to her, but she slipped away into another pipe. He thinks she's lost it."

"Even if she has, we can't abandon her," Drefan said. "We owe her our lives."

"I don't think she'll let anything living get near her," Mercy said, and then gave him a speculative look. "Of course, she wouldn't be afraid of a dred. Especially one that was a little more human than the others."

Drefan turned his glidechair around. "I'll suit up."

I caught Mercy's arm. "That mindset that recorded Posbret's thoughts and feelings while the Sovant was inside him—you are going to destroy it."

"Do I have to?" She laughed as she saw my reaction. "Doc, I was bluffing. Cat ran the playback through a remote unit for us to view, and there was nothing recorded. It was completely blank." The amusement faded from her expression. "The Sovant didn't have any thoughts or feelings."

"But you let Davidov believe . . ." I shook my head. "That was a terrible thing to do."

"That," she corrected, "was what he really deserved."

Reever and I went down into the tunnels with Drefan to help look for the Odnallak. We started at the substation, where my husband used the water temperature sensors to check each pipe.

"Here." He pointed to one section where the water was twenty degrees warmer than anywhere else under the colony.

Drefan's halo glowed green as he bent down to look at the schematic. "There's an old retention reservoir under the pipes there. The original colonists built it for their children to play in."

We went to the reservoir, and Reever and I stayed back out of sight while Drefan went in. There was no sign of Tya, but he lowered himself down to sit by the reservoir, as if he meant to wait.

An outlet valve on one of the pipes turned, and a long, gray figure slid out and dove into the standing water. She swam toward Drefan and then hoisted herself out, rising to face him as he stood.

I wrapped my arms around my waist. They looked exactly as the drednoc and the vral had in my nightmares.

"What are you doing down here, drone?" Tya reached for the drednoc's central panel, and then went still as Drefan raised his face shields and revealed himself to her. "You."

"Me." He caught her arm when she tried to dive back into the reservoir. "I want to talk to you."

"I have nothing to say to you, Terran."

"That's a shame, because I have a lot to tell you." He released her. "I never knew about the slaves being used in my mines, Tya. Had I known, I would never have allowed it."

"Why would you care about slaver meat?" Her orange eyes regarded him steadily. "They made you a wealthy, rich man."

"No amount of credit is worth a single life." He stepped back from her. "It's why I never tried to escape from the mines after I was made a slave. I believed that it was justice for what had been done in my name."

"Then you are a fool."

"I made friends with the other miners. I saw how they lived, and struggled. I watched them suffer, and some of them die in stupid accidents. I came to the point when I would have done anything for them." He lifted his artificial arm. "I should not have survived the accident that crushed my limbs. I didn't want to. It was supposed to be my final penance."

"I started to like it," Tya said in a hollow, faraway tone. "Killing other slaves. I couldn't wait to get onto the sand. It was the only time I felt alive. That's why I cast down my sword. Not because I was a coward. Because they made me into a killer. When they tied me up and started beating me, I knew I would die. I welcomed it. And then Davidov came."

"Mercy took me in," Drefan said. "She wouldn't let me go."

"Do you know what I can do, Terran?" The white lights in her hair swirled around her, and changed her shape into that of Alek Davidov. "I can read your thoughts and shape myself into what you despise." She shifted a second time, growing into the burned, tortured image of Posbret. "What you dread." The lights spun again, and she became a mirror image of Drefan, his body trapped in ill-fitting prosthetics. "What you most fear."

"I prefer your true form."

Tya spun herself into her tall, ghostly shape. "Why do you bother with me?" she asked, turning away from him. "I am broken, useless. A coward. I couldn't even let Davidov kill me with his poison."

"I hated my body so much I tried to make myself into a drone." Drefan looked down at his armored chassis. "I built this place so that I could use the games to take slaves from their owners and give them new lives. But my anger and my self-hatred will never leave me. The only time I feel alive is when I'm the drednoc, and I can fight simulations. I remove all the safeties."

She stared at him. "So do I."

"Davidov is gone," he told her, "and he will never bother you again. You are free to leave Trellus."

Tya's hair coiled around her face, hiding her expression. "I have nowhere to go. My people are scattered across the galaxy, and they would have no use for an Odnallak who will not use fear. Other species do not understand my kind and would attack me, or would try to control and use me, as Alek did."

"You could stay here, with me." Drefan held out his gauntlet. "I understand you, Tya. I will protect you. Perhaps together we can at last find some peace."

For a long moment the Odnallak said nothing, and then she took a deep breath. "Will I have to become a Hsktskt again?"

Drefan smiled. "Never, unless you want to."

"I hate them, you know." Slowly she took his hand. "I will stay."

I let out the breath I was holding, and then took Reever's hand and silently retreated.

It took a few more days of caring for the wounded and helping repair the damage to the domes before Reever and I felt ready to leave Trellus. Mercy came to our quarters early that day with a parting gift.

"This is an old Aksellan mining map for this

quadrant that my parents and their friends brought with them," she said, spreading out the fragile, cracked sheet of plas on our table. "They bought it off a trader, and used it to pick the site for the colony."

"It is an interesting relic," my husband said.

"It's a little more than that. These maps were never archived because the Aksellans didn't want anyone else using their surveys. Most of them were destroyed when they left the quadrant and moved on to richer territories. This one was probably stolen." Her mouth quirked. "The occupied worlds are marked with symbols for species, type of climate, and mineral content." She pointed to one planet with a dark triangle marked beside it. "That is the symbol for the black crystal."

I looked at the map. There were hundreds of tiny planetary systems depicted, and thousands of black triangles. It was a survey that must have taken centuries to complete.

"I want you to have it." Mercy rolled it up carefully, replaced it in the tube she had brought, and handed it to me. "All I ask in return is that you promise never to tell anyone about Tya and Swap."

I exchanged a look with Reever. "We would do that without the map, Mercy."

"Then let it be a bon voyage present." She slung an arm around my shoulders and gave me a hug.

We made our last stop at Gamers central control.

Keel sat in Drefan's glidechair and monitored the games, while Cat prepared some sort of beverage.

The new prosthetic eye I had fitted for it glittered as it turned its head to greet us. "I was hoping you'd drop in. Come out onto the hover view, Cherijo. You're going to love this."

Cat handed me a server of a bubbly liquid. "Champagne," he said as he passed more of the same to Reever and Mercy. "Terran fermented–fruit juice, used for celebrations. It's vile, but if you breathe through your mouth, drinkable."

I sipped some of the drink, forgot to breathe through my mouth, and sneezed. "What are we celebrating?"

Mercy touched the side of her server to mine. "Life, Doc. Life."

Cold air kissed my face as we entered the grid, which had been programmed to simulate a very familiar-looking ice world. Towering plateaus of blue and white loomed against a kvinka-torn sky. Below us a series of snow bridges, methane fields, and ice caves formed an elaborate playing field.

The humanoid who entered with a dozen guards wore the garb of a slaver. He swatted the frosty air with an oversized sword and far too much enthusiasm.

"What are you waiting for?" he bellowed at Keel. "Initiate the program."

I looked over at the drednoc who stepped out from one of the largest ice caves. His halo threw a circle of purple light on the ice. The jlorra beside him was a massive female who lowered her head and growled, her blue claws digging into the snow crust, her orange eyes burning as if from a fire within. A beautiful icestone collar glittered around her neck.

The drednoc briefly rested one of his gauntlets on the top of the feline's head, and I smiled as I saw her rub against his palm. Then they began walking slowly toward the gamer and his guards.

I glanced at Keel's console, and saw that the slaver and his guards were the simulations. "An interesting game."

Keel grinned. "We hope it will appeal to the real slavers who stop by the colony."

"We need a toast," Mercy said. "Duncan, will you do the honors?"

"To life," Reever said, raising his champagne. "And to those who choose to live it."